Perry

**HODDER AND
STOUGHTON**
Ltd., London

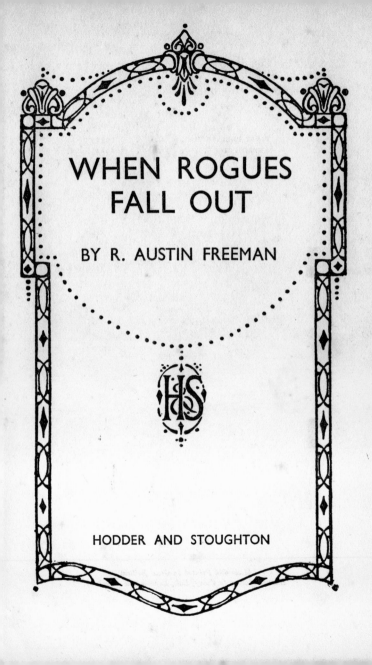

WHEN ROGUES FALL OUT

BY R. AUSTIN FREEMAN

HS

HODDER AND STOUGHTON

FIRST PUBLISHED 1932
REPRINTED 1934

011311

Made and Printed in Great Britain.
Hazell, Watson & Viney, Ltd., London and Aylesbury.

4212452

TO MY FRIEND
LADY ADAMS
FOR AULD LANG SYNE

Contents

BOOK I
THE THREE ROGUES

Chapter I — The Backsliding of Mr. Didbury Toke

THERE is nothing so deceptive as a half-truth. The half that is true has a certain suggestive power that lends to the other half a plausibility and a credibility that it does not possess in its own right. This interesting psychological fact was realized, at least subconsciously, by Mr. Didbury Toke. For Mr. Toke was a collector of antique and other works of art, a connoisseur and a dealer. He really was. It was not a pose or a pretence. He was a *bona fide* collector, and a connoisseur who had that genuine love of fine and beautiful works that is the indispensable condition of real connoisseurship. But Mr. Toke was also a fence. And that was where the illusory element came in. Any person who, not being a known collector and a recognized dealer, should have been seen, as he frequently was, in the company of definitely shady characters, would inevitably have attracted the attention of the guardians of the law. But everyone knows that the really enthusiastic collector must needs seek his quarry where it is most likely to be found ; and there is no need to watch him, for no crook or fence would be so foolish as to sell doubtful merchandise to a collector who is going to expose it forthwith in his show-cases, or a dealer who is going to offer it in the open market. So Mr. Didbury Toke went about his lawful occasions unmolested and unsuspected, and, under the cover of them, did a little unlawful business if it happened to come his way.

It came his way pretty often in these latter days.

But this was a comparatively new development. For many years he had carried on his activities in the most scrupulously correct manner. And so he might have continued to the end, but for some exceptional circumstance. We are all, indeed, the creatures of circumstance. But circumstances are not entirely beyond human control. Their control is, however, largely proportionate to our control of ourselves. And that was where Mr. Toke had failed. At a critical moment he found himself unable to resist a sudden temptation. But let us have done with generalities and consider the circumstances in detail.

The descent to Avernus is proverbially easy ; and, in practice, it is usually somewhat gradual. But there are exceptions ; and the case of Mr. Didbury Toke furnishes an example. For his start upon that famous decline was the result of an incident quite unforeseen and, to a certain extent, beyond his control. At any rate, the determining cause—or perhaps we should say the predisposing cause—was a convulsion of nature for which he certainly could not be held responsible ; being, in fact, no less than a thunderstorm. Mr. Toke did not like thunderstorms. Few of us do ; especially when they come on us in the open country, in which the only refuge visible is the illusory shelter offered by scattered hedgerow elms.

At the moment Mr. Toke was pursuing his way along the rather unfrequented road that led from the village in which his house was situated to the neighbouring market town of Packington. As he walked at an easy pace on the grass verge of the road, his thoughts were pleasantly occupied by reflections on a little windfall that he had recently picked up at a country auction; so much so that his immediate surroundings received but the vaguest attention. Suddenly, he was aroused from his meditations by a low rumble from the far distance behind him, and, turning sharply, became aware of an obvious inkiness of the sky, and, low down, an arched edge of blackness surmounting a pale area in which, even as he looked, jagged streaks of light shot up from the dim horizon.

Mr. Toke looked about him uneasily. He had passed no habitation, so far as he could remember, for the last mile; and Packington lay some two miles farther on. But, clearly, it was useless to think of turning back. His only chance of shelter, apart from the treacherous elms, was in some possible inn or cottage that might lurk unseen by the roadside ahead. Accordingly, he resumed his progress in that direction, mending his pace appreciably as his ears were smitten by a sound as if a Brobdingnagian tea-tray had been kicked by a Titanic foot.

Swiftly Mr. Toke padded along the solitary, inhospitable road while the leaves of the elm trees shivered audibly and elemental bangings from behind announced the approach of the storm. And then, just as the first big drops began to fall with an audible plop on the earth, a slight turn of the road revealed a cottage, hitherto hidden by a clump of trees. It was but a humble labourer's dwelling, timber-built and roofed with thatch, but to Mr. Toke's eagerly searching eyes it was more grateful than a baronial mansion. As a resounding crash from behind mingled with the hiss of a sudden deluge, he frantically unfastened the button of the little gate and darted up the path to the small porch that sheltered the door. Nor did he come as a mere suppliant doubtful of his welcome; for, on the jamb of the door hung a small board bearing the single word "TEAS." It was a laconic announcement; but brevity is the soul of wit; and to Mr. Toke it was as a charter of freedom conferring the right to enter unquestioned.

The door was opened in response to his rather urgent
thumps by an elderly labourer, who looked first at Mr.
Toke and then at the sky, as if he suspected the former
of some responsibility for the unfavourable state of
the weather. But he uttered no word ; and, as the
rain was playing freely on Mr. Toke's back, that
gentleman proceeded bluntly to state his wants.

" Can I have some tea ? " asked Mr. Toke.

The man seemed surprised at the request. " Tea,
you wants," said he. He took another critical survey
of the landscape, and then replied cautiously : " I'll
ask th' old woman."

As " th' old woman " was plainly in view, sitting by
the fire and obviously attentive to the conversation,
the precaution seemed hardly necessary. In fact, she
anticipated the question.

" Why, certainly, Tom ; I can get the gentleman a
cup of tea if he wants one." She rose stiffly from her
chair and cast an enquiring glance at the kettle which
reposed in unpromising silence on the hob.

" You have a notice by your door that you supply
teas," Mr. Toke ventured to remark.

" Yes," the master of the house admitted ; " that
there board was put up by my darter. She's gone and
got married, so we don't do much in that line nowadays.
Never did, in fact. Oo's coming out 'ere for tea ? "

Mr. Toke agreed that the road was not actually
congested, and, meanwhile, under the guidance of his
host, squeezed himself past an obstructive table
towards a Windsor arm-chair which he distinguished
with some difficulty in the pervading gloom. For,
now that the door was closed, the room was almost in
darkness, the small window, obscured by dirt and
invading creepers, admitting only a fraction of the
feeble light from the inky sky.

" Seems as if we was going to have a bit of rain," the

host remarked, by way of making conversation. Mr. Toke agreed that there was a suggestion of moisture in the air, and ventured to express the hope that it would do the country good.

" Ay," said his host, " a bit of rain is allers useful at this time o' year. In reason, mind yer. Yer don't want it a-comin' down like brickbats, a-flattenin' down the crops. A nice, soft, steady rain is what ye wants for the land. Keeps it miste, d'ye see."

Mr. Toke assimilated this lucid explanation as he watched the old woman coaxing the unresponsive kettle with sticks of firewood. By degrees, his eyes were becoming accustomed to the obscurity. Already, he had converted the sound of harsh, metallic ticking into the visual impression of a drum clock, perched on the mantelshelf, and now let his glance wander questingly round the dim interior. It was not an idle glance. By no means. Not, it is true, that he was ordinarily much concerned with the simple domestic antique. But all is fish that comes to a collector's net ; and experience had taught him that if " Honesty lives in a poor house, like your fair pearl in your foul oyster," so was it occasionally with the treasures that the past has bequeathed to the present. So Mr. Toke had made it a rule of life to " keep his weather eyelid lifting " even in the most unlikely surroundings.

" Main lucky for you, it is," remarked his host, as a resounding crash shook the door and made the window-frames rattle, " that you struck this house in time. There ain't another this side of The Rose and Crown, and that's a good mile and a half further on down the road. You'd a-caught it proper if you'd a-been out in it now."

" Yes, indeed," said Mr. Toke. " Holy water in a dry house is better than this rain-water out of doors."

His host did not, apparently, recognize the quotation, for he looked at him suspiciously, and replied in a somewhat surly tone :

" There ain't no holy water in this house. We're Baptisses, we are."

" Ha," said Mr. Toke ; " I was merely repeating an old saying. And there is some truth in it, you know."

" So there may be," was the grudging reply. " I don't hold with none of them there superstitions. Lord ! Look at that ! "

" That " was a blinding flash that flooded the room with violet light, and was instantly followed by a shattering crash directly overhead, as if some aerial three-decker had fired a broadside straight down the chimney. The instantaneous flash, followed by what seemed to the dazzled eye a period of total darkness, left Mr. Toke with a strangely vivid impression of the cottage interior, in which all its details were clearly visible : the seated figure of his host, the old woman, standing by the fire, the tea-pot poised in her hand, the little dresser with its modest crockery set out in an orderly array, and one or two pictures on the wall. But all these things lay, as it were, on the margin of his field of vision, seen, indeed, but only half-consciously perceived. For it happened that, at the moment of the flash, Mr. Toke's eyes had been fixed upon a dim square patch of paleness that was just barely discernible in the darkest corner of the room, and he had been speculating on the nature of the object to which it appertained. The flash solved that problem. The pale, square patch was the dial of a long-case clock. Anyone could have seen that much. But Mr. Toke saw a good deal more. It is true that the object was seen only for an infinitesimal fraction of a second (plus a further sixteenth of a second for what the physiologists call " the persistence of visual impressions "), and that in that instant of time it had revealed little more than a dark silhouette. But a silhouette may be highly significant. It was to Mr. Toke. The square-headed hood, flanked by twisted pillars, the slender body, the low plinth, taken together, suggested a date before the time of good Queen Anne. There were, indeed, two hands—pointing to an impossible hour and clearly indicating that the clock was not a " going concern "—but there was nothing incongruous in this, for two-handed clocks and even eight-day movements, were made before the dawn of the eighteenth century.

But what really did worry Mr. Toke was the appearance of the dial. It was obviously white. Now the seventeenth-century clock-maker had a soul above a painted dial. If this dial was painted, as it appeared to be, there were two possibilities ; either the old dial had been barbarously covered with paint, or, at some time, the clock had fallen into the hands of a Philistine and had its original movement replaced by a new one.

It was a momentous question, and Mr. Toke debated it anxiously as he stirred his tea and kept up a rambling conversation with his host. Of course, it was none of his business—at least one would have said so. But one would have been wrong. Mr. Toke intended to make it his business. There are, indeed, some who maintain that to strike a keen bargain with an ignorant man who happens to possess some valuable object is a base act almost tantamount to robbery. This was not Mr. Toke's view. He held most emphatically that the expert was fully entitled to the usufruct of his knowledge. And there is something to be said for this point of view. A man does not become a connoisseur without the expenditure of time, effort, and money ; and as to the person who, by chance inheritance, happens to possess a Rembrandt or a Leonardo and elects to use it as a tea-tray or to cover up a damp place on the

wall, it is not easy to grow sentimental over his rights.
After all, the base collector rescues the treasure from
imminent destruction, and preserves it for the benefit
of mankind at large.

At any rate, Mr. Toke, recalling the fugitive vision
of that elegant silhouette, kept an acquisitive eye on
the dim, pale square, which, like the grin of the Cheshire
cat, persisted when all else had vanished, and cast
about for some mode of strategic approach to the
subject. Presently his host, all unconsciously, gave
him an opening.

" You takes your tea early," he remarked (it had just
turned half-past three).

Mr. Toke pulled out his watch and glanced at the
drum clock on the mantelshelf.

" Is your clock right ? " he asked.

" Ay—leastways as near as I can tell. I sets him
by the carrier's cart. He go past every morning at
nine o'clock, sharp."

" Ha," said Mr. Toke, " and does it keep good time
—the clock, I mean ? "

" Ay, he do that ; wunnerful good time he keeps.
And I only give three shillings for him, brand noo."

" Really," said Mr. Toke. " It's surprising how
cheap clocks are nowadays."

" Ay," agreed the host, " times has changed. It's
what they calls progress. Now, that old clock in the
corner, he wasn't never bought for three shillings ;
no, nor for three pund."

Mr. Toke stared into the dark corner indicated, as if
he had not noticed the clock before. But the corner
was less dark now ; for, with the last crash, the storm
seemed to have spent its wrath, and now a gleam of
sunshine stole in at the window and so brightened up
the room that the shape of the clock became distinctly
visible.

" No," Mr. Toke concurred, " there were no three-shilling clocks in the days when that was made. Have you had it long ? "

" Had him from my old woman's grandfather. And he had him from the squire what he was coachman to. So he wasn't made yesterday. He's like my old woman and me : he's one of the has-beens."

" Does it keep good time ? " Mr. Toke asked, regardless of the wildly erroneous position of the hands.

His host chuckled. " Don't keep no time at all. Won't go. My darter's husband has a tinker at him now and again—he's a plumber and gas-fitter by trade —but it ain't no use. Th' old clock's wore out. Takin' up room to no purpose. Chap offered me five shillin' for him, and I'd a-took it. But my old woman said no. So we kep' him."

" It wasn't a very liberal offer," Mr. Toke remarked.

" That's what I thought," said the old woman. " 'Twasn't enough for a good old clock, even if it won't go. I said so to Tom at the time."

" Well," growled Thomas, " who's a-going for to pay good money for a clock what won't even tick ? "

Mr. Toke decided that the time had come to open negotiations.

" There are such people," said he. " I have a friend who has quite a fancy for old clocks. He would probably be willing to give you a couple of pounds for it."

" Then," said Thomas, " I'd be glad if you'd send him along this way. What d'you say, Susan ? "

" Two pounds 'ud be very useful," replied the old woman. " But I doubt if he'd give it when he see the clock. It be terrible old."

Mr. Toke rose and strolled across to the corner. The light was now quite good, and at close quarters it was possible to make out the details. And at some of those details Mr. Toke's gorge rose, and he half regretted the liberality of his offer. The venerable time-piece had received the most shocking treatment from some Vandal. The case was encrusted with varnish, apparently applied with a tar brush, and the brass dial had received a thick coat of white paint. Yet, through the treacly depths of the varnish and the layer of paint, other details were faintly discernible which he noted with deep satisfaction.

The clock had been an aristocrat in its day. The dark wood of the case was richly ornamented with marquetry, and a framed panel seemed to enclose some initials and a date, though Mr. Toke could not actually decipher them. But their presence hinted at a possibly traceable history, which would greatly enhance the value of the piece. A glance at the dial showed it to be undoubtedly the original one. The corner ornaments —simple cherubs' heads—were quite characteristic of the period, as were the hour and minute figures, where they were distinguishable, and the hands, though their form was obscured by a thick coat of black enamel paint, showed the simple elegance that marks the work of the earlier makers. Mr. Toke, seeking in vain to decipher the maker's name, was reassured. Perhaps, after all, the plumber's contribution did not go beyond the paint and the varnish.

" Do you happen to remember the name of the squire who originally owned the clock ? " Mr. Toke enquired.

" His name was Hawkwood," the old woman replied. " Sir John Hawkwood."

Mr. Toke made a mental note of the name and announced : " I am inclined to think that my friend would be willing to give a couple of pounds for this clock, if you are prepared to sell it."

Thomas was undoubtedly prepared to sell, and said

so with some emphasis ; and the old lady opined that two pounds would be more useful than the clock.

" Very well," said Mr. Toke, " then we will consider the matter settled. How am I to get the clock to my house ? "

" Where is your house ? " the practical-minded Thomas demanded.

" I live at Hartsden Manor ; just outside the village."

" I knows him," said Thomas. " A tumbledown old house just alongside the old church what is shut up. 'Tain't fur from here. A couple of mile. I could run th' old clock down in my barrer."

" When ? " asked Mr. Toke.

" Now, if yer like. I suppose yer pays on delivery ? "

" Certainly. When I receive the clock, you'll receive the money."

With this stimulus, Thomas awoke to strenuous activity. The clock was hauled out of its corner, and, while Mr. Toke detached the pendulum and secured the weights in a packing of spare garments, old Susan went in search of a blanket, and Thomas retired to fetch the " barrer." In a few minutes all was ready. The clock, decently swathed in the blanket, and faintly suggesting an impending inquest, was tied firmly on the barrow and Thomas signified that the procession was ready to start.

The journey to Hartsden was, for the most part, uneventful. One or two wayfarers on the road greeted the barrow and its burden with surprised grins, and, at the entrance to the village, a group of schoolboys, just released from bondage, formed up into an orderly procession and followed the barrow, two by two, with bare and bowed heads and unseemly giggles ; a proceeding that attracted unnecessary attention, and added appreciably to the gaiety of the neighbourhood for the time being.

" Passel o' grinnin' fules," said Thomas, casting a resentful and contemptuous glance at the little party of smiling bystanders as he drew up at the gate of the house while Mr. Toke unfastened it to admit him to the short drive. As the gate swung open, he stooped to grasp the handles of the barrow at the moment when one of the juvenile mourners advanced, with his handkerchief held to his eyes, to drop a dandelion on the shrouded clock.

The business was soon concluded to mutual satisfaction. The clock was conveyed to a disused room at the back of the house and deposited on a rough table. Then Mr. Toke wrote out a receipt in such terms as amounted to a formal conveyance of the property, and, when the vendor had subscribed his sign manual, two sovereigns were laid on the table.

" Thank ye, sir," said Thomas, transferring them to his pocket. " I hopes the clock will suit your friend. I shouldn't like to think of it being left on your hands."

" He'll have to take it now that I have paid for it," replied Mr. Toke. " But you needn't worry. He'll be quite satisfied."

In point of fact, the " friend " was more than satisfied. A rapid inspection showed that the case was in excellent condition under the crust of varnish ; and through the latter, it was now possible to see that the dark walnut was adorned with marquetry of a richness unusual in such early work. For, in the strong light, the date was clearly legible as well as the initials, grouped in a triangle around a heart—J. H. M. 1692, the H being uppermost, and, as Mr. Toke reasonably surmised, representing the name, Hawkwood. The dial and hands, too, were of appropriate style and of the same excellent workmanship ; and on the former could now be deciphered, through the paint : " Robert Cooke, Londini, fecit."

From this general, preliminary inspection Mr. Toke proceeded to the consideration of details. He had already noticed that the case was closed at the bottom. Now, on opening the door, he observed a partition closing the interior space at an appreciably higher level. This was rather remarkable, for the position of this upper partition was such as possibly to interfere with the proper fall of the weights. But what was still more remarkable was the way in which it was secured. There were four screws ; but, though the wood of the partition appeared to be old, the screws certainly did not. Their bright, clean heads seemed to shout, " Nettlefold."

Mr. Toke was quite interested. Between those two partitions there must be a space. That space might be an ancient hiding-place. But the screws hardly supported that view. At any rate, the question could soon be set at rest. And the first turn of the screwdriver settled it. The readiness with which the screw turned suggested a touch of tallow ; and a greasy stain on the wood around the hole was clear confirmation. The other three screws followed with the same ease, and then, by inserting a bradawl into one of the holes, it was possible to prise up the loose partition.

Now, whether this had or had not been an ancient hiding-place, it was quite clear that the contents were modern ; consisting of a parcel wrapped in undeniable newspaper. Mr. Toke lifted it out, and, having cut the string, carefully opened it. And then he got the surprise of his life. There were several layers of paper, the innermost being of clean tissue paper ; and, when the last of these was turned back, there was revealed to Mr. Toke's astonished gaze a magnificent diamond necklace and a still more magnificent pendant.

For some moments he stood staring at the gorgeous bauble, lost in amazement. Then a slow grin stole

over his face. Now he understood how it was that the
" tinkerings " of the plumber and gas-fitter had failed
to make the clock go. " My darter's husband " had had
other fish to fry. But that estimable artisan seemed
to have taken unnecessary risks, for the door had a
lock. Apparently it was not in working order, and the
key was missing (perhaps in the plumber's possession).
Common prudence would have suggested a repair to the
lock. But, possibly, it had been left for fear of attract-
ing attention. Thomas was not, it had seemed, gifted
with a peculiarly enquiring mind. Perhaps the
plumber had adopted the more prudent course.

But the obvious question arose, What was to be
done ? Mr. Toke believed that he recognized the necklace. He thought that he recalled a daring daylight
robbery at a great London house when the thief had
entered a bedroom by way of a stack-pipe while the
family were at dinner and got away unseen with a
diamond necklace—presumably this very one—said to
be worth £20,000. There would therefore be no difficulty in discovering the owner. Indeed, there was no
need for him to do anything of the kind. All that was
necessary was to report the discovery to the police.
And this was what occurred to Mr. Toke as the obvious
thing to do.

But was it so very obvious, after all ? Mr. Toke
looked at the necklace, and somehow the obviousness
of that course of action seemed to grow less. In the
course of his rather varied life, Mr. Toke had been
connected for a year or two with the diamond and gem
trade. That tended strongly to influence his point of
view. It was not that he was a great judge of gems.
He was not ; though, of course, he could price a stone,
approximately. But the vital fact, in regard to the
present transaction, was that he knew the ropes. The
man who had stolen this jewel had been reduced to the

necessity of hiding it until such time as he should find a " fence " who would take the incriminating treasure off his hands and ask no questions. And what would that fence pay him for it ? No more than a paltry fraction of its real value. Now he, Mr. Toke, could dispose of it at something like its market price.

He looked at it with a calculating eye. It was a fine necklace. Probably report had not greatly over-estimated its value. Every stone in it was a valuable stone. But there was no one of those fine brilliants that was of spectacular value. Not one of them was of a size that would involve questions or possibly lead to identification. He could safely deal with any of them in the ordinary market.

And, after all, why not ? He had not stolen the necklace. So far as he was concerned, it was a case of treasure trove, pure and simple. So he told himself, casuistically trying to smother his not very lively scruples. Of course, he knew quite well that he was contemplating a theft. But, although, up to this time, he had been at least conventionally honest, he was, if not actually avaricious, highly acquisitive by nature, as is apt to be the case with collectors. He had the passion to possess ; and, even if he had been unable to dispose of these diamonds, he would still have been reluctant to give them up.

The conflict in his mind was not a long one. There were the diamonds—ten thousand pounds' worth of them, at a moderate estimate—staring him in the face and inviting him to accept the gifts of Fortune. There was absolutely no danger. The transaction was as simple and safe as an ordinary commercial deal. Suppose the plumber should denounce him to the police. It was wildly improbable ; but suppose he did ? Well, who was going to prove that the diamonds were ever there ? The plumber's unsupported testimony would go for nothing ; and apart from him, there was, presumably, no one who had any knowledge of their whereabouts—unless it was " my darter." But neither of these was in a position to swear that the diamonds were in the clock-case when it was removed from its late owner's custody. Mr. Toke's position was impregnable. He simply knew nothing about the matter.

But he was not going to leave it at that. No sooner had he taken the fateful resolution to treat this gorgeous derelict as treasure trove than the inevitable psychological effect began to manifest itself. The contemplation of a criminal act immediately began to generate the criminal mentality. Safe as the enterprise was, he was going to make it safer. The tracks, already confused, must be further confounded. His intention had been to clean the case himself. He was a fairly expert french polisher. Not that he had contemplated french polishing this old case. On the contrary, his intention had been to un-french-polish it. But now he realized the inexpediency of meddling with it at all. It should go, just as it was, for treatment to some third party. Thus would the issues be further confused.

Having made his decision, he acted promptly. The very next day he conveyed the clock to a roomy closed car that he had lately adopted, and bore it up to town. There he deposited the movement at the premises of a reliable " chamber worker " in Clerkenwell for a careful overhaul, and then carried the case to Curtain Road and handed it to a skilful cabinet-maker with the instruction that it was to be cleaned and wax-polished, but left structurally intact, with the exception of any trifling repairs that might be unavoidable. The lock was to be repaired and fitted with a key of the correct pattern according to the date on the panel.

When he had done this, Mr. Toke felt that he had made his position unassailable. He allowed himself to hope that he would be left in undisputed possession of his treasure trove. But his hopes were tempered by a suspicion that he had not heard the last of the worthy Thomas's too-ingenious son-in-law. And subsequent events justified his suspicions.

Chapter II   *Enter Mr. Hughes*

It was a little over a week after his acquisition of the
clock that Mr. Toke's forebodings began to be realized.
On that day, about eleven in the forenoon, his housekeeper, Mrs. Gibbins, came to him as he sat in his study
writing letters, and announced with something of an
air of mystery that a man wished to see him.

" A man ? " Mr. Toke repeated. " Do you mean a
gentleman ? "

Mrs. Gibbins made it extremely clear that she did
not.

" Did he say what his business was ? "

" No, sir. I asked him, but he said he wanted to
see you on private business. He wouldn't say what it
was. He is waiting in the hall. I told Margaret to
keep an eye on him." (Margaret was Mrs. Gibbins's
niece and functioned as housemaid.)

" Well," said Mr. Toke, " I suppose you had better
bring him in here. But I can't imagine who he can
be " ; which was not perfectly candid on Mr. Toke's
part. He had a strong suspicion that the visitor would
turn out to be an exponent of the plumbing and gas-
fitting arts. And even so it befell. When Mrs. Gibbins
returned, she was accompanied by a somewhat seedy
stranger of truculent aspect, whose appearance suggested a Labour agitator or a working man of strongly
political leanings.

" Well," said Mr. Toke, when the housekeeper
had retired, " what is it that you want to see me
about ? "

His visitor crept towards him with an air of mystery and secrecy, and replied impressively :

" It's about a clock what you bought off of my father-in-law, Mr. Hobson."

" Yes," said Mr. Toke, " I remember. An old clock, a good deal out of repair. Yes. What about it ? "

" Well, you see, Mr. Hobson hadn't got no right for to sell you that clock. 'Twasn't his for to sell. That clock belongs to my wife. It was give to her as a wedding present."

Mr. Toke reflected rapidly. It would be perfectly practicable to restore the clock, since its contents were now securely concealed in an undiscoverable hiding-place. The clock, itself, valuable as it was, had become, by comparison, negligible. Nevertheless, Mr. Toke's strongly acquisitive temperament made him reluctant to disgorge. Besides, to what purpose should he restore the clock ? Its return, empty, would not dispose of the business. It was not the clock but the necklace that this worthy craftsman was seeking. And then there was the practical certainty that his statement was a barefaced untruth. No ; there was nothing to be gained by an attempt to compromise.

" This is very unfortunate," said Mr. Toke ; " but I am afraid you will have to settle the matter with Mr. Hobson. He has the money. I have no doubt that, if you put it to him, he will hand it over to you."

" But my wife don't want to sell the clock, nor more don't I."

" Ha," said Mr. Toke, " that is a pity ; because, you see, the clock has been sold. I bought it in a perfectly regular manner, and I have Mr. Hobson's receipt for the price of it."

" But don't I keep telling yer that old Hobson hadn't no right for to sell it ? "

Mr. Toke admitted that the matter had been mentioned. " But," he continued, " that is really not my concern. You must settle the affair with your father-in-law."

" Ho, must I ? Fat lot of good it 'ud be talking to him. No, Mister, I'm going to settle with you, I am. You've got my clock, and you're going to hand it over. I've got the barrer outside."

Mr. Toke complimented him on his providence, but declined to consider the demand.

" Look here," the stranger exclaimed in a threatening tone, " if you don't want any trouble, you just hand that clock over. I'm going to have it, you know. I'm going to make you hand it over. See ? You think I can't, but I tell you I can."

" I am sure you can," Mr. Toke agreed. " That is just my point. If the clock is yours, you can compel me to return it. All you have to do is to go to your solicitor, give him proof of your title to the property and instruct him to recover it in the ordinary way. He will make no trouble about it."

" Gawd ! " exclaimed the other. " I don't want all that trouble and fuss. And I don't want no solicitors. I shall just inform the police."

" Yes," said Mr. Toke, " you could do that. If your father-in-law did actually sell a clock that was not his property, he undoubtedly was guilty of a criminal act. You might prosecute him. So might I, for obtaining money from me by false pretences. But you would have to prove that the clock was yours, in any case. It would be less trouble to instruct a solicitor, and you would avoid the scandal."

Mr. Toke's calm, detached attitude seemed rather to nonplus his visitor, for the latter stood for some time gazing at him, breathing hard but uttering no word. At length he resumed, in a milder, even pacific tone :

" I don't want to make no trouble for old Hobson, seeing as he is my wife's father. And I don't want no truck with solicitors. I'll tell you what I'll do. You hand me back that clock, and I'll give you the two quid what you paid for it. I can't say no fairer than that."

But Mr. Toke shook his head regretfully. " I am sorry, Mr. —— I didn't quite catch your name——"

" My name is Dobey, Charles Dobey, if you want to know."

" Thank you. I was saying that I am extremely sorry that I can't accept your offer. But, to begin with, the clock is not here ; and as I have already spent a substantial sum of money on it, I should not be prepared to sell it at the price that I gave for it."

" What do you mean about spending money on it ? " Mr. Dobey asked with evident uneasiness.

" Well, you see," said Mr. Toke, " in the first place, I had to send the case to a cabinet-maker's——"

" What ! " gasped Dobey. Then, controlling himself, he demanded, huskily : " What was the cabinet-maker going to do to it ? There wasn't nothing the matter with the case."

" Nothing structural," Mr. Toke agreed. " But it wanted a clean up. I told him to clean off all the old varnish and put on a slight wax polish. That was all. And I have had the movement put in order. So you see, the clock is now worth a good deal more than I gave for it."

" And where is it now ? " Mr. Dobey asked, gloomily.

" I have sent it to Messrs. Moore and Burgess, the eminent auctioneers, and I understand that it will be put up for sale next Thursday—a week from to-day."

Mr. Dobey reflected on this statement with an expression compounded of dejection and bewilderment. And,

meanwhile, Mr. Toke looked him over, critically. He
was not much to look at. He presented none of those
interesting " stigmata " that distinguish the criminal
countenance in the plates of Lombroso's treatises. He
was just a common " low-grade " man of the type that
may be seen by the dozen, taking the air in the exercise
yard of any local prison ; with darkish red hair and—
rather unusually—a nose to match ; hands suggestive
of deficient washing rather than excessive labour and a
noticeably shifty and furtive cast of countenance.

At length he pulled himself together for a final
effort.

" This is all very well, you know, Mister, but I
can't allow you to put up my clock to auction just as
if it was your own. You'll have to get it back ; and
I'll make you an allowance for what you've spent
on it."

" I'm afraid I can't agree to that," said Mr. Toke.
" You seem to be forgetting that, at present, I am the
legal owner of that clock. The receipt that I hold
establishes my ownership ; and if you claim that the
clock is yours, it is for you to produce evidence of
ownership. You haven't done that, you know ; and,
if you haven't any papers to prove that it was given
to your wife, I don't think you would be able to
do it."

" I could swear a affidavit," said Mr. Dobey.

" M'yes," agreed Mr. Toke. " But you have to be
a bit careful about affidavits. There is such a thing
as perjury, you know. I shouldn't recommend an
affidavit."

Mr. Dobey received this advice with a bewildered
stare. He could make nothing of it. Mr. Toke's
bland, impersonal attitude left him, for the moment,
speechless. At length, he asked, lamely :

" Well, what am I to do ? I ought to be able

to get my own clock back—leastways, my wife's clock."

" So you are," said Mr. Toke. " There's nothing to prevent you from going to the auction and bidding."

For some moments Mr. Dobey was too much overcome to be capable of any reply. At last, he exclaimed, hoarsely :

" Well, I am blowed, I reely am. You've got the blinkin' sauce to tell me to go to the blinkin' auction and buy in my own clock. And you to take the money. I never heard the likes of it ! "

" I merely threw out the suggestion," said Mr. Toke. " I thought you were anxious to get the clock. You could always sell it and get your money back, you know."

Futile as the suggestion seemed, it was craftily conceived ; and Mr. Toke, furtively watching his visitor, saw that it had taken effect. The aggressive expression faded out of Mr. Dobey's countenance and gave place to one indicative of reflection.

" Where do these auction blokes hang out ? " he asked after a longish pause.

Mr. Toke took out from his letter case a card on which was inscribed, " MR. DIDBURY TOKE, 151 QUEEN SQUARE, BLOOMSBURY. TUESDAY AND FRIDAY, 11 to 5, OR BY APPOINTMENT." On the back of this he wrote the address of the auctioneers, and handed it to Mr. Dobey ; who, having read what was written, turned the card over and studied the printed inscription.

" I'll have to think over this," he remarked gloomily ; and then, as if a new idea had struck him, he demanded : " What is the name of the cabinet-maker what did the clock up ? "

" His name," said Mr. Toke, writing on a slip of paper as he spoke, " is Levy, Maurice Levy, and his place is in Curtain Road."

"Sounds like a sheeny," Dobey remarked, disparagingly.

"He is, as you have guessed, of the Jewish faith," Mr. Toke admitted. "A most excellent workman and a thoroughly honest man."

"Ho," said Mr. Dobey, in a tone of obvious scepticism. But he seemed to get some comfort from the description, nevertheless. He gazed reflectively at the slip of paper for a while, and then, slowly and reluctantly, rose.

"Well," he remarked in an aggrieved tone, "this ain't what I expected, but I suppose there's no use staying here chin-waggin' to no purpose."

He moved dejectedly towards the door, and Mr. Toke piloted him to the hall and launched him with a suave "Good morning" from the front door, watching him with a faint smile as he slouched down the short drive. He was not dissatisfied with the result of the interview. His subtle hint had evidently taken effect. And, though there would certainly be trouble if Dobey really bought the clock, it would be better so than that some other purchaser should have his house burgled, with the possibility of a capture and awkward explanations.

On the following Wednesday, the day before the sale, Mr. Toke arrived betimes at the rooms of Messrs. Moore and Burgess to watch the company of dealers and connoisseurs who had gathered to view the goods that were to be sold on the following day. There were two large rooms, connected by a wide doorway ; and, immediately opposite the doorway, the clock was standing, ticking solemnly in proof of its perfectly restored health. Mr. Toke halted before it and surveyed it with not unpardonable pride. By the joint efforts of Mr. Levy and the Clerkenwell artist, the shabby outcast that had cumbered the floor of Thomas

Hobson's cottage had been restored to its rightful status as an aristocrat among clocks. The fine, dark walnut case with its rich marquetry had emerged from the crust of varnish as a butterfly comes forth from its pupa-shell ; the brass dial with its cherub-heads and its silver hour-circle had been cleansed of the paint, and yet not cleansed too much, and the hands once more showed the fine, simple workmanship of their period.

Mr. Toke stood and let his eyes travel over its revived beauties with the genuine pleasure of the connoisseur, congratulating himself on having been the means of rescuing it from its unworthy surroundings and the risk of destruction. But, even as he gloated, he kept a watchful eye on the entrance through which new-comers were constantly pouring in ; and it was, perhaps, just as well that he did ; for, even as he held the narrow door of the clock open and peered in to see that the partition had not been tampered with, the countenance of Mr. Dobey came into view among the little crowd of new arrivals.

Now there was really no reason why Mr. Toke should have made any secret of his presence in the rooms. As a collector, it was quite natural that he should be there. But recent transactions had engendered in him a new furtiveness and secrecy. He didn't want Dobey to see him, and he did want to keep an eye on Dobey. Accordingly, having shut the clock-case, he made his way, as well as the crowded state of the rooms would let him, through the doorway into the other room, and looked about for some means of concealment. A large French armoire seemed to offer the best cover, for, from the shadow behind it, he could get a good view of the adjoining room in a large mirror.

Here, then, he established himself, and soon the bereaved artisan came into view. He was quite respectably dressed, and would have been unnoticeable but for the self-consciousness which caused him to move stealthily and suspiciously among the crowd. Very soon he spied the clock and crept up to it with ill-assumed unconcern. Mr. Toke watched him with grim amusement. Evidently, the changed appearance of the clock puzzled him considerably. The distinctive characteristics, now so striking, had been hidden by the varnish, and were unfamiliar to him, He stared at the clock, and then gazed about in search of another. But this was the only clock in the room. Finally, after a furtive glance to right and left, he ventured to open the door of the case and peer in. Then, evidently, some chord of memory was struck. No doubt the four Nettlefold screws were old friends. At any rate, he closed the door with an air of decision, and once more began to look about him furtively and uneasily, while Mr. Toke watched expectantly to see what his next move would be.

For some time Dobey crept to and fro rather aimlessly, gazing at the exhibits, but keeping in the neighbourhood of the clock, and Mr. Toke had the feeling that he was waiting for someone. And so it turned out, presently. The meeting was singularly unostentatious, but Mr. Toke, watching narrowly, noted the mutual recognition. The new-comer was a well-dressed man, obviously of a superior class to Mr. Dobey, who walked in confidently, and, having looked round, glanced at the catalogue that he held and then walked straight up to the clock. He stood before it and surveyed it critically, point by point ; tried the lock, opened the door of the case, gazed into the interior and reclosed it. And it was at this moment that the meeting took place. There was no sign of recognition ; but, as the stranger stood inspecting the clock, Dobey sidled up, and for a moment stood by his side. Nothing appeared to be said, but the stranger made an entry in his catalogue. Then Dobey moved away, and, after a few vague glances at some of the exhibits, faded away towards the entry and vanished into the outer world.

With the disappearance of Mr. Dobey, concealment became no longer necessary. Mr. Toke emerged boldly, and made his way into the other room with the purpose of getting a closer look at Mr. Dobey's friend. The circumstances were favourable for getting, at least, an unobserved back view ; and the observant Mr. Toke, beginning with a minute inspection from the rear, arrived at the decision that the unknown wore a wig. It was an exceedingly good wig ; so good and well-fitting as to suggest a bald or shaved head underneath. Having made this interesting observation, Mr. Toke contrived to obtain a view of the stranger's face. It impressed him as a rather curious face ; but he presently realized that the peculiarity of expression was due to the absence of eyebrows. Either they were naturally deficient or they had been shaved off. The presence of the wig suggested the former, but the meeting with Mr. Dobey made the latter possibility quite conceivable. At any rate, the dark-brown wig, with eyes to match, and the curiously blank forehead, rendered the stranger easy to recognize ; which was satisfactory, as Mr. Toke intended to keep an eye on him, if, as seemed likely, he should turn up at the sale on the following day.

And turn up he did. Mr. Toke, keeping a bright look-out, saw him come in, catalogue in hand, and select a seat well in view of the auctioneer. Mr. Toke saw him fairly seated and then found a place for himself, where he could command an uninterrupted view of the stranger without making himself conspicuous. As he was not going to bid, he had no need to be in a position to catch the auctioneer's eye.

His vigil was not unduly prolonged, for the clock came early in the list. As the number approached, he watched the wigged stranger ; but his queer, blank face showed no sign of uneasiness. He watched the proceedings stolidly, and did not even glance at his catalogue. Evidently, he was not a jumpy man.

At length the fateful number was reached. The auctioneer cleared his throat and announced, not without gusto :

" Long-case clock by Robert Cooke of London, dated 1692, in a case of fine walnut wood, enriched with elaborate marquetry. A most exceptional lot, this, gentlemen. It is really a museum piece. I have never seen a clock of this early period in such perfect condition. It is virtually untouched. With the exception of a modern partition in the bottom of the case, there are no restorations or repairs. It is in the very condition in which the maker turned it out. And I understand that an authentic history accompanies it. The initials on the case are those of Sir John Hawkwood and the Lady Margaret, his wife. Now, gentlemen, what shall we say for this unique clock ? "

Almost before he had finished speaking, a voice answered :

" Fifty pounds."

Mr. Toke grinned. This was, in effect, an ultimatum. The speaker meant to have the clock, and made no secret of his intention. But he was not the only pebble on the beach, as the vulgar saying has it. His challenge was immediately taken up by another enthusiast.

" Fifty-five."

" Sixty."

" Sixty-five."

The bids followed one another with hardly a

moment's interval, and the price hopped up by fives until it reached a hundred and ninety. Then there was a slight slackening ; but still the bidding went on, though at a reduced pace. And all the time the gentleman in the wig sat gazing stolidly before him and uttering not a word. Mr. Toke began to be uneasy. Was he not going to bid, after all ? Had he merely come to get the name of the purchaser with a view to a subsequent burglary ? That was an unpleasant possibility. Not that it mattered very much ; but, still, Mr. Toke didn't want a burglary. No one could say what disagreeable results might follow. But at this point his anxieties were dissipated by a sudden activity on the part of the wigged gentleman. The price had reached two hundred and five, and, after the last bid, a somewhat lengthy pause occurred. The auctioneer repeated the bid, solemnly, and his hand stole towards his hammer. But at this moment, the wigged stranger looked at the auctioneer and nodded.

" Two hundred and ten," the latter chanted, and repeated the refrain three times with increasing emphasis. But now there was no answer. The appearance of a new competitor at the eleventh hour was too much for the others. After a long and anxious pause, the hammer came down with a sharp rap and Mr. Toke drew a deep breath.

The name of the wigged gentleman, it transpired, was Hughes. As soon as he had communicated this fact, he rose and walked over to the clock and stood for a while surveying it with apparent satisfaction. Then he turned the key in the lock, put it in his pocket and sauntered out of the room ; and, as the purchase of the clock left Mr. Toke with no further interest in the proceedings, he also presently rose and left the premises. And, as he wended his way to his office, he speculated, not without a shade of anxiety, on the probabilities of the immediate future. Messrs. Hughes and Dobey were going to suffer a somewhat severe disappointment. It was not likely that they would suffer in silence. He had a strong presentiment that he had not heard the last of that necklace or of its quondam owners. As to Dobey, he was a negligible ass. But Mr. Hughes was in a rather different class. His conduct at the auction showed considerable judgment and self-restraint. He was clearly a gentleman who knew his own mind ; a man of courage and resolution.

Mr. Toke was rather sorry that Mr. Hughes had come into the affair.

LOVERS of paradox assure us that it is the unexpected that happens. Perhaps they are right. But the unexpected holds no monopoly. Sometimes the expected happens. It did, for instance, on a certain Friday afternoon—the very day, in fact, after the auction. On that day, in accordance with the announcement on his cards, Mr. Toke was in attendance at his professional premises. At the moment he was seated at the writing-table in the inner room—it was hardly an office—writing one or two letters. He was quite alone, for he had no clerk or secretary. He had no use for one, since his business was entirely personal and his transactions few, though the amounts involved were usually substantial. So there he sat, writing his letters, but by no means engrossed with the matter thereof.

To tell the literal truth, Mr. Toke was just a shade nervous. The auction had not gone quite according to plan. He had reckoned on Mr. Dobey, whereas he now had to deal with Mr. Hughes ; which was a slightly different proposition. Accordingly, he sat, making shift to write, but with an attentive ear on the outer door.

It was within a few minutes of five o'clock, and he was preparing for a scrupulously punctual departure, when the expected happened. The outer door opened, and, through the slight opening of the door communicating with the outer room, he saw a man enter. He rose, and, stepping out into the other room, found himself confronting Mr. Hughes. The visitor looked at him critically and affirmed :

" I wish to see Mr. Didbury Toke."

" Fortunate man ! " said Mr. Toke. " Your wish is realized even as you utter it. In what way can I be of service to you ? "

" I should like to have a few words with you in private," was the reply.

" Again," said Mr. Toke, with genial facetiousness, by way of keeping up his spirits, " you are favoured. For here we are, *solus cum solo*, with none to supervise, as the poet expresses it. You can say anything you like and no one will be the wiser."

He led the way into the inner room, and, shutting the communicating door, indicated a chair adjoining the writing-table, resumed his seat at the table, and looked expectantly at his visitor.

" I have come to see you on behalf of Mr. Charles Dobey," said the latter. " My own name is Hughes."

" I hope Mr. Dobey is not unwell," said Mr. Toke.

" He is not," was the reply ; " but he wished me to act on his behalf, as being more experienced in business affairs. The matter is this : a short time ago you purchased from a certain Thomas Hobson an antique clock. Dobey states that the clock was actually his property, but I am not going into that. The point is, that there was certain property, which certainly was Dobey's, concealed in that clock. He had been in the habit of using it as a safe."

" What an extraordinarily stupid thing to do ! " exclaimed Mr. Toke.

" I agree," said Mr. Hughes. " But he did. He stowed this property in a cavity between two partitions, the upper of which was secured with screws."

" Was this property of any considerable value ? " Mr. Toke asked.

" I understand that it was."

" Dear me ! " exclaimed Mr. Toke, " I wish I had known. May I ask what was its nature ? "

" I understand that it consisted of jewellery," replied Mr. Hughes. " But the point is, that it has disappeared. Acting on Dobey's instructions, I bought the clock, and Dobey removed the partition in my presence. The cavity underneath was empty."

" Dear me," said Mr. Toke. " Was it, indeed ? Now, I wonder how it can have disappeared."

" Dobey assumes that you removed it, and it seems a reasonable supposition. I have come to ask you what you propose to do about it."

Mr. Toke leaned back in his chair, and, placing his finger-tips together, looked steadily at Mr. Hughes. He had, indeed, been looking at him throughout the interview, and, as the light from the window fell full on the queer, rather sinister face, he had been able to study it advantageously. I use the word " study " advisedly ; for at the first glance he had been aware of a faint stirring of memory. Mr. Toke had an exceedingly good memory for faces ; and, although this face was strange to him, yet, as he looked, it seemed to set some chord of memory vibrating.

" May I ask what leads you to suppose that I removed this property ? " he asked, without any sign of resentment.

" It is obvious enough," Hughes replied. " The property was there when the clock came into your possession, and it isn't there now."

" But," protested Toke, " you seem to be overlooking the number of hands through which the clock has passed. There is the cabinet-maker, the clockmaker who fitted the movement to the case, and various unknown persons who had access to it at the auction rooms."

" And there is yourself, the only one of the lot who happens to have the means of disposing of valuable jewellery."

" That is quite true," Mr. Toke agreed. " If Dobey had offered me the jewellery, I could certainly have disposed of it to advantage. Unfortunately, he did not. And you must see that my professional standing has no bearing on the question as to who found the jewellery, assuming it to have been really there. The fact is that I, of course, saw the partition, and I saw that it had no business to be there. But I make it a rule, when I buy a piece with the intention of selling it, to leave it exactly as I find it. And I instructed the cabinet-maker to make no structural changes in the case ; otherwise, he would, no doubt, have removed the partition, as it might be thought to stand in the way of the weights. Still, it might be worth while to ask him if he did remove it."

" I have," said Mr. Hughes, " and he states very positively that he did not. And I believe him."

" So do I," said Mr. Toke. " He is a most respectable man, and would, I am sure, have reported to me if he had made any discovery. And so, I think, would the clock-maker. If the property was really there, it must have been abstracted by someone after it was delivered at the auction rooms."

Mr. Hughes received this statement in gloomy silence, but with a lowering of the brows—or, at least, of the region where the brows should have been—that plainly expressed his unbelief. But he did not leave it at mere facial expression. After a somewhat lengthy pause, he said, in low, emphatic tones :

" Look here, Mr. Toke, all this evasion is no good. You have got those jewels. It is of no use your telling me that you haven't. I am perfectly sure that you have."

" Very well," Mr. Toke replied calmly, " then there is no more to be said. You have your legal remedy, you know."

" You know that we have nothing of the sort," replied Hughes. " I realize that you can stick to them if you like. The question is, do you intend to hold on to them, or are you willing to make some sort of arrangement with Dobey ? "

Mr. Toke reflected. Once before, when he had discovered the jewels, he had stood at the cross-roads ; and he had taken the wrong turning. Now he stood at the cross-roads again. Should he share the loot with these two rascals, or should he accept the gifts of Fortune and snap his fingers at them ?

It was a momentous question ; more momentous than he knew. If he could have looked into the future and seen the consequences that hung on his decision, that decision might have been very different. But Mr. Toke was like the rest of us. He could be wise enough after the event. But the future was a matter of guess-work. And it is always possible to guess wrong. Probably Mr. Toke guessed wrong on this occasion. At any rate, he made the fateful decision ; and the future was to show that it was the wrong one.

" I cannot be committed to any opinions that you may have formed," said he. " As to these jewels, I feel no conviction that they were ever there. Mr. Dobey is a plumber and gas-fitter. Now, what has a gas-fitter to do with valuable jewels ? "

" We need not go into that," Mr. Hughes said, brusquely.

"Very true. We need not," Mr. Toke agreed. "There is certainly a particular kind of gas-fitter who comes into the possession of valuable jewels. But he is not an honest kind of gas-fitter, whose word could be accepted without proof. I am very doubtful about those jewels."

" Then I take it that you don't mean to make any kind of arrangement ? "

" I am willing to make one concession," Mr. Toke replied. " As I assume that you bought the clock for the purpose of recovering the jewels, I am ready to take it back at the price that you paid, subject to its being in the same condition as when it was sold."

" Well," said Hughes, " I suppose we must be thankful for small mercies. We don't want to drop a couple of hundred on an empty shell. I will accept your offer. The clock shall be delivered here in good condition next Tuesday, if that will suit you."

" It will suit me perfectly," replied Mr. Toke. " And as to payment ? Will a crossed cheque do ? "

" Certainly," Hughes replied ; and, for the first time, his rather unprepossessing countenance was illuminated by the ghost of a smile.

Mr. Toke was secretly surprised, but he concealed the fact and rejoined :

" One naturally prefers to draw crossed cheques. Shall I give the cheque to the person who delivers the clock ? "

" No," replied Hughes. " I will come with it, or soon after."

Mr. Toke nodded, and, rising as the other rose to depart, said facetiously, and perhaps a little untactfully :

" I am sorry that things have turned out so unsatisfactorily for Mr. Dobey ; but, if he had brought his heirlooms to me, instead of hiding them in a clock in someone else's house, we might have made some mutually satisfactory arrangement—that is, if he wished to dispose of them. You might mention the fact to him for his future guidance."

It was not a tactful thing to say, under the circumstances, and, for a moment, Mr. Hughes looked decidedly vicious. But, if he was an angry man, he was

also a politic man. He was not going to let temper
stand in the way of self-interest. Just as the great
difficulty of the murderer is the disposal of the body, so
the great difficulty of those who acquire unlawful goods
is the disposal of the loot. Now Mr. Toke undoubtedly
had the means of disposing of valuable property. Mr.
Hughes had not. For though, like Mr. Toke, he knew
the ropes, there were circumstances that hindered his
appearance in the places where precious things were
bought and sold. Therefore, to Mr. Toke's surprise,
instead of resenting the advice, he replied, dryly :

" He will be grateful for the tip. Shall I tell him
that you are prepared to waive the question of title
deeds ? "

Mr. Toke smiled blandly. " When I am offered
property for purchase," he said, " I assume that the
vendor is the owner. It is a reasonable assumption."

" Quite," agreed Hughes. " But suppose there
seems to be a flaw in the title. How would that affect
the transaction ? I suppose it would be a case of a
knock-down price, at any rate ? "

" My dear sir," said Mr. Toke, " you know very well
that property which is hampered by conditions that
hinder its sale in the open market is of less value than
property not so hampered. That has to be allowed for
in order to leave a reasonable profit to the purchaser.
But the allowance need not be excessive."

Hughes reflected with a calculating eye on Mr. Toke.
After a considerable pause, he said, rather suddenly :

" Look here, Mr. Toke. I want to ask you a plain
question. I don't know a great deal about Dobey's
affairs, but I fancy that he sometimes comes by odd-
ments of property—jewellery, for the most part—that
are not quite negotiable in the regular markets. I
don't know where he picks them up. It isn't my affair.
Now the question is, in plain language, would you be

prepared to take them off his hands and give him a fair price for them ? "

" If I bought them, I should give a fair price, allowing for difficulties of disposal. But I couldn't have Dobey coming here, you know, or at my private house."

" I realize that," said Hughes. " But that could be arranged. May I take it that you would be willing to buy the goods and ask no questions ? "

Mr. Toke was a little staggered by the bluntness of the phrase, but he answered with belated caution :

" My business, hitherto, has been of a strictly legitimate kind. My reputation in the trade is spotless. Still, if the affair could be arranged with absolute discretion, I might be prepared to consider a deal of the kind that you propose."

" Very well," said Hughes, " I will tell Dobey. And, if he should happen to pick up any chance trifles, we must consider how the negotiations could be carried out."

With this Mr. Hughes took his leave and departed with very mixed feelings. On the one hand, he was possessed by a murderous hatred of Mr. Toke. That the latter had the diamonds—that he had quietly annexed the product of an almost unique coup—he had no doubt. But he was equally sure that Mr. Toke's position was impregnable. By no means that he could think of could that discreet gentleman be made to disgorge. On the other hand, much to his surprise, Toke seemed quite willing to act as a receiver of stolen property. That was all to the good ; for Toke would probably pay better prices than the wretched pittances offered by the regular " fences." And he would be much safer to deal with, provided the transactions were kept on the discreet lines that both of them desired. So Mr. Hughes was not displeased, especially as the arrangement promised, sooner or later, to give him a chance to settle accounts with Mr. Toke.

The latter gentleman, left alone in his office, was also a little surprised at himself. After years of blameless dealing, he had suddenly proposed to embark on the perilous activities of the " receiver." Why this sudden change of outlook ? He was a little puzzled, though he dimly perceived the explanation ; which was, in reality, fairly simple. He had dismounted the diamonds from their settings, and had made an estimate of their marketable value. The amount that he could safely reckon on pocketing by their sale came out at the highly satisfactory figure of seven thousand pounds. Now, seven thousand pounds takes a great deal of earning by legitimate industry. Naturally he was impressed by this " easy money "—the immemorial lure that has drawn so many on to the broad road that leadeth to destruction. But the really potent influence was the fact that he was already in actual possession of stolen property, and making preparations to dispose of it. The first step had been taken ; and, in taking it, he had made a curious discovery. He had discovered that, apart from the attraction of easily won wealth, there was a certain element of excitement and adventure in the acquirement and sale of illicit property that was only feebly present in lawful dealing.

On the following Tuesday the clock was duly delivered, and Mr. Toke was in the act of winding it when Mr. Hughes arrived. His greeting was not effusive, nor was it in any way hostile. He merely stated that he had come for the cheque.

" A crossed cheque, you said, drawn to your own name, I suppose ? "

" Yes. Arthur Hughes."

Mr. Toke wrote out the cheque and handed it to Hughes with the remark :

" Well, you've got your money back, at any rate."

" Some of it," responded Hughes, adding : " Are you sure you won't reconsider the other little matter ? "

But Mr. Toke's heart was hardened. Already, in effect, he had his hand on that seven thousand pounds.

" If you mean the problem of the alleged lost property in the clock," said he, " I can only repeat that I know nothing about it, and that I am profoundly sceptical as to its having been there, at any rate when the clock came into my possession."

" Very well," said Hughes, " then we must leave it at that. And now as to the other matter—the question of your negotiating some of Dobey's unconsidered trifles. Have you considered the question of procedure ? "

" In a general way," replied Mr. Toke. " In the interests of us both, we must avoid jeopardizing my position as a reputable dealer. You realize that ? "

Hughes realized it perfectly. Not that he was in the least tender about Mr. Toke's reputation in the abstract, but he saw clearly that a reputable dealer could obtain, and pay, better prices than a common fence. He said so, and Mr. Toke continued :

" To that end, there must be as little contact as possible. I can't have Dobey coming here ; and the less you come here, yourself, the better. We must avoid leaving tracks."

" Certainly," Hughes agreed, " if you can see how to avoid leaving them."

" I think I can. We will go into that presently. But there is another point. We shall simplify matters a great deal if we try to treat one another quite fairly and honestly."

Mr. Hughes's thoughts turned, inevitably, towards

the despoiled clock, and he grinned openly and undisguisedly. Nevertheless, he assented to the proposition. Mr. Toke observed and interpreted the grin,
but continued, unabashed :

" What I mean is, that if the vendor and purchaser
are each content with actual, realizable values, contacts, even by post, will be reduced to a minimum."

Hughes nodded with the air of one waiting for further
details, and Toke continued :

" Supposing, for instance, Dobey submits a parcel of
goods with a specified price. Now, if that price is a fair
one it can be paid, and there is the end of the matter.
But if he makes an excessive claim, the goods must be
returned, or there must be a course of bargaining,
involving, in either case, an undesirable number of
contacts. Or, if he should submit a parcel for an offer,
and I make such an offer as, in my judgment, is the
best that is practicable ; if he accepts that offer
without haggling, again contacts are reduced to a
minimum. You see my point ? "

" Yes, and I agree in principle. One can't do more
until one sees how things work out in practice. How
do you suggest that samples should be submitted ?
You don't want them left by hand, and the post is not
very safe—an accident is always possible. Have
you any plan ? "

" A simple method occurs to me," said Mr. Toke.
" It is this. On receiving notice in some prearranged
manner that a sample is to be delivered, I draw my
car up at night in a quiet place, opposite a blank wall,
with the doors locked, but the rear window open. I
then leave it for a few minutes unattended. It would
be quite easy for a passer-by to drop a small parcel in
at the window unobserved and pass on. A few suitable
localities could be designated by numbers for greater
safety in making arrangements."

Mr. Hughes considered this proposal, and, on the whole, approved.

" It would work all right," said he, " provided both parties keep to the principle of a square deal. Otherwise, the party who dropped his goods into the other man's window would take a biggish risk."

" Quite so," agreed Mr. Toke. " That is why I emphasized the necessity for scrupulous fair dealing on both sides."

They spent some time in settling a few details and in arranging a simple code for use in unavoidable letters. Then Hughes rose as if to depart. But, as he was turning away from the table, he paused and then sat down again.

" There is one little affair that we might settle as I am here," said he. He unbuttoned his coat and from an inner pocket produced a little wash-leather bag. From this he extracted a ring set with a single large emerald and laid it down on the table.

" Any offers ? " he asked.

Mr. Toke took it up and examined it.

" A fine stone," he remarked, approvingly ; " a very fine stone. Well cut, too. These step-cut stones often have the table too large. I can offer you thirty pounds for this ring."

" It is worth a good deal more than that," said Hughes.

" It is," agreed Mr. Toke. " It might fetch sixty at a suitable auction. I will give you forty-five if I may sell it publicly and say where I got it. Is that possible ? "

" No," replied Hughes. " I am selling it on commission, and I don't know where the vendor got it."

" Then," said Toke, " thirty is the outside price. You see, this is an important stone. Someone is sure to have the particulars of it—the measurements and weight—so it could be identified. If I take it, I shall either have to have it re-cut or put it into store for a year or two. Still, you might get a better price from someone else."

Hughes, however, knew that he certainly would not ; having tried a fence, who offered him ten pounds. But he did not mention this fact. He merely replied :

" Very well. I suppose you know best. I'll take thirty, if you can't offer any more."

Accordingly the amount was paid—in cash—and Mr. Hughes took his leave.

.   .   .   .   .

We need not pursue the details of the subsequent transactions. The visible parties to those transactions were Toke and Hughes ; and, as both of them were reasonable men, the necessary conditions were loyally observed and everything went fairly smoothly. Toke made it a rule to give the best prices that were economically possible ; and these were so much better than those obtainable from the regular fences that Hughes found it practicable to purchase illicit goods from certain practitioners other than Dobey, with the result that Mr. Toke was almost embarrassed by the magnitude of the transactions. Yet it was all to the good. For the increased amount of capital at his disposal enabled him not only to make more important purchases in his own legitimate line, but to indulge in the luxury, dear to the true collector's heart, of keeping specially choice pieces which he would otherwise have had to sell.

But it had another effect ; and a very queer effect it was. There was a side to Mr. Toke's character which we have not had occasion to mention, because, in the ordinary affairs of life, it did not show itself. But the fact is, that there was in Mr. Toke's mental make-up a very definite streak of the miser. It was very strange.

In his daily conduct of the common business of life, and even in his domestic affairs, he was a perfectly normal man, with a banking account and investments, an ordered financial system, and a completely rational sense of values. Yet, behind it all was that queer mental twist ; and, when it showed itself, Mr. Didbury Toke was a miser—a genuine miser, too, of the real " Blackberry Jones " brand.

But perhaps it was not so very strange, after all. For Mr. Toke was a born collector ; and what is a miser but a collector of a rather irrational kind ? A collector whose joy is in mere possession, regardless of the qualities—other than intrinsic value—of the things possessed ? At any rate, there it was ; and it must be mentioned because certain consequences, directly traceable to it, have to be recorded hereafter. And, for the same reason, it is necessary to describe briefly the ways in which this queer trait manifested itself.

In the good old days before the war, Mr. Toke was accustomed to keep, in one of the rooms adjoining the gallery at the Manor House, in which his collection was lodged, a drawer filled with sovereigns. It was a secret hoard, not provided for current use, but, like the rest of the collection, a treasure to be enjoyed by mere gloating and contemplation. At night, when the gallery door was locked, he would bring it out and set it on the table. Then, in the genuine " Blackberry Jones " manner, he would sit himself down to gloat over its glittering contents, taking up handfuls of the shining coins or spreading them out on the table in rows or geometrical patterns.

Perhaps there was something to be said for this rather odd pursuit. The sovereign was a handsome coin, particularly as to the reverse, which displayed Pistrucci's magnificent St. George. But, though Mr. Toke was far from unappreciative of Pistrucci's masterpiece, it

was not that work of art which endeared the coins to
his heart, as subsequent events proved. For, in the
days that followed the war, he was compelled to make
inroads on his treasure to carry out some of his foreign
deals, and to furnish himself for his journeys abroad.
Gradually, the golden contents of the drawer dwindled,
until only a hundred or so of the coins were left.

It was at this point that the inflow of ill-gotten
wealth came to his relief. The parcels of jewellery
that Mr. Hughes dropped periodically in through the
window of his car consisted principally of " trade "
articles, which, however valuable intrinsically, were of
no artistic merit. Mr. Toke's procedure was to pick
out the stones and dispose of them through the ordinary
trade channels. Their sale yielded him a modest profit, and with this he was content, at least for a time.
But presently the gold mountings began to accumulate.
If the transactions had been lawful ones, he would
simply have taken these mountings to a bullion dealer
and realized the value of the gold. But the gold
mounts were precisely the most recognizable parts of
the " swag." It was quite impracticable to dispose of
them in the state in which they came to him.

Then he decided to melt them down ; and, to this
end, he provided himself with a small crucible furnace
that burned coke or charcoal—there was no gas at the
Manor House—and was fitted with a foot bellows. He
also obtained a few crucibles, one or two jewellers'
ingot moulds, and the necessary tongs and other imple-
ments ; and with these appliances he set to work to
reduce the miscellaneous collection of stoneless jewellery
to neat little ingots, each of which he carefully marked
with a punch to show its " fineness " in carats.

But even this did not quite solve the difficulty. For,
as we have seen, Mr. Toke was an eminently cautious
gentleman, and it was borne in on him that the sale of

gold ingots on a somewhat considerable scale was a proceeding that might, in the course of time, lead to inconvenient enquiries. He was known as a dealer in stones. But gold ingots were things that needed to be accounted for. He decided, at least for the present, not to run the risk.

So, by degrees, the ingots accumulated. But Mr. Toke was not disturbed. On the contrary, the larger his stock grew—and it grew apace—the less desirous did he become to dispose of it. For a curious change had come over him. Gradually, the affection that he had felt for the sovereigns transferred itself to the growing pile of ingots; and at nights, when he had turned out the surviving remnants of coins from the drawer, he would bring forth the ingots from the cupboard where they were secreted and lay them out on the table or build them up into little stacks. And as the stacks grew steadily in size and number, he would think of his partners and their mysterious activities with pleasant anticipations of yet further additions to his hoard; which was rapidly becoming more real to him than the less visible wealth that was represented by the figures in his bank books and his lists of investments.

Occasionally he found himself speculating on the part that Mr. Hughes played in this curious, unlawful business. Was he a receiver, pure and simple, or was he an actual operator? On the rare occasions when they met, Hughes maintained the most profound reticence. Mr. Toke's view was that Hughes and Dobey formed a small firm to which Hughes contributed the brains and power of contrivance, and Dobey the manual skill and executive ability.

Possibly he was right. At any rate, as we have said, all went well and smoothly, and Dobey, more fortunate than most of his fellow practitioners, continued to keep out of the clutches of the law.

In a remote corridor at the top of a large building in Holborn the rather infrequent visitors might have seen a door, glazed with opaque glass, on which was painted the name of Mr. Arthur Hughes. No further information was vouchsafed; but if the directory had been consulted it would have been ascertained that Mr. Hughes was a patent agent. His practice was not extensive; but still, on certain rare occasions, stray members of that peculiarly optimistic class, prospective patentees, discovered his existence by means of the directory aforesaid, and subjected him to a mild surprise by appearing in his office.

Their visits were not unwelcome; for, though the business that they brought was of little enough value, they rendered possible the keeping of books which could be produced in evidence of a *bona fide* industry.

The visitor, however, who appeared on a certain afternoon was not one of these clients, nor was he connected with the patent industry; being, in fact, none other than Mr. Didbury Toke. Mr. Toke was a good deal out of breath, having climbed the long staircase as a matter of precaution, and now sat panting across the table behind which Mr. Hughes was seated, regarding him with undisguised impatience.

" It's a devil of a way up," said Mr. Toke.

" It is if you are fool enough to walk," was the ungracious reply. " Why the deuce don't you use the lift ? "

" Well," Mr. Toke explained, " one is apt to meet

people in a lift, or at least be seen and possibly remembered, by the lift girl, at any rate. It is better to avoid contacts as far as possible."

" You're mighty careful," said Hughes, sourly. " You're glad enough to mop up the profits of our little enterprises, but you don't mean to take any of the risks."

" Not if I can help it," Toke admitted. " Why should I ? And what good would it be if I did ? "

The question was so obviously reasonable (since the safety of each member of the firm was essential to the well-being of the others) that Hughes was reduced to a non-committal snort ; and might have left it at that had not Toke rather untactfully added : " And I am not aware that you are in the habit of exposing yourself unnecessarily."

Mr. Hughes was apparently in a somewhat irritable state of mind, for he took needless umbrage at this remark.

" Oh," he exclaimed, " so you think so, too, do you ? "

" Too ? " repeated Toke, interrogatively.

" Yes. You are taking up the same position as that infernal Dobey."

" I hope not," said Mr. Toke. " But what is Dobey's position ? "

" In effect the same as yours. He says that he takes all the risks while we take most of the profits."

" I did not say that," Mr. Toke protested. " I admit that I keep out of harm's way to the best of my ability. And, really, I suppose, as a matter of fact, Dobey does take more risks than we do."

" Do you ? " snarled Hughes. " How do you know what risks I take ? "

Mr. Toke had to admit that he knew very little about the matter. " But," he continued, " there is no use in mutual fault-finding. We each have our respective parts to play, and each of us is indispensable to the others."

" That isn't Dobey's view," said Hughes. " I have discovered that he has been doing some jobs on his own, and what is worse, he has found some other market for the swag. He is a slippery devil. Thanks to me, he has been able to work in safety, and do uncommonly well. Now he thinks he knows all there is to know, and he is going to work on his own and stick to all the stuff that he collects—the ungrateful bounder ! "

Mr. Toke expressed his profound disgust at this base conduct of the unappreciative gas-fitter. " But, after all," he added optimistically, " I suppose he is not the only pebble on the beach."

" No," Hughes admitted, " but he is a pretty big pebble, from our point of view. We can't afford to lose his little contributions. But it is not only that. Now that he seems to have gone off on his own, and knows that I have spotted him, he may give us trouble, especially if he should get into a tight place. As I said before, he is a slippery devil. But he had better look out. If I see any signs of his making trouble, I shall make things most unpleasantly lively for him. However, he hasn't starved us out yet. I have got quite a nice little collection from another artist. Got it here, too. I don't usually bring stuff to this place, but I had to, on this occasion. So here it is, all ready for you to take away when we have settled preliminaries."

" Oh, dear ! " exclaimed Mr. Toke, " how very unfortunate ! I can't possibly take it now. I called to tell you that I am just starting on a longish tour on the Continent."

" Well, you'll just have to put off the start for a day. I can't have the stuff here, and I certainly can't store it while you are browsing about the Continent."

"But," protested Mr. Toke, "I have made all my arrangements. I have shut up the wing of my house where I keep my collection and sealed the doors, and I have notified my solicitor that I have started."

"I suppose you can alter your arrangements if you please. You are your own master."

Mr. Toke shook his head, and was about to add some confirmatory remarks when Hughes suddenly lost what little patience he had and broke out, angrily :

"Look here, Toke, you are going to take that stuff. You have got to. I am not going to keep it in store for months. Besides, I want the money for it. There is a hundred and fifty pounds' worth in this parcel. You can look at it now, and, if you are afraid to take it away with you, I will plant it in your car later."

"But," pleaded Toke, "I haven't got my car. I took it to the garage this morning to be overhauled and taken care of while I am away. I should have to go by train with the confounded stuff in a hand-bag."

Mr. Hughes was on the point of demanding what the occasion of the train journey might be, seeing that the "stuff" was presumably to be deposited either at Mr. Toke's bank or in his safe-deposit. That was how he had always understood that Mr. Toke secured his valuables. But the reference to the train journey seemed to offer a rather curious suggestion. And, Mr. Hughes being a decidedly reticent, not to say secretive, gentleman, refrained from either comment or question. But he stuck to his point, and continued to insist that the property must be transferred. If he had done so in a polite and tactful manner, all might have been well. Unfortunately, he adopted a bullying, hectoring tone that jarred heavily on Mr. Toke's already ruffled feelings. As a result, his customary suavity gave place to a slightly forbidding manner.

"I think," he said stiffly, "you misunderstand the

nature of our relations. I purchase from you at my convenience. You are addressing me as if I were some sort of subordinate, as you might address Dobey—who, by the way, doesn't seem to have found your manners endearing."

" He will find them a good deal less endearing if he doesn't take care, and so will you. Don't you come here with your damned superior airs. You are one of the firm, and I am the boss of the firm, and you have got to understand that."

" And suppose I don't accept that relationship ? Suppose I retire from the firm, as you call it, and wash my hands of you ? Would that suit you ? "

" It wouldn't suit you if the police got to know that the eminently respectable Mr. Didbury Toke had been doing a roaring trade in stolen gems."

Mr. Toke's face hardened. " It is a great mistake to utter threats," he said in a warning tone. And then, in total disregard of the admirable principle that he had just laid down, he continued : " And, in fact, it would not suit *you* particularly well if the police should be induced to take an interest in you."

" But they couldn't," retorted Hughes. " You couldn't prove anything against me. I've made it my business to see to that. In regard to this swag, the man who collected it is at one end and the man who marketed it—that's you—is at the other. I don't appear in it at all."

Mr. Toke smiled sourly. " I see," he said, quietly, " that you don't remember me. But my memory is better."

" What the devil do you mean ? " Hughes demanded angrily, but with a startled expression which he failed to control.

" Of course," Mr. Toke continued, calmly, " I am a good deal changed. So are you since the days when you used to have a sandy moustache and a bushy head of hair. But, all the same, I recognized you at the first glance " (which was not quite correct. It had taken him some three months to convert a vague sense of familiarity into a definite identification). " The sight of you carried me back to the time when I used to have connections with the assaying industry, and when a good deal was heard about a certain famous thumb-print."

He stopped rather abruptly—and wished that he had stopped sooner, as he noted the effect of his foolish speech. Hughes did not trouble to contest the state-ment, but sat gazing fixedly at the speaker ; and the concentrated malignity that expressed itself in that look brought Mr. Toke suddenly to his senses. The gentle art of making enemies is an art that is practised only by fools. But Mr. Toke was not a fool, and he cer-tainly did not want to make an enemy of Mr. Hughes. He saw clearly that reconciliation was the necessary policy, and proceeded forthwith to swallow his pride.

" This won't do, Hughes," he said in a conciliatory tone. " We are behaving like a couple of fools. Of course we sink or swim together. I understand that. I was annoyed at having my arrangements upset and lost my temper. Let us have a look at that stuff."

Without a word, Hughes rose and walked across to a small safe which he unlocked and threw open. From some inner recess in it he produced a parcel which he laid on the table. Then he stepped over to the door, and, having slipped the catch of the lock, came back and began methodically to untie the string of the parcel. When the various wrappings were loosened, there was exposed to view a miscellaneous collection of jewellery which Mr. Toke diagnosed as probably the pooled swag from several different robberies. He looked it over with tepid interest, being anxious chiefly to get the business over and bring the rather unpleasant interview to an end.

" Well," he said, " there's nothing sensational about it. You say you want a hundred and fifty for this lot. It's quite enough, but it isn't worth while to haggle over a trifle. I'll give you what you ask. I suppose a cheque won't do for you ? "

" No," Hughes replied gruffly, " of course it won't."

" It's infernally inconvenient," Toke grumbled. " This will eat up the greater part of the cash that I had provided for travelling."

He produced a fat wallet from his pocket, and sorted out its contents ; a process that was watched by Hughes with a curious, avid interest as he retied the string of the parcel.

" Fifteen tens," said Toke. " Will that do ? I would rather keep the fives for use on the road."

As Hughes made no reply, but silently held out his hand, Toke placed in the latter the sheaf of crisp, rustling notes, and closed his wallet, fastening it and returning it to his pocket.

" Now, Hughes," he said as he dropped the parcel into his hand-bag and put on his hat, " let us forget the nonsense that we talked just now and bury the hatchet. We shan't see each other again for a month or two. Don't let us carry away unpleasant memories."

He held out his hand genially, and Hughes, relaxing with an effort the grimness of his expression, took it and gave it a formal shake.

" I suppose," said he, " you will spend the night at Hartsden ? "

" No," replied Toke, " I can't do that. I want to catch the night—or rather early morning—train to Dover."

" You will have some trouble in making the various connections," Hughes remarked. " There aren't so very many trains to and from Hartsden. It is a pity that you didn't keep your car for another hour or two."

" Yes," Toke agreed reflectively. " I think you are right. The trains will be an awkward complication. I rather think that I will just get the car out again or borrow another. That will make me independent of trains."

" But what will you do with the car ? " asked Hughes, who was beginning to take an interest in Toke's movements.

" I dare say I shall be able to run it down to the garage. Or perhaps I shall be able to get a taxi driver to run it round from the station. It will only take him a few minutes."

" Yes," Hughes agreed, " that will be quite simple. And the car will enable you to take your own time. Much better than the suburban trains. Well, so long. I hope you will have a pleasant and profitable trip."

He gave a sort of valedictory grin—the nearest that he could get to the semblance of a friendly smile—and accompanied Toke out into the corridor, where he stood, watching the retreating figure of his associate in iniquity. And, even as he looked, the grin faded from his features and was replaced by a scowl of the most intense malice.

He went back into his office, still scowling forbiddingly, and with the air of one wrapped in profound thought. Which was, in fact, his condition. For Mr. Toke's indiscreet outburst had furnished him with the matter for anxious cogitation. That Toke could or would " blow on " the little transactions that took place between them had never occurred to him. Nor did it now. He had made his position at least as safe as that of Mr. Toke himself. Neither of them could effectively blow on the other. But now it appeared that Mr. Toke could, by merely uttering a few words

in the proper quarter, send him, Mr. Hughes, to a term
of penal servitude. This was quite a different affair.
The sudden appearance of Mr. Toke as a potential
accuser was, to put it very mildly, an extremely disagreeable surprise. Up to this time, Hughes had
believed that one person only in the whole world had
penetrated the very effective disguise with which a
natural affliction had furnished him as a free gift.
For Mr. Hughes's wig was, in any case, a necessity.
An attack of the complaint known as *Alopecia areata*
had produced large bald patches which had to be
covered up by a wig ; and this, together with the loss
of his eyebrows, and aided by the removal of his beard
and moustache, had so metamorphosed him that,
though he avoided all old haunts and old acquaintances,
he was almost completely secure from recognition.
But, as we have said, there was one person who had
appeared, at least, to suspect his identity, and whose
existence kept him in a state of constant watchfulness
and anxiety. And now there was another.

Mr. Hughes was not a scrupulous man ; and if he
was a cautious man, he was ready to take a present
risk for the sake of future safety. In the very moment
when Mr. Toke had foolishly proclaimed his power, he
had made a decision. He was not going to walk abroad
with this everlasting menace at his elbow. One
dangerous enemy was more than enough. Two were
more than could be borne. The plain fact was that
Mr. Toke knew too much ; and that fact pointed to the
obvious remedy. So much Hughes had decided even
while Toke was speaking. The rest was only a question of ways and means.

Apparently, this question also was in course of being
settled, for Mr. Hughes, after pacing up and down the
office for a few minutes, began, in a leisurely and
deliberate fashion, to make certain changes in his

3

visible characteristics that suggested a definite purpose. It is one of the compensations of being compelled to wear a wig that one can choose one's wig and even, on occasion, change it. Of this privilege Mr. Hughes proceeded to avail himself. From a locked drawer in a locked cupboard he took out a wig of a pronounced red and of a fluffy, rather ragged texture, strikingly different from the sleek, dark brown one that he was wearing. Having locked the door, he put on the new wig, and then produced from the drawer a reddish moustache, a small bunch of hair of the same colour, and a bottle of spirit gum. With some of the latter, he anointed the base of the moustache (which was not one of those artless devices used by the amateur actor, but a workmanlike affair, made by a regular theatrical wig-maker) and carefully affixed it to his upper lip with the aid of a small mirror.

When he had fixed it securely in position he cut off some wisps of hair from the bundle, and, having stuck them along the upper margin of the moustache, combed them over the latter and finally trimmed them off with scissors. The effect was extremely realistic ; and when, in the same way, a pair of darkish eyebrows had been attached, the transformation was complete.

But Mr. Hughes was too old a hand to trust a make-up, no matter how excellent, farther than was unavoidable. The afternoon was already merging into evening. Another half-hour and the dusk would have fallen. Then not even close inspection would penetrate the disguise. So Mr. Hughes proceeded with caution. Having tidied up the office, he put away the bottle and the other materials and appliances which he had been using, and was in the act of locking the cupboard when he seemed to remember something that he had forgotten, and hastily reopened the door. Then that something was searched for and found in another

locked drawer ; revealing itself as a sheath-knife of the
kind used by old-fashioned sailors (and commonly
known as a " Green river knife "), furnished with a
narrow waist-strap. Having slipped the knife inside
the waistband of his trousers, he secured it in place by
means of the strap. Then he took a glance at a time-
table and jotted down a few figures on a slip of paper
which he put in his pocket, after which he walked over
to the window and stood for a while, looking down
into the fast-emptying street.

Already the daylight was beginning to fade, and the
quiet of evening was settling down on the city. Judging that the time had come, he emerged cautiously
into the dim corridor, locked the door behind him and
set forth. Emulating Mr. Toke's discretion, he
avoided the lift, taking his way down the unfrequented
staircase, from the bottom of which he hurried along
the lower corridors, and so out into the street. Even
there he preserved his attitude of caution, threading
his way through the quieter back thoroughfares, and
maintaining that incessant watchfulness that has to be
habitual with those who are on unsatisfactory terms
with the law.

By the time that he reached the station the daylight
was visibly weakening. He walked confidently to the
booking-office, where he took a first-class single ticket
to Hartsden Junction, which, as he knew, was some
three-quarters of a mile from the hamlet which gave
it its name. He was by no means unacquainted with
the locality, for, if the truth must be told, he and
Dobey had reconnoitred the neighbourhood with the
idea of a possible nocturnal visit to Mr. Toke's premises
on some occasion when that gentleman was absent
on one of his periodical excursions abroad. That
visit had never been made, for the reason that Mr.
Toke had let it be very clearly understood that he

kept on those premises nothing but the "pieces" that formed his collection—porcelain figures, bronzes, and other objects, valuable enough in themselves, but of no use to merchants of the class to which Hughes and Dobey belonged. All negotiable property, he had explained, was kept securely in the strong room of his bank or in the safe that he rented at the safe-deposit establishment ; and this had seemed such an obvious precaution that both rascals had accepted the statement and abandoned the idea of the nocturnal raid.

But now, by the light of the admission that Mr. Toke had so incautiously made, that he was proposing to convey this parcel of stolen property to his house, evidently with the intention of leaving it there during his absence abroad, Mr. Hughes began to reconsider the situation. The main object of his journey was not irreconcilable with certain other transactions ; and, as he was borne by the fast express to the neighbourhood of Mr. Toke's residence, he turned over quite a number of interesting possibilities.

The night had definitely fallen when Mr. Hughes approached the hamlet of Hartsden by the road from the Junction. He looked about him with his habitual wariness, but there was little need ; for, as he passed through the single street, not a soul was to be seen, and, but for the lighted windows, the place might have been uninhabited. Beyond the hamlet the old manor house stood in dignified isolation, and adjoining it was the disused churchyard, enclosing the ruinous church —now also disused and replaced by a new building at the other end of the village.

It was towards the churchyard that Hughes directed his steps, making for the gateway without hesitation as if by a considered plan. On arriving there, he paused for a moment to glance down the road—of which the gateway commanded a clear view ; then he pushed open the rickety gate and entered. Slowly he walked along the narrow path that led to the church, looking back from time to time to see that he still had an uninterrupted view of the road. Presently the path turned slightly to the right, and, passing into the shadow of a great yew tree, was encompassed by darkness so complete that Hughes was able only with the greatest difficulty to grope his way along it. Here, by the side of a large sarcophagus tomb which stood between the yew tree and the wall, he stopped and looked about him. Finding that the road was now no longer in sight, he slowly retraced his steps until he was able once more to look out through the gateway along the road that formed the only approach to the village. And here he selected a spot where he could keep a look-out, secure from the observation of any chance wayfarer who might pass along from the village.

He was prepared for a long vigil, for it was possible that Toke might be delayed ; and, in any case, the car would take considerably longer to cover the distance than the fast train by which Hughes had travelled. To beguile the time, he produced his cigarette-case and took out a cigarette. But his habitual caution warned him not to light it in view of the road. Accordingly, he retired past the yew tree into the darkest corner of the churchyard, behind the great tomb, and there, crouching low against the plinth of the tomb, he struck a match, held it for a moment to the cigarette and blew it out. But even then he held the cigarette shrouded in his hand ; and when he returned to his look-out, he was careful to ensconce himself behind the tall headstone that he had selected as cover so that the glow of the cigarette should not be visible from outside.

But it was a tedious business, waiting in the gloom of the darkening churchyard for the coming of the man who could send him to penal servitude. And it was rendered none the more pleasant by a somewhat acute anxiety. For, though he had a perfectly clear purpose, the carrying into effect of that purpose could not be planned in exact detail. The precise method of procedure must be determined by Mr. Toke's actions; and these could not be foreseen.

Time ran on. One by one, the lights in the windows of the few houses that were visible from the churchyard went out, and the chime of the clock in the new church at the end of the village, borne faintly on the night air, told out quarter after quarter. It was just striking the hour of ten when Hughes, having lighted his sixth cigarette, came out from behind the sarcophagus tomb and crept back to his look-out; and at that moment the lights of a car came into sight far away down the road.

Hughes was not a nervous man. But the message that those glimmering lights conveyed to him set his heart thumping and his hands trembling so that the cigarette dropped unheeded from his fingers. It is one thing to contemplate an atrocious deed from afar, but quite another to feel the irrevocable moment of action drawing nigh. With a feeling of shuddering dread, but yet never for an instant abandoning his dreadful intent, he watched the lights gradually wax brighter until the approaching car was actually entering the village. Apparently it was fitted with a powerful but silent engine, for no throb or hum of mechanism was borne to his ears.

Suddenly the lights went out, and for a few moments the car was perceptible neither to eye nor ear. Then it became faintly visible as a dim spot of deeper darkness. Nearer and nearer it came, now growing into a defined shape, and recognizable as a large, closed car. Hughes craned out from behind the headstone to watch it as it passed the gate. But it did not pass the gate. Just as it reached the farther wall of the churchyard, it slowed down suddenly and turned off to the left and was instantly lost to view.

To Hughes, in his state of extreme nervous tension, this unexpected behaviour was highly disconcerting. He had assumed that Mr. Toke would drive up to his gate, get out, and open it, and then run the car up the drive to the door of the house. Much puzzled and somewhat alarmed, he crept out from behind the headstone and began to steal softly and cautiously down the path towards the gate. But he had gone only a few steps when he was startled by the sudden appearance of Mr. Toke within a few paces of the gate and walking briskly towards it with the evident intention of entering the churchyard.

Sweating and trembling from the sudden shock, Hughes staggered back to the headstone and crouched down behind it, cursing silently and for the moment overcome by terror. A step or two more and he must have been seen ; and who could say what would have happened then ? Toke could hardly have failed to grasp the situation ; and Toke was no weakling. It had been a near thing.

From his lurking-place he saw Mr. Toke, hand-bag in hand, walk up the path with the assured manner of a man who is making for a definite destination. When he had passed the headstone Hughes craned out to watch the retreating figure ; and, as it disappeared into the darkness under the yew tree, he rose and followed stealthily, crouching low to keep out of sight among the crowded tombstones. Presently he halted just at the edge of the patch of shadow and watched from the shelter of a crumbling tomb that was enclosed by an ivy-covered railing. From the impenetrable darkness under the yew tree there came a faint grinding or creaking sound. It lasted but a few moments, but, after a brief interval it was repeated. After yet another short interval, Hughes rose and came out from behind the railed tomb. Then he, too, disappeared into the darkness under the yew tree.

The minutes passed, but no sound came from that eerie corner of the churchyard over which the yew tree cast its sinister shadow. The clock of the distant church told out a quarter and then another. The reverberations of the bell had just died away when the silence was broken once more by that curious faint grinding or creaking sound. It was followed, almost immediately, by what sounded like a muffled cry. Again there was a brief space of silence. Then the grinding sound was repeated. And, after that, again silence.

The time ran on. Save for the murmur of the trees, as the leaves were gently stirred by the soft breeze, and the faint, indefinite voices of the night, not a sound disturbed the stillness that brooded over the church-yard. Away in the distance, the clock of the new church made its announcements to the sleeping village of the passage of the minutes that perish for us and are reckoned. But among the grey headstones and under the solemn yew tree, nothing stirred and no sound broke in to disturb the peace of the dead.

So the time passed, measured out impassively, quarter by quarter, by the distant chimes. More than an hour had slipped away since those two figures had been swallowed up in the dark cavernous depths under the yew tree, when the silence of the night was at last broken by the faint grinding creak. After the lapse of a few seconds, it was repeated. Then a figure appeared creeping stealthily out of the shadow and down the path towards the gate, which, as it emerged into the dim light, revealed itself as that of Mr. Hughes.

There was something curiously secret and furtive

in his demeanour. He walked slowly, setting down his
foot at each step with evident care to make no sound,
and every few seconds he paused to listen and look
about him. Thus he crept down to the gate, where
again he halted and stood, listening intently and gazing
into the darkness, first up the village street, and then
across at the old manor house, sleeping among its trees.
But it seemed that in the whole village there was no
living creature besides himself waking and moving.

From the gate he turned to the right, and, in the
same silent, furtive manner, stole along the wall of the
churchyard towards the place into which the car had
seemed to disappear. Short as the distance was, it
seemed interminable in the agony of suspense that
possessed him. For the car was indispensable. It
had been the keystone of his plan—the appointed means
of safety and escape. But suppose it had been seen,
or, still worse, taken away ! The fearful possibility
brought the sweat afresh to his already clammy brow,
and set his trembling limbs shaking so that he staggered
like a drunken man.

At length he reached the corner of the wall. Beside
the churchyard ran a narrow, leafy lane, enclosed
between the high wall and a tall hedge-row, and as
dark as a cellar. He peered desperately into the dense
obscurity, but at first could see nothing. With
throbbing heart he stole up the lane as quickly as he
dared, still craning eagerly forward into the darkness,
yet still careful not to trip on the rough ground.
Suddenly he gave a gasp of relief ; for, out of the darkness ahead, a shape of deeper darkness emerged, and,
as he hurried forward, he recognized the big covered
car with which he had had so many dealings in the
past.

Shaken as he was, he still had all his wits about him,
and he realized that there must be no false start.

3*

Once he was on the move, he must get straight away from the neighbourhood. It would never do to be held up on the road by any failure of the engine or other occasion of delay. Accordingly, he went over all the working parts with the aid of a small electric lamp that he produced from his pocket and satisfied himself that all was in order. Then he threw the light back along the lane to see that the way was clear for steering out in reverse. That was the immediate difficulty. There seemed to be no room to turn round. He would have to back out ; and to back out at the first attempt.

At length he prepared for the actual start. Getting into the driver's seat, he switched on the lights and the ignition and pressed the electric starter. Instantly, the silence was shattered by a roar that seemed fit to rouse the whole countryside, and brought the sweat streaming down his face. Still, though the hand that held the steering wheel shook as if with a palsy, he kept his wits under control. The lane was practically straight and the car had been run straight in. By the dim light of the rear lamp he could see through the rear window well enough to back the car down the lane to the road.

At last, he was out in the open, as he could see by the light from the front lamps shining on the corner of the churchyard wall. He put the steering-wheel over and started forward, now quite noiselessly, through the village street and so out on to the London road.

.   .   .   .   .

It was getting on for two o'clock when he drove into the small car-park attached to the garage.

" Late, ain't you ? " said the night watchman. " They told me Mr. Toke was going to bring her back by half-past eleven. Did he miss his train ? "

" No," replied Hughes. " He caught his train all

right. It was my fault. I had to go somewhere else
and couldn't bring her along any sooner."

"Well," was the philosophical response, "better
late than never."

"Very much better," Hughes agreed. "Good
night—or rather, good morning."

He paused for a moment to light a cigarette, and then
walked out into the street and was lost to sight.

BOOK II
INSPECTOR BADGER DECEASED

MR. SUPERINTENDENT MILLER was by no means an emotional man. He had his moments of excitement or irritation, but in general he was a person of a calm exterior, and gave the impression of one not easily ruffled. That was my view of him, born of years of intimacy. But the Superintendent Miller whom I admitted to our chambers in response to a somewhat peremptory knock was a new phenomenon. His flushed, angry face and lowering brow told us at once that something quite out of the ordinary had occurred, and we looked at him expectantly without question or remark. Nor was there any occasion for either ; for, without seating himself or even taking off his hat, he came instantly to the point.

" I want you two gentlemen to come with me at once, if you can. I've got a car waiting. And I want you to bring all your wits and knowledge to bear on this case as you never brought them before."

Thorndyke looked at him in surprise. " What is it, Miller ? " he asked.

The Superintendent frowned at him fiercely, and replied in a voice husky with passion : " It is Badger. He has been murdered. And I look to you two gentlemen as officers of the law to strain every nerve in helping us to bring the crime home to the villain who committed it."

We were profoundly shocked ; and we could easily understand—and indeed share—his wrathful determination to lay hands on the murderer. It is true that

Inspector Badger had been no favourite with any of the three of us. His personal qualities had not been endearing. But now this was forgotten. He had been, in a sense, an old friend, if at times he had seemed a little like an enemy. But especially, he was a police officer ; and to a normally constituted Englishman, a police officer's life is something even more sacred than the life of an ordinary man. For the police are the guardians of the safety of us all. The risks that they accept with quiet, matter-of-fact courage are undertaken that we may walk abroad in security and rest at night in peace and confidence. Well may we feel, as we do, that the murder of a police officer is at once an outrage on the community and on every member of it.

" You may take it, Miller," said Thorndyke, " that we are at your command, heart and soul. Where do you want us to go ? "

" Greenhithe. That is where the body is lying and where the murder must have been committed. There is a fairly good train in a quarter of an hour, and the car will get us to the station in five minutes. Can you come ? "

" We must," was the reply ; and without another word Thorndyke rose and ran up to the laboratory to notify our assistant, Polton, of our sudden departure. In less than a minute he returned with his " research case " in his hand, and announced that he was ready to start ; and as I had already made the few preparations which were necessary, we went down to the car.

During our brief journey to the station nothing was said. As we arrived at the platform from the booking-office, the train came alongside, and the passengers poured out. We took up our position opposite a first-class coach, and, when the fresh passengers had all bestowed themselves and the train was on the point of starting, we entered an empty compartment and shut ourselves in.

" It is very good of you gentlemen," said Miller, as the train gathered speed, " to come off like this at a moment's notice, especially as I have not given you any inkling of the case. But there will be plenty of time for me to tell you all I know, which isn't very much at present. Probably we shall pick up some fresh details at Greenhithe. My present information is limited to what we have heard over the telephone from there and from Maidstone. This is what it amounts to.

" Yesterday morning poor Badger went down to Maidstone to look over a batch of prisoners for the assizes and see if there were any old acquaintances lurking under an alias. But principally his object was to inspect a man who had given the name of Frederick Smith, but whom he suspected of being a certain crook whose real name was unknown to us. We were a good deal interested in this man. For various reasons we associated him with a number of burglaries of a rather clever type—one-man jobs, which are always the most difficult to deal with if they are efficiently carried out. And we had something to go on in one case, for Badger saw the man making off. However, he got away, and neither he nor the stuff was ever traced. So our position was that here was a man whom we suspected of quite an important series of crimes, but who was, so to speak, in the air. He was not even a name. He was just a ' person unknown.' Whether we had his finger-prints under some name we couldn't guess, because nobody knew him by sight excepting Badger ; and his opinion was that the man had never been in custody, and couldn't be identified—excepting by himself."

" But," said I, " surely Badger could have put a description of him on record."

" M'yes," replied Miller. " But you know what Badger

was like. So beastly secretive. One doesn't like to
say it now, but he really didn't play the game. If he
got a bit of information, instead of passing it round for
the benefit of the force and the public, he would keep it
to himself in the hope of bringing off a striking coup and
getting some kudos out of it. And he did bring it off
once or twice, and got more credit than he deserved.
But to come back to this Maidstone business. Badger
gleaned something from the reports concerning the
prisoners there that made him suspect that this man,
Smith, might be the much-wanted burglar. So down
he went, all agog to see if Smith was the man he had
once got a glimpse of."

" I shouldn't think a recognition of that kind, based
on a mere passing glance, would have much value as
evidence," I objected.

" Not in court," Miller admitted. " But it would
have had considerable weight with us. Badger had a
devil of a memory for faces, and we knew it. That was
his strong point. He was like a snapshot camera.
A single glance at a face and it was fixed on his memory
for ever."

" Do you know if he recognized the man ? " Thorndyke asked.

" He didn't," replied Miller, " for the man wasn't
there. In some way he had managed to do a bolt ; and
up to the present, so far as I know, they have not been
able to find him. It is quite likely that he has got
clean away, for, as he was wearing his own clothes, he
won't be very easy to track. However, Badger seems
to have satisfied himself that the man was really the one
he was looking for—probably he thought he recognized
the photographs—and this morning he started for
Town with the papers—the personal description, photographs, and finger-prints—for examination and comparison at the Criminal Record Office. But he never

arrived ; and about eleven o'clock his body was found
near the middle of the Greenhithe tunnel. The engine
driver of an up train saw it lying across the rails on the
down side, and reported as soon as he got into Greenhithe. But it seemed that at least one train had been
over it by then. I gather that—but there ! I don't
like to think of it. Poor old Badger ! "

" No," Thorndyke agreed sympathetically. " It is
too horrible to think of. But still, as we have to investigate and ascertain what really happened, we must
put aside our personal feelings and face the facts,
terrible as they are. You spoke of his having been
murdered. Do you know if there were any signs,
apart from the mutilation caused by the train passing
over him, that he had met a violent death ? Is it clear
that it was not an accident ? "

" Quite clear, I think," replied Miller. " I know
nothing about the condition of the body, but I know
that there was no open door on the off side of the train
that he travelled by."

" That would seem to be conclusive," said Thorndyke, " if the fact can be established. But it isn't
always easy to prove a negative. A passenger, getting
into an empty compartment and finding the door open,
would naturally shut it and might not report the circumstance. The point will have to be enquired into."

" Yes," Miller agreed ; " but I don't think there is
much doubt. You must remember that the train
passed through Greenhithe station and past the signal
boxes both there and at Dartford. An open door on
the off side would be very noticeable from the down
platforms. Still, as you say, the point will have to
be settled definitely. Probably it has been by now.
We shall hear what they have to say when we get to
Greenhithe. But for my part I have no doubt at all,
door or no door. Badger was not the sort of fool who

leans out of the window of a moving train without
seeing that the door is fastened. It is a case of murder,
and the murderer has got to be found and dealt
with."

If the Superintendent may have seemed to have
formed a very definite opinion on rather slender evidence, that opinion received strong confirmation when
we reached Greenhithe. Awaiting us on the platform
were a detective sergeant and one of the senior officers
from Maidstone Prison. They had travelled up from
Maidstone together, apparently comparing notes and
making enquiries by the way.

" Well, sir," said the Sergeant, " I think we can
exclude the suggestion of accident, positively and
certainly. It was unlikely on the face of it. But we
have got some definite facts that put it out altogether.
This officer, Chief Officer Cummings, whose duties
include all matters relating to descriptions and records,
handed to Inspector Badger the papers relating to the
prisoner, Frederick Smith—finger-prints, description,
and photographs—and saw him put them into his
letter wallet. Now, I have been through that wallet
with the greatest care, and there is not a trace of any
of those papers in the wallet or in any of his pockets."

" Ha ! " exclaimed Miller in a tone of grim satisfaction, " that settles it. I take it, Cummings, that there
is no possible doubt that the Inspector had those
papers in his pocket when he started from Maidstone ?"

" Not a shadow of doubt, sir," replied Cummings.
" I gave him the papers, carefully folded, and saw him
put them into his wallet—just into the open wallet,
as they were too large to go into the pockets without
further folding. He stowed the wallet away in his
inside breast pocket and buttoned his coat. And I can
swear that it was in his pocket when he started, for I
walked with him to the station and actually saw him

into the train. He asked me to walk down with him,
as there were various questions that he wanted to put
to me respecting the prisoners, especially this man,
Smith."

" Yes," said Miller, " we shall have to have a talk
about Mr. Smith presently. But the fact that the
Inspector had those papers on his person when he got
into the train, and that they were not on the body,
makes it certain that he was not alone in the carriage."

" It does, sir," the Sergeant agreed. " But apart
from that, we have got direct evidence that he was not.
The station-master at Strood gave us the particulars.
The Inspector's train stopped there, and he had to get
out and wait a few minutes for the London train. The
station-master saw him standing on the platform, and,
as they knew each other, he went up to him, and they
had a few words together. While they were chatting
the London train came in and drew up at the platform.
Inspector Badger was just moving off to find a compartment when a man came along from the entrance.
As soon as the Inspector saw this man, he stopped
short and stood watching him. The man walked rather
quickly along the train, looking in at the windows, and
got into an empty first-class smoking compartment.
But the station-master noticed that, before he got in,
he looked into each of the adjoining compartments,
which were both empty. As soon as he had got in and
shut the door after him, the Inspector wished the
station-master ' Good morning,' and began to saunter
slowly towards the compartment that the stranger had
got into. A few paces away from it he stopped and
waited until the guard blew his whistle. Then he
walked forward quickly and got into the compartment
where the strange man was."

" Could the station-master give you any description
of this man ? "

"No, sir. No description that would be of any use. He said he was a middle-aged man of about medium height, not noticeably stout or thin, moderately well-dressed in a darkish suit, and wearing a soft felt hat. He thought that the man had darkish red hair and rather a red nose. But that isn't very distinctive. And he thought he was clean-shaved."

"Did you ask him if he would know the man again if he saw him?"

"I did, sir, and he said that he might or he might not, but he didn't think he would, and he certainly wouldn't swear to him."

The Superintendent emitted a growl of dissatisfaction, and, turning to the Chief Officer, asked: "What do you say, Cummings? Does the description suggest anything to you?"

The officer smiled deprecatingly. "I suppose, sir, you are thinking of Frederick Smith, and it does seem likely. Smith certainly has darkish red hair and a reddish nose. And he is about that age and about that height and he hasn't got a beard, and when I last saw him he was wearing a darkish suit and a soft felt hat. So it might have been Smith. But as the description would apply to a good many men that you might meet, it isn't much good for identification."

"No," growled Miller, "not enough details. And now that the finger-prints and detailed description are gone, it might be difficult to prove his identity even if we should get hold of him."

"It isn't as bad as that, sir," said Cummings. "As it happens, luckily, we have a duplicate of the finger-prints, at least of some of them. The officer who took the finger-prints made rather a mess of one of the rolled impressions. So he had to waste that form and start over again. Fortunately, the spoiled form wasn't destroyed. So we've got that, and of course we've got the negatives of the photographs, and the officer who took the description can remember most of the items. There will be no difficulty in proving the identity if we can get hold of the man. And that ought not to be so very difficult, either. There are several of us who have seen him and could recognize him."

The Superintendent nodded. " That's all to the good," said he ; " but before we can recognize him we've got to find him. The train didn't stop here, I understand."

" No, sir," the Sergeant replied. " The first stop after Strood was Dartford. We've been over there, but we had no luck. There were a lot of people waiting for the train, so the platform was pretty crowded, and it was not easy to see who got out of the train. None of the porters noticed any first-class passengers getting out, though there must have been one, for a first-class ticket was collected—from Maidstone."

" Maidstone ! " exclaimed Miller. " Well, that couldn't have been our man. He came on to the Strood platform from the entrance."

" So the station-master says. But the booking-office clerk there doesn't remember issuing any first-class ticket, or any ticket at all to Dartford."

" Hm," grunted Miller. " Looks rather as if he didn't get out at Dartford. May have chanced it and gone on to London. We must have all the tickets checked. Did you make any enquiries from the ticket collector ? "

" Yes, sir. But it was no go. He hadn't noticed any of the passengers particularly. Two or three of the men who passed out answered the station-master's description more or less. Of course they would. But he didn't really remember what any of them was like, and he couldn't say whether either of them was a first-class passenger. I suppose he just looked at the tickets and didn't see anything else."

"Yes," Miller agreed. "But we will go into this matter presently. We mustn't keep these gentlemen waiting." He turned to Thorndyke and asked : "What would you like to do first, Doctor ? I suppose you will want to inspect the tunnel, and I should like you to take a look at the body."

"The body has been examined, sir," said the Sergeant, "by one of the local doctors. He was rather cautious in his opinions, but I understood that he found no marks of violence—no wounds or injuries excepting the accidental ones."

"Where is the body ? " the Superintendent asked.

"In an empty store, sir, down below. They put it there out of sight until it could be moved to the mortuary."

Miller looked at us enquiringly, and Thorndyke reflected for a few moments.

"I think we had better take the tunnel first and see if we can pick up any traces from which we can gather a hint. It isn't very likely. The inside of the carriage, if we could have identified and examined it, would have been more hopeful as a source of information. However, the carriage is not available and the tunnel is. Will it be safe to explore it now ? "

As he asked the question he glanced at the station-master, who took out his watch and consulted it.

"There is a down train due in a couple of minutes," said he. "We had better let that go through. Then the line will be clear for a full hour on the down side."

"You have pretty long intervals," Miller remarked.

"We have," the station-master admitted, "but they will be a good deal shorter when the electrification is completed. At present only the steam trains come on from Dartford. There goes the signal."

We waited until the train had drawn up at the platform, discharged its two or three passengers and proceeded on its way. Then we walked on to the end of the platform, descended to the permanent way, and, marching in a procession, headed by the stationmaster, along the rough side-path, presently entered the mouth of the tunnel, advancing along the space between the down-side rails and the smoke-blackened wall.

There is always something rather eerie about a tunnel, even a comparatively short and straight one like that at Greenhithe, in which the light is never completely lost. It is not the obscurity only or the strange reverberating quality that the vaulted roof imparts to the voice. The whole atmosphere is weird and uncanny, there is a sense of remoteness from the haunts of living men, heightened by the ghostly, whispering sounds which pervade the air, confused and indistinguishable echoes from the far-away world of light and life.

The light from the entrance followed us quite a long way, throwing our indefinitely elongated shadows into the twilight before us until they were lost in the deeper gloom ahead. Gradually, the warm glow of the station-master's lantern and the whiter circles of light from the electric lamps carried by Thorndyke and the Superintendent replaced the dwindling daylight and told us we were approaching the middle of the tunnel. The combined lights of the three lamps illuminated the ground with a brilliancy that was accentuated by the encompassing darkness, lighting up the rails and sleepers and the stones of the ballast, and bringing into view all the little odds and ends of litter that had been jettisoned from passing trains ; scraps of newspaper, match-boxes, spent matches, cigarette-ends—trivial by-products of civilized human life, insignificant and worthless, but each scanned attentively by six pairs of eyes.

It was in the heart of the tunnel that Miller remarked —in a hollow voice with an accompaniment of chattering echoes :

" Someone has chucked away a pretty good cigar. Shocking waste.   He hasn't smoked a quarter of it."

He spoke feelingly, for it was just the type of cigar that he favoured : a big, dark-coloured cigar of the Corona shape.   Thorndyke let the light from his inspection lamp fall on it for an instant, but he made no reply, and we continued our slow progress.   But, a few moments later, I suddenly missed the light from his lamp (we were marching in single file and he brought up the rear of the procession), and, looking round, I saw that he had gone back and was in the act of picking up the cigar with his gloved left hand.   As he evidently did not wish his proceedings to be noticed by the others, I continued to walk on at a slightly reduced pace until he overtook me, when I observed that he had carefully enclosed the cigar in two of the seed envelopes that he invariably carried, and was now tenderly wrapping it in his handkerchief before disposing of it in his breast pocket.

" Any special significance in that cigar ? " I asked.

" It is impossible to say," he replied.   " A half-smoked cigar must have some significance.   It is for us to see whether it has any significance for us."

The answer was a little cryptic and left me with the suspicion that it did not really disclose the motive for his evidently considered act.   To one unacquainted with Thorndyke and his methods of research, the salving of this scrap of jetsam must have appeared entirely foolish, for there seemed no more reason for taking and preserving this cigar than for collecting the various empty match-boxes and cigarette-packages that lay strewn around.

But I knew Thorndyke and his ways as no one else knew him. I knew that it was his principle to examine everything. But the word " everything " has to be construed reasonably. There was always some selection in the objects that he examined ; and I had the feeling that this cigar had presented to him something more than its mere face value.

So I reflected as we walked on slowly, scanning the ballast by the light of our lamps. But no other object came into view to engage our attention until we reached the spot where the tragedy had occurred. Here we halted with one accord and stood looking down in silence at the gruesome traces of the disaster. Miller was the first to break the silence.

" There seems to have been a lot of blood. Doesn't that suggest that he was alive when the train went over him ? "

" Yes," replied Thorndyke, " in a general way, it does. But we shall be able to judge better from an examination of the body." Then, turning to the station-master, he asked : " How long could he have been lying on the line when the down train came along ? "

" Not more than a minute," was the reply. " Perhaps not that. The two trains passed in the tunnel."

" And how was the body lying ? You came with the search party, I think ? "

" Yes, I directed the search party. The body was lying across the rails slantwise with the feet towards the Greenhithe end. It was lying nearly on its back. But, of course, the train passing over it may have changed its position. Still, it is rather curious that the feet should have been pointing that way. If a man steps out of a moving train, his feet come to the ground and catch, and he flies forward head first. The position of the body almost seemed to suggest that he fell out head downwards."

" Yes," agreed Thorndyke. " But there isn't much in it, for he certainly did not step out. And a man who falls out by the unexpected opening of the door may fall in almost any position. Have you had any detailed report from the driver of the down train ? "

" Yes. I had a talk with him when he brought the train back from New Brompton. But he had very little to tell. He never saw the body at all, and he wouldn't have known of the accident if it hadn't been for the chance that the fireman happened to look over the near side of the foot-plate and caught just a passing glimpse of a pair of feet sticking out from under the engine. He shouted out as soon as he saw them, but of course there was nothing to be done. It was a fast train, and it couldn't have been pulled up in its own length, even if that would have been any good."

" And where did he pass the up train ? "

" He was just passing the rear of it when the fireman shouted."

" Did he notice any open door ? "

" No. But that is not to say that there was not an open door. He didn't really see the other train at all. They had just opened the furnace door and the light from that must have dazzled him. It was the light from the furnace reflected from the roof and walls of the tunnel that enabled the fireman to see the body."

" It is unnecessary to ask in what part of the train Badger was travelling," said Thorndyke. " He must have been near the front unless it was a very long train."

" It was rather a long train," said the Sergeant. " The station-master at Strood told us that, though he couldn't say exactly how many coaches there were.

Of course, we can easily find out, and we shall have to. But he was able to tell us where Inspector Badger's compartment was. It was right up in front, in the second coach—rather an unusual position for a first-class compartment."

While this interrogation was proceeding, we had been walking on slowly towards the east end of the tunnel, scrutinizing the ground as we went but without any further result. We now came out into the open in a deepish cutting, and, on the station-master's advice, continued our examination of the permanent way as far as Swanscombe Halt; but nothing came into view that threw any light on the tragedy. At the halt we waited a few minutes for an up train that was then due, in which we travelled back to Greenhithe; an arrangement that not only saved time and effort, but gave Thorndyke the opportunity of observing, with his head out of the window, the conditions of light prevailing in the tunnel and the visibility of one part of the train from the others.

As we came out on to the platform at Greenhithe, Miller looked wistfully at my colleague.

"Did you think of having a look at the body, Doctor?" he asked, adding: "I should feel more satisfied if you would. A local doctor hasn't had the experience of criminal cases that you and Dr. Jervis have."

"I don't suppose that the local doctor would have missed any signs that bore on the cause of death," said Thorndyke. "But still, an additional examination is at least an extra precaution. Perhaps the station-master will direct someone to show us the way."

The station-master elected to show us the way himself, and preceded us down the stairs. Reluctantly, I followed Thorndyke, leaving the others on the platform; and, as I descended the stairs, I was, for the first time in my professional life, conscious of a shrinking repugnance to the atmosphere of tragedy and death. After all, a doctor has his human feelings. It is impossible to look on the mutilated corpse of an old acquaintance as the mere " subject " of an investigation. But, as a matter of fact, I took no part in the actual examination. I saw that the body still lay on the tarpaulin-covered stretcher and that part of the clothing had been removed, but I stood aloof by the door, leaving the inspection to Thorndyke ; who evidently realized my state of mind, for he made his examination in silence and with no suggestion that I should join him.

One thing, however, I did observe, and with considerable surprise. When he had completed his examination of the body, he opened his research case and took from it the portable finger-print outfit that formed part of its permanent equipment. Taking out the ready-inked copper plate and a couple of cards, he proceeded, in his neat, methodical way, to make a set of ten prints, one of each digit.

" Why are you taking his finger-prints ? " I asked. " Does anything hinge on them ? "

" Not at present," he replied. " But it is possible that some finger-prints may be found ; and, if they should be, it might be very important to be able to say whether they were or were not Badger's. So I am securing the means of comparison while they are available."

Thus stated, the motive for the proceeding seemed reasonable enough ; but yet the explanation left me wondering if there was not something more definite in Thorndyke's mind. And this vague suspicion was strengthened when, as I helped him to repack the research case, I saw him deposit in it, and pack with extreme care, the derelict cigar which he had picked up in the tunnel. But I made no comment, and as the gruesome business was now completed, I took up the research case and led the way out of the store.

"Apparently," he said as we ascended the stairs, "the local practitioner was right. There are no signs of any injuries that might have been inflicted before he fell on the line. But one thing is clear. He was certainly alive when the train ran over him and for at least a few seconds after."

"Then," said I, "it might really have been an accident."

"So far as the appearances and condition of the body are concerned, it might. But if there was another person in the compartment and that person has not reported an accident, the probabilities are overwhelmingly in favour of either a crime or what we may call an incriminating misadventure."

"What do you mean by an incriminating misadventure?" I asked.

"I mean a misadventure which would probably not have been accepted as such. Miller believes that the other passenger was the escaped prisoner, Frederick Smith. Suppose that Miller is right. Suppose that Badger recognized the man and tried to arrest him. That the man resisted and a struggle occurred. I don't see why it should unless Badger had handcuffs with him and tried to put them on. But suppose a struggle to have occurred, in the course of which the door became unfastened and Badger fell out. That would have been a pure misadventure. But it is not likely that the man would have reported it, for he would realize the improbability of his statement being believed. He would trust rather to the probability of his presence in the carriage being unknown."

"I have no doubt that he would," I agreed, "and wisely, too. For no one would believe his statement.

He would be charged with murder and most probably
convicted. But you don't entertain the possibility
of a misadventure, do you ? "

" As a bare possibility, yes. But it is wildly improbable ; and still more so if those documents were
really in Badger's pocket and have really disappeared.
That is a crucial point. For, if it is certain that they
were removed from the wallet, that is not only evidence
of a conflict having taken place, but suggests in the
strongest possible way that Badger had been rendered
unconscious or helpless. But that suggestion at once
raises the question, How was he rendered unconscious
or helpless ? The state of the body seems to exclude
physical violence such as throttling or a knock on the
head. Yet it is difficult to think of any other means."

" Very difficult," I agreed, " particularly in the
alleged circumstances—the casual and unexpected
meeting of two men in a railway carriage ; and if one
of those men was, as the theft of the documents seems
to imply, a man just escaped from prison, the difficulty
is still greater. Such a man would, presumably, be
unprovided with anything but his fists ; indeed, the
mystery is how he could have procured his ticket."

" Yes," Thorndyke assented, " that calls for explanation. But we must not mix up hypothesis and fact.
Miller assumes that the man was the prisoner, Smith,
and it is possible that he was. But we must not let
that possibility influence us. We have to approach the
inquiry with a perfectly open mind."

As he concluded, we came out on to the platform,
where we found our friends awaiting us. In a few
words Thorndyke communicated to them the results of
his inspection, at which Miller was visibly disappointed.

" It is an extraordinary thing," said he. " Badger
was a pretty hefty fellow and a skilled wrestler and
boxer. I can't imagine even a strong man putting him

out through the door unless he had disabled him
first. And, in any case, you would expect to find some
signs of a scrap. Did you propose to make any
further examination ? "

" It doesn't seem very necessary," Thorndyke replied. " But perhaps you might like me to be present
when the local doctor does the post-mortem. There
are other possibilities besides gross physical injury."

" That is what I was thinking," said Miller ; " and
I *should* be glad if you could be present at the post-
mortem. Then I could feel satisfied that nothing had
been overlooked. I understand that the inquest is to
be held to-morrow afternoon at four o'clock and the
post-mortem at two. Can you manage that ? "

" I shall have to, if you think it important," was
the reply.

As Miller was making grateful acknowledgments,
the station-master approached to convey to us the
welcome tidings that a fast train to London was due in
a few minutes.

" Are you coming back with us, Superintendent ? "
Thorndyke asked.

" I may as well," Miller replied. " The Sergeant will
carry on with the case, and I must set some inquiries
going at the London end. And, by the way, Cummings,
are you returning to Maidstone to-day ? "

" Yes, sir," answered the Chief Officer. " I shall
take the next train back."

" Then," said Miller, " you had better have those
finger-prints of Smith's photographed and send either
the photographs or the original up to Headquarters
with the portrait photographs and the personal description. See to it at once, for we may want the
information at any moment. In fact we want it
now."

" Very well, sir," replied Cummings. " I expect the

4

photographs have been done already, but in any case, I will see that you get them some time to-morrow."

The short remaining interval was occupied by Miller in the delivery of detailed instructions to the Sergeant. Then the train came hissing into the station, and Thorndyke, Miller, and I took our places in a compartment to which we were escorted by our three coadjutors.

ON the way up to Town little was said on the subject
of our investigation and that little was mainly contributed by Miller. Thorndyke, unwilling as he
always was to go far beyond the ascertained facts,
maintained a tactful reticence tempered by a sympathetic interest in the Superintendent's comments
and suggestions.

" What I can't understand," said Miller, " is how
that fellow managed to get Badger out of the door.
It wouldn't be easy in the case of an ordinary man, but
in the case of a man like Badger—a trained police
officer and a pretty hefty one at that—it seems incredible."

" It would seem," I suggested, with little conviction, " that he must have been taken unawares."

" But how could he ? " retorted Miller. " He knew
that he was shut in with an escaped prisoner and that
the other man probably knew that he knew it. You
can take it that Badger would have watched him like
a cat with a mouse. And the other fellow would have
had to get the door open. That's rather a noticeable
proceeding. No ; when you think of the circumstances,
it seems impossible that Badger could have been
caught off his guard, and in a tunnel, too, of all places.
What do you say, Doctor ? "

" I agree with you," replied Thorndyke, " that it
seems impossible that Badger could have been put out
by mere physical violence."

" Are you quite sure that there were no signs of any

injury ? No bullet wound or marks of a life-preserver or sand-bag, or anything of that sort ? "

" I think I can say positively," Thorndyke answered, " that there was no bullet wound and no bruises on the head, though I shall examine the body more minutely to-morrow when I attend at the post-mortem. As to a sand-bag, that would probably leave no external marks. But it is an infinitely unlikely weapon to be used in a railway carriage, even in a tunnel. The carriage was presumably lighted like this one ; and although that lamp gives a mere glimmer, hardly visible in daylight, the carriage would not be dark enough to make the use of a sand-bag practicable."

" No," Miller agreed, " it wouldn't. I was just feeling around for some sort of explanation. What about chloroform ? Have you considered that ? "

" Yes," replied Thorndyke, " and I think we can exclude it. At any rate I could discover no trace of it. But, as a matter of fact, it is really not practicable to administer chloroform forcibly to a strong man. The whiff from a handkerchief, producing instant unconsciousness, appertains to fiction. In practice the forcible use of chloroform involves a rather prolonged struggle, and results in very characteristic marks on the skin around the mouth and nose. There were no such marks in this case, nor any other signs whatever."

" Then," Miller rejoined disconsolately, " I'm done. There must be some sort of explanation, but I'm hanged if I can think of one. Does anything occur to either of you gentlemen ? "

For my part, I was as much in the dark as the Superintendent and had to admit it ; and Thorndyke, as I expected, refused to commit himself to any speculative opinions.

" There isn't much use in theorizing at this stage,"

said he. " We want more facts, and we want confirmation of the assumptions that we have been treating as facts. For instance, the identity of the man who was seen to get into the carriage at Strood."

" M'yes," Miller agreed reluctantly. " I don't think there's much doubt, but, as you say, a little direct proof would be more satisfactory. Probably we shall get some more details in the course of a day or two. Meanwhile, I'm afraid I've taken up a lot of your time to very little purpose. We don't know much more than we did when we started."

" Apparently we do not," Thorndyke admitted. " But I don't regret the expedition. It was desirable for our own satisfaction to go over the ground at once and make sure that we had not missed anything."

" I'm glad you take that view, Doctor," said Miller, " but, all the same, you've got mighty little for your pains ; nothing, in fact, excepting what you have gleaned from your examination of the body, and that doesn't seem to help us much."

" It doesn't," Thorndyke agreed. " But we must not forget that negative evidence has its value. The exclusion of one possibility after another leaves us eventually with the one that has to be accepted."

Miller received this rather academic observation without enthusiasm, remarking, truly enough, that the early stages of that sort of investigation were apt to be a little discouraging. " Possibly," he added, " something new may come out at the inquest, though it isn't likely. And it is just possible that, when we get those finger-prints from Maidstone, we may find that we are dealing with a known criminal. But even that would not prove the fact of the murder."

" As to that," said I, " if it can be proved, as apparently it can, that this man was alone with Badger in the compartment when the disaster occurred, that will create a pretty strong presumption of murder."

" No doubt," agreed Miller. " But presumption is a different thing from proof. If he should give a plausible account of an accident—such as leaning out of the window of an unfastened door—we shouldn't believe him, but we couldn't disprove his statement, and you might find it hard to get a jury to convict. If there is any doubt, the accused is entitled to the benefit of it. What we want is something in the way of positive evidence ; and all that we have got is that certain documents have apparently been taken from the person of the deceased."

" I should call that pretty weighty positive evidence," said I, " especially as the documents included the suspect's finger-prints and description. What do you think, Thorndyke ? "

" I think," he replied, " that we shall be in a better position to form opinions after the inquest, when we shall know what facts are really available. And, speaking of the inquest, Miller, what is to be done with regard to notes of the evidence ? Are you employing a shorthand reporter, or shall I bring or send my own man ? "

" I don't see that either is necessary," replied Miller. " We can get a copy of the depositions if we want one."

" That may meet your requirements," said Thorndyke, " but it may not suit me so well. I think I will send a reporter of my own, and you can have a copy of the notes if you have any use for them."

The Superintendent accepted this offer with suitable acknowledgments, and the subject dropped for the time. As the train moved out of London Bridge Station, however, I ventured to raise another subject of more immediate interest, at least to me.

"What are we going to do in the matter of food, Thorndyke?" I asked. "Does Polton know when to expect us?"

"Obviously not," was the reply, "as we did not know ourselves. I told him that we should get some food on the way, and I suggest that the Coffee Room at the Charing Cross Hotel will be the best place to stoke up. Perhaps the Superintendent will join us."

"Very good of you, Doctor," said Miller, "but I think I must get on to my office to finish up one or two odds and ends. Possibly we shall travel down together to-morrow, but, if not, we shall meet at the inquest. By that time I shall probably have seen those finger-prints from Maidstone."

Accordingly, we separated at Charing Cross, Miller striding away towards the entrance while Thorndyke and I made our way to the Hotel Coffee Room, where, with one accord, we demanded whatever might be ready at the moment. The long fast that our various activities had entailed had disposed us both to find a better use for our jaws than conversation. But as the entrée dish emptied, and the level in the claret bottle sank, my interest in our quest revived and I began cautiously to put out feelers. It had been evident to me that Thorndyke was not prepared to accept Miller's interpretation of the facts, and the question that I asked myself—and by implication put to him— was, Had he any alternative theory? But my feelers felt nothing but a steady, passive resistance to discussion, which, however, was not entirely unilluminating; for long experience of Thorndyke had taught me that when he was more than usually uncommunicative, he had something up his sleeve.

Now, could he have anything up his sleeve on the present occasion? Was there something that he had noticed and the rest of us had overlooked? Naturally,

I could not be sure, but there had been so little to see that it seemed hardly possible. His examination of the body could not have yielded any fact that he had not disclosed. It was quite unlike him to withhold any observed fact when he made a report. As I turned over the events of the day, I could recall only two that seemed to involve any obscurity or uncertainty. Thorndyke had taken the dead man's finger-prints. I did not see why. But it was a simple and reasonable proceeding and Thorndyke's explanation had seemed adequate. But was it possible that he had something more definite in his mind ?

Again, he had picked up a half-smoked cigar in the tunnel. That I could make nothing of. I could imagine no possible bearing that it could have on the case. The subsequent taking of the finger-prints suggested a suspicion that the cigar had been smoked by Badger. But supposing it had ? What light could that fact conceivably throw on the crime ? I could perceive no relevancy at all. Nevertheless, the more I reflected on these two incidents, the more strongly did I suspect that they were connected with something definite in Thorndyke's mind ; something connected with Badger's finger-prints, or even with those of the other man—which would, indeed, furnish highly relevant and important evidence.

That suspicion deepened when, on our arrival at our chambers, he made his way straight up to the laboratory with an air of evident purpose. There we found our laboratory assistant, Polton, apparently engaged in a post-mortem examination of the dismembered remains of a clock. He greeted us with a crinkly smile of welcome, and, scenting some more alluring activity, abandoned the autopsy and slipped off his stool.

" Is there anything that you are wanting, sir ? " he

asked, as Thorndyke ran a seeking eye along the shelves.

" Haven't we a holder for objects that are to be photographed ? " Thorndyke enquired.

" Yes, sir.   The stand forceps," was the reply ; and, opening a cupboard, Polton produced an appliance somewhat like an enlarged edition of the stage forceps of a naturalist's microscope—a spring holder supported on a heavy foot and furnished with a universal joint. As Polton set the appliance down on the bench, Thorndyke opened his research case, and, taking from it the envelope containing the cigar, extracted the latter with a pair of forceps and fixed it in the jaws of the holder, which grasped it near the pointed end.   Anticipating the next move, I repaired to the cupboard and brought forth an insufflator, or powder spray, and a wide-mouthed bottle filled with a fine, white powder, both of which I placed on the bench without remark. Thorndyke acknowledged the attention with a smile, enquiring :

" What are the odds that we draw a blank ? "

" You are gambling on the chance of finding Badger's finger-prints ? " I suggested.

" It is hardly a gamble, as we don't stand to lose anything," he replied.   " But I thought it worth while to try.   There is at least a possibility."

" Undoubtedly," I agreed.   " And the probability is not so very remote.   What I don't see is the relevancy of their presence or absence.   Does it matter to us or to anybody else whether Badger was or was not smoking a cigar when he met his death ? "

" That question," he replied, " we may leave until we see what luck we have.   The might-have-beens certainly do not concern us."

As he was speaking, he filled the container of the insufflator with the white powder, and, starting the

4*

bellows, blew a jet of powder on to the cigar, turning the latter round by degrees until every part of it was covered with a white film. Then, swinging up the arm of the holder until the cigar was upright, he took a little box-wood mallet that Polton had picked out of a rack and handed to him, and began rapidly and lightly to tap the foot of the holder. As the slight concussions were transmitted to the cigar, the film of powder on its surface crept gradually downward, uncovering the dark body by degrees, but leaving a number of light-coloured patches where the powder had adhered more closely. Slowly, as the tapping continued, the loose powder became detached until only the lightest dusting remained ; and meanwhile the light patches grew more distinct and defined, and began to show faintly the characteristic linear patterns of finger-prints. Finally, Thorndyke blew gently on the cigar, rotating it as before by means of the universal joint. And now, as the last vestiges of the loose powder were blown away, the finger-prints—or at least some of them—grew suddenly quite clear and distinct.

Polton and I pored eagerly over the curious markings (though it had been almost a foregone conclusion that some finger-prints must appear, since somebody had held the cigar in his fingers) while Thorndyke once more opened his research case and took from it a couple of cards, each bearing five finger-prints and each inscribed with the name of Inspector Badger. Laying the two cards on the bench beside the holder; he took a magnifying glass down from a nail on the wall and carefully examined through it first the prints on the card and then those on the cigar. After several prolonged comparisons he seemed to have reached a conclusion, though he made no remark but silently handed me the glass.

I began with a thorough inspection of the prints on

the cards. They were beautifully distinct, having been skilfully executed with finger-print ink, and showed, with the sharpness of an engraving, not only the ridge-pattern but the rows of tiny white dots on the black lines which represented the mouths of the sweat glands. When I had to some extent memorized the patterns, I turned my attention to the cigar, selecting first a rather large print which looked like that of a thumb. It was slightly blurred as if the thumb had been damp, but it was quite legible ; and when I compared it with the two thumb prints on the card, I recognized it pretty confidently as that of the left hand.

Having reached a positive result, no further examination was worth while. But before giving my decision, I handed the glass to Polton, who took it from me with a crinkle of satisfaction and bent eagerly over the cards. But I think he had already made his observations with the naked eye, for, after a very brief inspection, he delivered his verdict.

" It's a true bill, sir." He pointed at the large print with a pencil and added :

" That is Mr. Badger's left thumb."

" That was my opinion, too," I said in confirmation.

" Yes," Thorndyke agreed, " I think there is no doubt of it, though it will have to be verified by a detailed comparison of the separate characters. But it establishes a *prima facie* case. There are a number of other, less distinct prints, but we need not examine them now. The important thing is to secure a permanent record which can be safely handled. How many photographs shall we want, Polton ? "

" You will want to show every part of every finger-print free from distortion," said Polton, stating the problem and slowly rotating the cigar as he spoke. " Six photographs would do it at a pinch, but if it is important, I should do twelve and make it safe. That

would give you about four views of each finger-
print."

"Very well, Polton," said Thorndyke, "we will
make twelve exposures. And if you have the plates
ready, we will get them done at once."

As the making of twelve exposures promised to be a
tedious business and my assistance was not required,
I took one or two sheets of paper from the rack, and,
laying them on the work-bench, proceeded to occupy
myself usefully in drawing up a summary of the day's
experiences and the facts, such as they were, which
had transpired during our investigations. But they
were few and apparently not very significant, so that I
was not long in coming to the end of my summary ;
when I laid down my pen and transferred my attention
to Thorndyke's proceedings.

It was evident that the discovery of Badger's thumb-
print had not exhausted his interest in the derelict
cigar, for, as each negative was developed and washed,
he brought it to the bench, and, holding it over a sheet
of white paper under the lamp, scrutinized it through
his lens and compared it with the prints on the cards.
I did not quite understand the object of this detailed
comparison, for the identification of the one print had
established the fact that the cigar had been smoked by
Badger, whatever the significance of that fact might be.
The identification of further prints seemed rather like
flogging a dead horse. Eventually I was moved to
make a remark to that effect.

"That is true enough," said he, "but we have to
get all the information that our material will yield.
As a matter of fact, I am not looking for the remainder
of Badger's prints ; I am looking to see if there are
any prints which are not his."

"And are there ? "

"Yes, there is at least one and a problematical

second one, but that is practically obliterated by the heat from the burnt end. The other is a fairly clear print, apparently a thumb ; and it is certainly not either of Badger's thumbs."

" From which, I presume, you infer that the cigar was given to Badger by someone else ? "

" That is the reasonable inference ; and as he was alone with another man in the carriage, the further inference is admissible that the giver of the cigar was that other man. That, however, is only a probability which will have to be considered in relation to the other facts."

" Yes," I agreed. " It might have been given to him at Maidstone to smoke in the train. I don't see how you are to prove either view, or that you would be much forrarder if you did."

I was, in fact, rather puzzled by the intense interest that Thorndyke displayed in this cigar. For, surely, nothing could be less distinctive or more hopeless for purposes of identification than a commodity which is manufactured in thousands of identical replicas. But as Thorndyke must necessarily realize this, I could only suppose that there was some point the significance of which I had overlooked ; and with this probability in my mind, I followed my colleague's proceedings closely in the hope that the point which I had missed would presently emerge.

When the last of the negatives had been developed and examined, Thorndyke took the cigar out of the holder and wiped it clean of all traces of the powder.

" That," he remarked, " is the advantage of carrying out these investigations ourselves. If Miller had seen those finger-prints, he would have insisted on annexing the cigar to produce as an ' exhibit ' at the trial—if there ever is one. Whereas our photographs, properly attested, are equally good evidence, and the cigar is at our disposal for further examination."

The advantage was not very obvious to me, but I discreetly abstained from comment, and he continued :

" It is a rather unusual cigar ; considerably above the ordinary dimensions. The part which remains is five inches and an eighth long. Judging by the thickness—a full three-quarters of an inch—the complete cigar was probably well over six inches in length. How much over we can't say. There are some enormously long cigars made for civic banquets and similar functions."

" No doubt," said I, " a cigar merchant could identify the type and give us the actual dimensions."

" Probably," he agreed.   " But it is enough for us to note that it was an exceptionally large cigar and pretty certainly an expensive one. And then, as if the size were not enough, there is the strength of the tobacco. The appearance of the leaf tells us that it is an uncommonly strong weed. Taking the size and the strength together, it would be rather more than enough for an ordinary smoker."

All of this was doubtless true, but it seemed to have no bearing on the question as to how Inspector Badger had met with his death. I was still puzzling over Thorndyke's apparently irrelevant proceedings when I received a sudden enlightenment. Having finished his examination of its exterior, Thorndyke laid the cigar on the bench and with a long thin knife, cut it cleanly lengthwise down the middle. The action set a chord of memory vibrating, and incidentally engendered in me a desire to kick myself. For, years ago, I had seen Thorndyke cut open another cigar.

" Ha ! " I exclaimed. " You are thinking of that poisoned cheroot that Walter Hornby sent you."

" That we inferred to have been sent by him," Thorndyke corrected. " We were pretty certainly right, but we had no actual proof. Yes, it seemed possible that this might be a similar case."

I looked closely at the cut surfaces of the two halves. In the case of the cheroot, the section had shown a whitish patch where the alkaloid—it was aconitine, I remembered—had dried out of the solution. But nothing of the kind was visible in these sections.

" I don't see any signs of the cigar having been tampered with," said I. " There doesn't seem to be any trace of a hypodermic needle, as there was in the cheroot, or any crystals or foreign matter of any kind."

" As to the needle," said Thorndyke, " the heat and the steam from the burning end would probably obliterate any traces. But I am not so sure of the absence of foreign matter. There is certainly no solid material, but the whole of the inside has a greasy, sodden appearance which doesn't seem quite natural, and the smell is not like that of a normal cigar."

I picked up one of the halves and cautiously sniffed at it.

" I don't make out anything abnormal," said I. " It is devilish strong and rather unpleasant, but I can't distinguish any smell other than that of virulently rank tobacco."

" Well," said Thorndyke, " there is no use in guessing. We had better ascertain definitely. And as the foreign matter, if there is any, appears to be a liquid, we will begin by making an attempt to isolate it."

He glanced at Polton, who, having put the negatives to drain, had now reappeared and was casting wistful glances at the divided cigar.

" Will you want any apparatus prepared, sir, or any reagents ? " he asked.

" A fairly wide-mouthed ten-ounce stoppered bottle

and some sulphuric ether will do for the start," replied
Thorndyke ; and as Polton went to the chemical side
of the laboratory in search of these he laid a sheet of
paper on the bench, and, placing on it one of the halves
of the cigar, proceeded to cut it up into fine shreds.   I
took possession of the other half and operated on it in
a similar manner ; and when the whole cigar had been
reduced to a heap of dark-brown, clammy " fine-cut "
tobacco, we shot it into the bottle, which Thorndyke
then half-filled with ether.

" This is going to be a long job," I remarked, looking
a little anxiously at my watch.   " This stuff ought to
macerate for two or three hours at least."

" We need not complete the examination to-night,"
Thorndyke replied, reassuringly, as he gave the bottle
a shake.   " If we can decide whether there is or is not
any foreign substance present, that will be enough for
our immediate purposes ; and we ought to be able to
settle that in half an hour."

Thorndyke's estimate seemed to me rather optimistic, unless—as I was disposed to suspect—he had
already decided that some foreign substance was
present and had formed some opinion as to its nature.
But I made no comment, contenting myself with an
occasional turn at shaking the bottle or prodding the
mass of sodden tobacco with a glass rod.

At the end of half an hour, Thorndyke decanted off
the ether—now stained a brownish yellow—into a
beaker which he stood in a pan of warm water to hasten
the evaporation, while Polton opened the windows and
door to let the vapour escape.

" It's an awful waste of material, sir," he remarked,
disapprovingly.   " We ought to have done this in a
retort and recovered the ether."

" I suppose we ought," Thorndyke admitted, " but
this is the quicker way, and time is more precious than

ether. Dr. Jervis wants to get done and go to bed."

As he was speaking, we all watched the beaker, in which the liquid dwindled in bulk from minute to minute, growing darker in colour as it grew less in volume. At length it was reduced to a thin layer at the bottom of the beaker—less than half a teaspoonful —and as this remained unchanged in volume, and the odour of ether became rapidly less intense, it was evident that evaporation had now ceased. Thorndyke took up the beaker, and, having smelled the contents, turned it from side to side to test the fluidity of the liquid ; which flowed backwards and forwards somewhat sluggishly like a thinnish oil.

" What do you say it is, Jervis ? " he asked, handing the beaker to me.

" Probably a mixture," I replied. " But it smells like nicotine and it looks like nicotine, excepting as to the colour ; and as it has been extracted from a cigar, I should say that it is nicotine, stained with colouring matter."

" I think you are right," he said, " but we may as well confirm our opinions. The colour test will not answer very well owing to the staining, but it will probably work well enough to differentiate it from coniine, which it resembles in consistency, though not very much in smell. Can we have a white tile, Polton, or the cover of a porcelain capsule ? "

From the inexhaustible cupboard Polton produced a small white, enamelled tile which he laid on the bench, while Thorndyke picked up a glass rod which he dipped into the liquid in the beaker and then touched the middle of the tile, leaving a drop on the white surface.

" I have rather forgotten this test," said I, leaning over the tile, " but it seems to me that this drop shows quite a distinct green tint in spite of the staining. Is that what you expected ? "

" Yes," he replied. " The green tint is characteristic of nicotine. Coniine would have given a pink colour. But we had better try Roussin's test and settle the question quite definitely. We shall want two test tubes and some iodine."

While Polton was supplying this requisition, Thorndyke took up a clean filter paper and laid it on the drop of liquid on the tile, which it immediately soaked up, producing an oily spot of a distinct green colour.

" That," said he, " further supports the suggestion of nicotine. But it is not conclusive in the way that a chemical test is."

Once more I had the feeling that he was flogging a dead horse, for there seemed to be no reason whatever for doubting that the liquid was nicotine. However, I kept this view to myself, taking the opportunity to refresh my memory as to the procedure of Roussin's test, while Polton followed the experiment with breathless interest.

It was quite a simple test. Into one test tube Thorndyke dropped a few particles of iodine and poured on them a small quantity of ether. While the iodine was dissolving, he poured a little ether into the other test tube, and, with a pipette, dropped into it a few minims of the liquid from the beaker. When the iodine was dissolved, he poured the solution into the other tube. Almost immediately a brownish-red precipitate separated out and began to settle at the bottom of the tube.

" Is that according to plan ? " I asked.

" Yes," he replied. " The result is positive, so far, but we must wait a few minutes for the final answer to our question. If this liquid is nicotine, the precipitate will presently crystallize out in long, slender needles of a very characteristic colour—ruby red by transmitted light and dark blue by reflected light."

He stood the test tube in a stand, and, seating himself on a high stool, proceeded to fill his pipe, while Polton stationed himself opposite the test tube stand and kept an expectant eye on the little mass of sediment. Presently I saw him pick up the magnifying glass, and, having drawn down an adjustable lamp, make a closer inspection. For three or four minutes he continued to watch the test tube through the glass, assisting his observations by placing a sheet of white paper upright behind the stand. At length he reported progress.

" It is beginning to crystallize—long, thin blue crystals."

" Try it against the light," said Thorndyke.

Very slowly and carefully, to avoid disturbing the formation of the crystals, Polton lifted the tube from its stand and held it between the lamp and his eye.

" Now they are red," he reported, " like thin splinters of garnet."

I took the tube from his hand and examined the growing mass of fine, needle-like crystals, crimson against the light and deep blue when the light was behind me, and then passed it to Thorndyke.

" Yes," he said when he had verified our observations, " that is the characteristic reaction. So now our question is answered. The liquid that we extracted from the cigar is nicotine."

" Well," I remarked, " it has been a very interesting experiment, and I suppose it was worth doing, but the result is not exactly sensational. Nicotine is what one might expect to extract from a cigar, though I must say that the amount is greater than I should have expected, especially as we haven't got the whole of it."

Thorndyke regarded me with an indulgent smile.

" My learned friend," said he, " has allowed his toxicology to get a little rusty, and thereby has missed the point of this experiment. It is not a question of quantity ; there ought not to have been any nicotine at all."

As I gazed at him in astonishment and was beginning to protest, he continued : " The nicotine that we dissolved out with the ether was free nicotine. But there is no free nicotine in a cigar. The alkaloid is combined with malic acid. If this had been a normal cigar, we should have got no free nicotine until we had treated the cigar—or a decoction of it—with a caustic alkali, preferably caustic potash."

" Then," I exclaimed, " this nicotine had been artificially introduced into the cigar."

" Exactly. It was a foreign substance, although it happened to be a natural constituent of a cigar. Probably it was injected into the open end with a hypodermic syringe. But at any rate there it was ; and I think that its presence disposes of Miller's question as to how Inspector Badger was put out of the carriage on to the line."

" You think that he was suffering from nicotine poisoning ? "

" I have no doubt of it. We have seen that he smoked at least an inch of this cigar. The cigar contained naturally anything up to 8 per cent. of combined nicotine, part of which would pass into the smoke. To this had been added not less than half a fluid drachm of free nicotine. Now, when we consider that the lethal dose of nicotine is not more than two or three drops, and that more than that amount must have been contained in the part that was burned, we are pretty safe in assuming that the smoker would have been reduced, at least, to a state of physical helplessness."

" You have no doubt that he was alive when the train went over him ? "

" No. But though he was undoubtedly alive, I think it quite likely that he was moribund. He had apparently taken nearly, if not quite, the full lethal dose."

" It is a little surprising," I remarked, " that he went on smoking so long ; that he did not grow suspicious, seeing that he knew who his fellow passenger was, as apparently he did."

" I don't think it is very surprising," replied Thorndyke. " The procedure had been so well calculated to avert suspicion. Let us suppose—as probably happened—that the stranger produces a cigar-case. There are two cigars in it—one, no doubt, bearing a private mark. The stranger takes the marked cigar and holds out the case to Badger. Now Badger, as we know, usually smoked a pipe, but he was very partial to a cigar, and he preferred a strong one. He would certainly have taken the cigar and would have been impressed by its strength. Probably, owing to the presence of the free nicotine, the cigar would not have burned freely. He would have had to draw at it vigorously to keep it alight, and so would have drawn into his mouth a large amount of the vaporized nicotine.

" Presently he would begin to feel unwell, but at first he would feel nothing more than ordinary tobacco-sickness, and before he had time to become suspicious, he would be in a state of collapse. Nicotine, you will remember, is probably, with the exception of hydrocyanic acid, the most rapid of all poisons in its action."

" Yes ; but if Badger was really in a moribund state, it would seem that it was a tactical mistake to throw him out on the line. If the murderer had simply sat him up in a corner and got out at the next station, no suspicion of any crime would have arisen. The body might not have been observed until the train reached London, and when it was discovered and examined, death would have appeared to have been due to natural causes, or to excessive smoking, if the nicotine poisoning had been detected."

" I don't think that would have done, Jervis," Thorndyke replied. " Your plan would have involved too many contingencies. The next stop was at Dartford—a fairly busy junction. Someone might quite probably have got in there and seen the murderer getting out. And again, Badger might have recovered. You can usually tell when a man is dead, but it is difficult even for an expert to be certain that an insensible man is dying. No, this man was taking no risks, or as few as possible. And he was a desperate man. Probably, Badger was the only officer who knew him, and he was aware of the fact. His safety depended on his getting rid of Badger."

" I gather," said I, " that you don't accept Miller's view as to the identity of the other passenger. It struck me that he was rather jumping at conclusions."

" He was, indeed," Thorndyke agreed, " in a most surprising manner for so shrewd and experienced an officer. It was a positive obsession. I never entertained the idea for a moment, for, apart from the total absence of evidence, it bristled with impossibilities. The man was a runaway prisoner. He was, it is true, wearing his own clothes, but he would probably have no hat and his pockets would almost certainly be empty. How could such a man have got a first-class ticket ? And how could he have got away from Maidstone to make his appearance so promptly at Strood ? The thing is inconceivable.

" But we had better adjourn this discussion. It is past midnight, and Polton is yawning in a way that threatens us with the job of reducing a dislocation of the lower jaw. The rest of the nicotine extraction can wait till the morning, if it is necessary to pursue the question of quantity. The actual amount is of no great consequence. The presence of free nicotine is the essential fact, and we have established that."

"And thereby," said I, as the meeting broke up, "prepared quite a pleasant little surprise for Superintendent Miller."

As I undressed, and for the short time that I lay awake, I revolved in my mind the amazing events of the evening ; and in the morning, no sooner was I in possession of my waking senses than the question presented itself afresh for consideration. What was it that had impelled Thorndyke to secure and preserve that cigar ? It had looked like a mere chance shot. But all my knowledge and experience of Thorndyke and his ways was against any such explanation. Thorndyke was not in the habit of making chance shots. Moreover, the act had been deliberate and considered. He had seen the cigar by the instantaneous flash of the lamp ; he had walked on for a few paces, and then he had slipped on a glove and gone back to pick up the cigar and bestow it in his pocket with evident care. In those few instants of reflection, something must have occurred to him to suggest the incredible possibility that had been turned into ascertained fact in the laboratory. Now, what could that something have been ?

When we met at the breakfast-table, I proceeded without delay to present my problem for solution.

" I have been wondering, Thorndyke," said I, " what made you pick up that cigar. Evidently, the results of the examination were not entirely unexpected."

I could see that my question, also, was not unexpected. But he did not reply immediately, and I continued :

" That cigar was perfectly normal to look at. Yet it seems as if some intuition had suggested to you the possibility of its amazingly abnormal qualities. It is an utter mystery to me."

" I pray you, Jervis," he replied, smilingly, " not to accuse me of intuitions. I have always assumed that intuitions are for those who can't reason. But let us consider the circumstances surrounding that cigar. We will take first the *prima facie* appearances, disregarding, for the moment, our own personalities and our special knowledge and experience.

" Here was a cigar which had been lighted and thrown away, less than half-smoked. Now, its condition offered evidence, at a glance, of some sudden change in the state of mind of the smoker. That would be true even of a cigarette. Normally, a man either wants a smoke or he does not. If he does, he lights the cigarette and smokes it. If he does not, he doesn't light it. But if he lights it and then throws it away, that act is evidence of a change of purpose ; and that change is almost certainly determined by some change in his circumstances or surroundings.

" But what is true of a cigarette, which costs about a penny, is more emphatically true of a cigar of an expensive type, which must have cost at least half a crown. There must have been some definite reason for its having been thrown away. But within a few yards of the place where the cigar was lying, a man had been murdered. There had been two men in a smoking-compartment. If deceased had been smoking a cigar, he would obviously not have finished it ; and the same is almost certainly true of the other. Hence there was an appreciable probability that this cigar had some connection with the murder. But, since a cigar which has been smoked is practically certain to bear finger-prints, it would have been reasonable in any case to secure the cigar and see, if possible, whose finger-prints it bore.

"So much for the general aspects of the incident—which I should have thought would have been obvious to Miller. We, however, were not concerned only with the general aspects. We had special knowledge and special experience. I have told you how, in the early days of my practice, when I had little to do, I used to occupy myself in the invention of crimes of an unusual and ingenious kind and in devising methods of detection to counter them. It was time and effort well spent ; for each crime that I invented—and cir-cumvented—though it was imaginary, yet furnished actual experience which prepared me to deal with such a crime if I should encounter it in real life. Now, among the criminal methods which I devised was the use of a cigar as the means for administering poison."

"Yes," said I, "I remember ; and very fortunate it was for you that you did. The fact that the possi-bility was in your mind probably saved your life when our friend, Hornby, sent you that poisoned cheroot."

"Exactly," he agreed. "The imaginary case had the effect of a real case ; and when the real case occurred, it found me prepared. And now let us apply these facts to the present case. You heard Miller's sketch of the tragedy as he had heard it told through the telephone, and you will remember that he put his finger on the point that most needed explanation. How had Badger been put out of the carriage on to the line ? According to the report, no gross injuries had been found. He had not been shot or stabbed or bludgeoned. He seemed simply to have been thrown out. Yet how could such a thing be possible ? A Metropolitan police-officer is a formidable man, and Badger was a fine specimen of his class—big, powerful, courageous, and highly trained in the arts of offence and defence. He could not have been off his guard, for he knew that he was travelling with a criminal and must have been prepared for an attack. How then could he have been thrown out? That was Miller's difficulty, and it was a real one, assuming that the report had given the true facts.

" The train journey down gave us time to think it over. That time I employed in turning over every explanation that I could think of. Since direct violence seemed to be ruled out, the only reasonable supposition was that, in some way, Badger must have been rendered insensible or helpless. But in what way? You heard Miller's suggestions; and you could see that none of them was practicable. To me, it appeared that poison in some form was the most likely method. But how do you set to work to poison a man in a railway carriage?

" I considered the various methods that were physically possible. The most obvious was to offer a drink from a flask. That would be effective enough— but not with a detective inspector of the C.I.D. Badger would have refused to a certainty; and poisoned sweets would have been still more hopeless. Then the possibility of a poisoned cigar occurred to me. The idea seemed a little extravagant; but, still, the method had actually been used within my own experience. And there was no denying that it would have met the case perfectly. The offer of a cigar would have appeared, even to a cautious police officer, a quite unsuspicious action. And we know that Badger liked a cigar and would almost certainly have accepted one. So, in spite of the fact that, as I have said, the suggestion seemed rather far-fetched, I made a mental note to keep the possibility in mind.

" At Greenhithe the absence of any traces of violence was confirmed. Then we went into the tunnel; and behold! almost the first object that we notice is a half-smoked cigar. There was not much need for intuitions."

I admitted a little shamefacedly that there was not. It was the old story. An item of knowledge or experience that was once in Thorndyke's mind was there for ever; and what is more, it was available for use at any moment, and in any set of circumstances. I had not this gift. My memory was good enough; but I had not his constructive imagination. I could only use my experiences when analogous circumstances recurred. The poisoned cheroot had come by post. Thereafter, I should have looked with suspicion on any cigar that arrived by post from an unknown source. But Thorndyke had the idea in his mind, ready to apply it to any new set of circumstances. It was a vital difference.

Having settled this question, I passed on to another that had exercised my mind a good deal.

" You seem," I said, " to have decided pretty clearly how the actual murder was carried out. Have you carried the matter any farther? Have you any theory of the general *modus operandi* of the crime? "

" Only in quite general terms," he replied. " I think we are forced to certain conclusions. For instance, the fact that the murderer had the poisoned cigar available compels us to assume that the crime was not only premeditated but very definitely planned. My impression is that poor Badger was under a delusion. He thought that he was stalking a criminal, whereas, in fact, the criminal was stalking him. I suspect that he knew what was going on at Maidstone, and that he kept Badger in sight. I believe that he saw him into the train at Maidstone and travelled with him in that train to Strood."

" There seem to be at least two objections to that theory," said I. " To begin with, he could hardly have avoided being seen at Maidstone. For, leaving Badger out of the picture, there was Cummings, who certainly knew him by sight and would surely have spotted him at the station."

" I see," said Thorndyke, " that you are adopting Miller's view that the murderer was the man Smith. That view seems to me quite untenable. I have never entertained it for a moment."

" You are not forgetting the resemblance between the two men ? That both men had red hair and a noticeably red nose ? It would be a remarkable coincidence, if they were different men."

" Very true," he agreed. " But don't let us lose sight of the collateral circumstances. If we assume that this was a carefully planned murder, as it appears to have been, we have to be on the look-out for such ordinary precautions as a murderer would probably take. Now a red nose with red hair is a rather uncommon combination ; and, as you say, its occurrence in two men in these peculiar circumstances would be a remarkable coincidence. But there are such things as wigs and rouge and grease-paint ; and these are just the circumstances in which we might look to see them used. The very simplest make-up would do. Consider how easy it would have been. Supposing a dark man with close-cropped hair gets into an empty carriage at Maidstone. Just before reaching Strood, he slips on a red wig and gives his nose an infinitesimal touch of rouge. On arriving at Strood, he hops out, and at once makes for the stairs leading to the subway. There, or elsewhere, he waits for the arrival of the London train, and, when it comes in, he emerges, boldly, on to the platform, and lets himself be plainly seen."

" But don't you think Badger would have spotted the wig ? " I objected.

" I feel pretty sure that he would," Thorndyke replied. " But why not ? The stranger was there for

the express purpose of being spotted. And you notice
a further use that the make-up would have had. For,
after the murder, he could have doffed the wig and
cleaned off the rouge ; and forthwith he would have
been a different person. The description of him, as he
had been seen at Strood, no longer applied to him. He
could show himself boldly at Dartford and leave no
trace. What is the second objection ? "

" I was thinking of the fact—if it is a fact—that he
took the risk of stealing Smith's finger-print papers
from the body. It was a very serious risk. For if he
had been stopped and searched and they had been
found on his person, that would have convicted him
of the murder beyond any question. And, moreover,
the very fact that they were taken furnishes evidence
of murder and effectually excludes the possibility of
misadventure. The taking of such a risk points to a
very strong motive. But they were Smith's finger-
prints ; and if he were not Smith, what strong motive
could he have had for taking them ? "

" Admirably argued," Thorndyke commented. " But
perhaps we had better postpone the consideration of
that point until we have actually ascertained that the
papers were really taken from the body. The point
is of importance in more than one respect. As you
very justly remark, the taking away of these papers
converts what might have been accepted as a misadventure into an undeniable murder. And the man
who took them—if he did take them—could not have
failed to realize this. You are certainly right as to the
strength of the motive. The question that remains to
be solved is, What might have been the nature of that
motive ? But I think we shall have to adjourn this
discussion."

As he spoke, I became aware of footsteps ascending
the stairs, and growing rapidly more audible. Their

cessation coincided with a knock at the door, which I instantly recognized as Miller's. I sprang up and threw the door open, whereupon the Superintendent entered and fixed a mock-reproachful eye on the uncleared breakfast-table.

"Well, gentlemen," he said, by way of greeting, "I thought I would just drop in and give you the news in case you were starting early. You needn't. The post-mortem is fixed for two-thirty, and there is nothing else for you to do."

"Thank you, Miller," said Thorndyke. "It was good of you to come round. But, as a matter of fact, we are not going—at least, I am not, and I don't think Jervis is."

The Superintendent's jaw dropped. "I am sorry to hear that," said he in a tone of very real disappointment. "I was rather banking on your getting us something definite to go on. We haven't got much in the way of positive evidence."

"That," Thorndyke answered, "is why we are not going. We have got some positive evidence; and we think—and so will you—that we had better keep it to ourselves, at least for the present."

The Superintendent cast an astonished glance at my colleague.

"You have got some positive evidence!" he exclaimed. "Why, how the deuce—— but there, that doesn't matter. What have you discovered?"

Thorndyke opened a drawer and produced from it a pack of mounted photographs and the two cards bearing Badger's finger-prints, which he laid on the table.

"You may remember, Miller," he said, "pointing out to me in the tunnel that someone had thrown away a half-smoked cigar."

"I remember," the Superintendent replied. "An uncommon good weed it looked, too. I had half a mind to pick it up and finish it—in a holder, of course."

" It's just as well that you did not," Thorndyke chuckled. " However, I picked it up. I thought there might possibly be some finger-prints on it. And there were. Some of them were Badger's. But there were some others as well."

" How were you able to spot Badger's finger-prints ? " Miller demanded in a tone of astonishment.

" I took the records from the body," Thorndyke replied, " on the chance that we might want them."

Miller stared at my colleague in silent amazement.

" You are a most extraordinary man, Doctor," he exclaimed, at length. " You seem to have the gift of second sight. What on earth could have made you—— but there, it's no use asking you. Are these poor Badger's prints ? "

" Yes," Thorndyke answered, " and these are the photographs of the cigar with the prints developed on it."

Miller pored eagerly over the photographs and compared them with the prints on the cards.

" Yes," said he, after a careful inspection, " they are clear enough. There is poor old Badger's thumb as plain as a pikestaff. And here is one—looks like a thumb, too—that certainly is not Badger's. Now we are going to see whose it is."

He spoke in a tone of triumph, and as he spoke, he whisked out of his pocket, with something of a flourish, a large leather wallet. From this he extracted a blue document and spread it out on the table. On it, among other matter, were four sets of finger-prints— the " tips " of the two hands, both sets complete, and the two sets of " rolled impressions," of which those of the right hand consisted only of two perfect impressions and a smear. Miller confined his attention principally to the tips, glancing backward and forward from them to the photographs, which were spread out on the table. And, watching him, I was sensible of a gradual change in his demeanour. The triumphant air slowly faded away, giving place, first to doubt and bewilderment, and finally to quite definite disappointment.

" Nothing doing," he reported, handing the paper to Thorndyke. " They are not Smith's finger-prints. Pity. I'd hoped they would have been. If they had been, they would have fixed the murder on him beyond any doubt. Now we shall have to grub about for some other kind of evidence. At present, we've got nothing but the evidence of the station-master at Strood."

Thorndyke looked at him with slightly raised eyebrows.

" You seem," said he, " to be overlooking the importance of those other finger-prints. If they are not Smith's, they are somebody's ; and the person who made them is the person who gave Badger that cigar."

" No doubt," Miller agreed. " But what about it ? Does it matter who gave him the cigar ? "

" As it happens," Thorndyke replied, " it matters a great deal. We have analysed that cigar and we found that it contained a very large dose of a deadly volatile poison."

Miller was thunderstruck. For some moments he stood, silently gazing at Thorndyke, literally openmouthed. At length, he exclaimed in a low, almost awe-stricken tone :

" Good God, Doctor. This is new evidence with a vengeance ! Now we can understand how poor old Badger was got out on to the line. But, how in the name of fortune came you to analyse the cigar ? "

" There was just the bare possibility," Thorndyke replied. " We thought we might as well make the trial."

5

Miller shook his head. "It's second sight, Doctor. There's no other name for it. It looks as if you had spotted the poison in the cigar as it lay on the ground in the tunnel. You are a most astonishing man. But the question is, how the deuce he got hold of that cigar."

"Who?" demanded Thorndyke. "You don't, surely, mean Smith?"

"Certainly I do," Miller replied, doggedly. "Who else?"

"But," Thorndyke protested with a shade of impatience, "you have just ascertained, beyond any reasonable doubt, that the cigar was given to Badger by some other person."

But the Superintendent was not to be moved from the conviction that apparently had possession of his mind. "Those other prints," he insisted, "must be the prints of the man from whom Smith got the cigar. We shall have to find out who he is, of course. But it is the murderer we want. And the murderer is Frederick Smith, or whatever his real name is."

Thorndyke's sense of humour apparently got the better of his vexation, for he remarked with a low chuckle:

"It seems odd for me to pose as the champion of finger-print evidence. But, really, Miller, you are flying in the face of all the visible facts and probabilities. There is absolutely nothing to connect the man Smith with that cigar."

"He may have worn gloves," suggested Miller.

"He may have worn a cocked hat," retorted Thorndyke. "But there is no reason to believe that he did. Why do you cling to the unfortunate Smith in this tenacious fashion?"

"Why," rejoined Miller, "look at the description on

his paper and then recall what the station-master at Strood said."

Thorndyke took up the paper and read aloud :

"'Height, 67 inches ; weight, 158 pounds ; rather thick-set, muscular build. Hair, darkish red ; eyes, reddish brown ; complexion, fresh ; nose, straight, medium size, rather thick and distinctly red.' Yes, that seems to agree with the station-master's description. I see that he gives no address, but describes himself as a plumber and gas-fitter."

"Probably that is right," said Miller. "A considerable proportion of the men who take to burglary started life as plumbers and gas-fitters. Their professional training gives them an advantage."

"It must," I remarked a little bitterly, recalling the ravages of a gas-fitter on my own premises. "There seems to be a natural connection between gas-fitting and house-breaking."

"At any rate," said Thorndyke, who was now inspecting the photographs—one profile and one full face—"the description fits the man's presumed avocation, without insisting on the gas-fitting. It is a coarse, common face. Not very characteristic. He might be a burglar or just simply a low-class working-man."

"Exactly," the Superintendent agreed. "It's the sort of mug that you can see by the dozen in the yard at Brixton or in any local prison. Just a common, low-grade man. But that hasn't much bearing on our little problem."

"I don't think I quite agree with you there, Miller," said Thorndyke. "The man's general type and make-up seem to have a rather important bearing. We are dealing with a crime that is distinctly subtle and ingenious, and which seems to involve a good deal more knowledge than we should expect an ordinary working-

man to possess. The face fits the assumed character
of the man ; but it does not fit the crime. Don't you
agree with me ? "

" I'll not deny," the Superintendent conceded,
grudgingly, " that there is something in what you say.
Probably, we shall find that there was some man of a
different class behind Smith."

" But why insist upon Smith at all ? The poisoned
cigar is the one solid fact that we have and can prove.
And, as you have admitted, we have not a particle of
evidence that connects him with it. On the contrary,
the evidence of the finger-prints clearly connects it with
someone else. Why not drop Smith, at least provisionally ? "

Miller shook his head with an air of resolution that I
recognised as hopeless.

" Theory is all very well, Doctor," he replied, " and I
realise the force of what you have pointed out. But
you remember the old story of the dog and the shadow.
The dog who let go the piece of meat that he had in
order to grab the other piece that he saw reflected in the
water was a foolish dog. I'm not going to follow his
example. This man, Smith, was seen to get into the
carriage with Badger. He must have been in the
carriage when Badger was killed ; and no one else was
there. If he didn't murder Badger, it's for him to
explain how the thing happened. And I fancy he'll
find the explanation a bit difficult."

Thorndyke seemed, for a moment, inclined to
pursue the argument. But then he gave up the
attempt to convince the Superintendent and changed
the subject.

" What was the charge against Smith ? " he asked.

" He was charged with uttering counterfeit paper
money," Miller replied. " It was a silly affair, really.
I can't think how the magistrate came to commit him.

It seems that he went into a pub in Maidstone for a drink and tendered a ten-shilling note. The publican spotted it at once as a bad one and he gave Smith in charge. At the police station he was searched and two more notes were found on him. But they were both genuine and so was the rest of the money that he had about him. His statement was that the note had been given to him in change, and that he did not know that it was bad ; which was probably true. At any rate, I feel pretty sure that the Grand Jury would have thrown out the bill. He was a mug to complicate matters by bolting."

" So, as an actual fact, there is no evidence that he was a criminal at all. He may have been a perfectly respectable working-man."

" That is so," Miller agreed rather reluctantly, " excepting that Badger seemed to have been satisfied that he was the crook that he had been on the look-out for."

" As he never saw the man," said Thorndyke, " that is not very conclusive. Do you know how the escape was managed ? "

" Only in a general way," replied Miller. " It doesn't particularly concern me. I gather that it was one of those muddles that are apt to occur when prisoners are wearing their own clothes. Got himself mixed up with a gang of workmen. But he'd better have stayed where he was."

" Much better," Thorndyke agreed with some emphasis. " But, to return to the case of the unknown man who prepared the poisoned cigar, I think you will agree with me that we had better keep our own counsel about the whole affair."

" I suppose so," answered Miller. " At any rate, I think you are right to keep away from the inquest. The coroner might ask you to give evidence, and then you'd have to tell all you know, and the story would be in every blessed newspaper in the country. I take it you are prepared to swear to the poison in that cigar ? "

" Certainly ; and to produce the poison in evidence."

" And you are going to let me have a photograph of those finger-prints ? "

" Of course. There is a set ready for you now, including two of Badger's. And, as to those from the cigar, it is just possible that you may find them to be those of some known person."

" It's possible," Miller admitted, " but I don't think it very likely."

" Nor do I," said Thorndyke, with a faint smile ; by which I judged that he realized, as I did, that Miller's suspicions, even in the matter of the cigar, were still riveted on the elusive Smith.

" With regard to this paper of Smith's," said Thorndyke, as he handed Miller the set of photographs that had been reserved for him ; " I should like to take a copy of it for reference. A photographic copy, I mean, of the portraits and the finger-prints."

Miller looked a little unhappy. " It wouldn't be quite in order," he objected. " An official document, you know, and a secret one at that. Is it of any importance ? "

" It is impossible to say, in advance," replied Thorndyke. " But I shall be working at the case on your behalf, and in collaboration with you. It might be important, on some occasion, to be able to recognize a face or a finger-print. Still, if it is not in order, I won't press the matter. The chances are that the copy will never be needed."

But Miller had reconsidered the question. He was not going to put any obstacles in Thorndyke's way.

" If you think a copy would be helpful," said he,

" I'll take the responsibility of letting you have one. But I can't let the document go out of my possession. Can you take it now ? "

" Yes," Thorndyke replied. " It will be only a matter of a minute or two, to make one or two exposures."

Without more ado, he took the document and went off with it to the laboratory. As he disappeared, the Superintendent commented admiringly on the efficiency of our establishment.

" Yes," I replied, with some complacency (though the efficiency was none of my producing), " the copying camera is a great asset. There it is, always ready at a moment's notice to give us a perfect facsimile of anything that is set before it—an infallible copy that will be accepted in any court of law, But you have quite as good an outfit at the Yard."

" Oh yes," Miller agreed, " our equipment and organization are good enough. But, in a public department, you can't get the flexibility and adaptability of a private establishment like yours, where you make your own rules and use your own judgment as to obeying them. This can't be the Doctor, already."

It was, however. Thorndyke had just made the exposures and left the development to be done later. He now returned the document to the Superintendent, who, having carefully bestowed it in his pocket with the photographs, rose to take his departure.

" I hope, Doctor," he said, as he shook hands with Thorndyke, " that I haven't seemed unappreciative of all that you have done. That discovery of yours was a most remarkable exploit—a positive stroke of genius. And it has given us the only piece of real evidence that we have. Please don't think that I'm not grateful."

" Tut, tut," said Thorndyke, " there is no question

of gratitude. We all want to catch the villain who murdered our old friend. Are you going to the inquest ? "

" No," replied Miller. " I am not wanted there ; and, now that you have given me this new information, I feel, like you, that I had better keep away, for fear of being compelled to let the cat out of the bag. You said you were sending a shorthand reporter down to take notes for you."

" Yes," said Thorndyke ; " Polton has made all the arrangements, and has told our man to type the notes out in duplicate so that you can have a copy."

" Thanks, Doctor," said Miller. " I think they may be useful, after all, particularly the station-master's evidence concerning the man he saw at Strood."

" Yes," agreed Thorndyke. " It will be a great point if he can recognize the prison photograph—and an almost equally great one if he cannot."

I seemed to gather from the Superintendent's expression that he did not view the latter contingency with any great enthusiasm. But he made no rejoinder beyond again wishing us " Good morning," and at length took his departure, escorted to the landing by Thorndyke.

WHEN Thorndyke re-entered the room, closing the oak door behind him, he appeared to be in a thoughtful and slightly puzzled frame of mind. For a minute or more, he stood before the fireplace, filling his pipe in silence and apparently reflecting profoundly. Suddenly he looked up at me and asked :

" Well, Jervis ; what do you think of it all ? "

" As to Miller ? I think that he has his nose glued to the trail of Mr. Frederick Smith."

" Yes," said he. " The Smith idea almost amounts to an obsession ; and that is a very dangerous state of mind for a detective superintendent. It may easily lead to a bad miscarriage of justice."

" Still," I said, " there is something to be said for Miller's point of view. The man who got into the train at Strood did certainly agree, at least superficially, with the official description of the man Smith."

" That is quite true," Thorndyke admitted. " The report of the evidence at the inquest will show what sort of description the station-master is prepared to swear to. But I don't feel at all happy as to Miller's attitude. We shall have to watch events closely. For we are deeply concerned in this investigation. And it will be just as well if we go over the facts that are known to us and consider what our own attitude must be."

He took up a pencil and a note-block, and, dropping into an easy chair, lit his pipe and opened the discussion.

" I think, Jervis," he began, " we are justified in
assuming that the man who got into the carriage at
Strood is the man who murdered Badger."

" I think so," I agreed. " That is, if we assume
that it was really a case of murder. Personally, I have
no doubt on the subject."

" I am assuming that the document was really in
Badger's pocket when he started, and that it was not
there when his body was examined by the sergeant.
The inquest notes will confirm or exclude those
assumptions. At present, our information is to the
effect that they are true. And if they are true, the
document must have been taken from Badger's pocket;
and that fact furnishes *prima facie* evidence of murder.
But if Badger was murdered, the Strood man must be
presumed to be the murderer, since no other possibility presents itself. Hence, the question that we have
to settle, or at least to form a definite opinion on, is,
Who was the Strood man ?

" Now, our information is to the effect that he had
red or reddish hair and a noticeably red nose. But
the man Smith has dark-red hair and a noticeably red
nose. Then it is possible that the Strood man may have
been Smith. But mere coincidence in these two
characteristics does not afford positive evidence that
he was. For two men resembling one another in these
respects might be otherwise very different."

" That is so," said I. " But you must admit that
it is a rather remarkable coincidence. And you have
often pointed out, with great justice, that coincidences
call for very careful consideration."

" Precisely," said he. " And that is what I am going
to insist on now. We have to note the coincidence
and ask ourselves what its significance may be. It is,
as you say, a quite remarkable coincidence. Neither
of these peculiarities is at all common. If you were to

examine any considerable collection of men, such, for example, as a battalion of infantry, how many men with dark-red hair would you find in it ? Not more than one or two. Perhaps not one. But, of the one or two, or say half a dozen, that you found, how many would have noticeably red noses ? Most probably none. Improbabilities become rapidly cumulative as you multiply the characteristics that are postulated as appearing coincidently.

" The position, then, in regard to the Strood man is this : In two salient personal characteristics, he resembled the man Smith. That resemblance can be accounted for by three hypotheses, one of which must be true :

" 1. That the Strood man was Smith.

" 2. That he was another man who happened to resemble Smith.

" 3. That he was another man who had been purposely made up or disguised so as to resemble Smith.

" Those are the only possibilities, and, as I said, one of them must be true. Let us take them in order and consider their respective probabilities. We begin with the first hypothesis, that the Strood man was Smith. Now, in order to judge of the probability of this, we have to consider what we know of the personality of Smith and of the Strood man respectively, and to decide whether what we know of the one is compatible with what we know of the other.

" Now, what do we know of Smith ? First, we have the fact that he described himself as a plumber and gas-fitter. As that description seems to have been accepted by the prison officials, we may assume that it fitted his appearance and manner ; and we see that his face is of the type characteristic of the lower class of working-man. We know, further, that he had just escaped from prison, and that he was known and could have been recognized by several persons at the prison, including Chief Officer Cummings. It is probable that when he escaped, his pockets were empty and he may have been hatless.

" Now as to the Strood man. It is almost certain that he had a first-class ticket ; that he travelled from Maidstone in Badger's train, and, if so, he must have been on the platform at Maidstone at the same time as Badger and Cummings. He carried in his pocket a cigar which had been treated with a poison which is practically unprocurable commercially and which he must almost certainly have prepared himself. Now, Jervis, does it seem to you possible that those two descriptions could apply to one and the same person ? "

" No," I replied, " it certainly does not, though you omitted to mention that Smith is probably a burglar."

" That is not known to us, though I admit that it is not improbable. But it really has no bearing. Even if we knew that he was a burglar, all the obvious discrepancies would remain. I submit that the hypothesis that the Strood man was the escaped prisoner, Smith, must be rejected as untenable.

" We pass on, then, to the next possibility, that the Strood man was not Smith, but was a man who happened to resemble Smith in these two physical characteristics. In order to state the probabilities, it is necessary to note that the Strood man was apparently in this train with the premeditated purpose of murdering a police officer, and that a few hours previously a man with dark-red hair and a noticeably red nose had escaped from a Maidstone prison and was still at large. Bearing in mind the rarity of this combination of physical characters, what do you think of the probability of the coincidence ? "

" Well," I replied, " obviously, the chances against

are a good many thousands to one. But that is not quite the same thing as certainty."

"Very true, Jervis," he agreed, "and very necessary to remember. It is by no means safe to apply the laws of chance to individual cases. A prize of £30,000 in a lottery or sweepstake necessarily implies sixty thousand ten-shilling tickets, of which all but one must be blanks; so that the chances against any ticket-holder are fifty-nine thousand nine hundred and ninety-nine to one. Nevertheless, in spite of that enormous adverse chance, someone does win the prize. You are quite right. Long odds against do not exclude a possibility. But, still, we have to bear the odds in mind; and, if we do, we shall be very indisposed to accept this coincidence.

"We are left with the third hypothesis: that the Strood man was an unknown man, deliberately disguised or made up to resemble the escaped prisoner, Smith. This suggestion, though it has certain positive elements of probability, has also certain weighty objections, as I have no doubt you have noticed."

"I see one objection," said I, "that seems to exclude the suggestion altogether. If the Strood man had made up to resemble Smith, he must have had the means with him, provided in advance. He couldn't have gone about, habitually, with a red wig and a bottle of rouge in his pocket. But the escape of Smith was a contingency that couldn't have been foreseen. If we accept the idea of the make-up, we have to suppose that, after hearing of Smith's escape, this man was able to provide himself with the wig and the rouge. That seems to be quite incredible."

Thorndyke nodded, approvingly.

"Very true," said he. "My learned friend has made a palpable hit. It is a very serious objection, and, as you say, it appears, at the first glance, to be insuperable—to render the hypothesis quite untenable. But if you consider the circumstances more thoroughly, you will see that it does not. The probability is that we are dealing with one of those combinations of chance and design that are always so puzzling and so misleading. Let us exercise our imaginations a little further and make one or two more hypotheses. Let us suppose that this man had already decided to avail himself of Smith's conspicuous peculiarities and to personate him to that extent—presumably for some unlawful purpose. He would then have had the wig and the rouge in readiness. Suppose that he is staying in Maidstone, perhaps keeping a watch on Smith. Smith, however, is in custody, with the certain result that his personal peculiarities will be noticed in detail and recorded. This will make him much better worth personating. If the stranger is keeping a watch on Smith, he will know about the prosecution, and he will know that there is a good chance of an acquittal. Suppose, now, at this point, two unforeseen events happen : Smith makes his escape, and then Badger turns up in Maidstone. The stranger has, as the murder pretty clearly proves, some strong reason for getting rid of Badger. But here is a set of unforeseen circumstances that creates a first-class opportunity. The apparent impossibility of the disguise is an additional favourable factor."

I was impressed by my colleague's ingenuity and said so, perhaps with some faint suggestion of irony in my tone.

" Of course," I hastened to add, " all that you suggest is quite possible. The trouble is, that it is quite imaginary. There is not a particle of direct evidence to suggest that it is true—that what you postulate as having possibly happened, really did happen."

" No," Thorndyke admitted, " there is not. It is

hypothesis, pure and simple. So far, I do not contest your objection. But I remind you of our position. We have three hypotheses which represent all the imaginable possibilities. One of the three must be the true one. But we have already excluded two as being quite untenable on the grounds of extreme improbability. The third is admittedly difficult to accept ; but it is far less improbable than either of the other two. And you notice that, if we make the assumptions that I suggest, what follows presents a high degree of probability. I mean that a man, setting out to commit a murder, under circumstances in which he must be seen in the company of his prospective victim, would be taking a very ordinary precaution if he should so alter his appearance that a description of the murderer would not be a description of himself. And if he had the opportunity to make up so as to resemble some other person, and that other person an escaped prisoner, it would be very much to his advantage to take it. How great the advantage would be, we can see for ourselves by the attitude of our old friend, the Superintendent."

" Yes, by Jove ! " said I. " The deception, if it is one, has operated most effectively on Miller. And, if your suggestion is correct, it will explain another rather incomprehensible thing—I mean the taking from the body of the prison record. That naturally suggested that the murderer was the man whose description was on the stolen document. In fact, my impression is that it is the document as much as the personal resemblance that is sticking in Miller's gullet."

" I think you are right," said Thorndyke. " At any rate, the combined effect of the two facts—the theft of the document and the personal characteristics—is undoubtedly responsible for his state of mind. But, to return to our discussion, I think that, out of the three

hypotheses from which we have to choose, we are
forced to adopt the third, at least provisionally : that
the man who murdered Badger is not Smith, but is
some unknown man who had deliberately made up to
the end that he might be mistaken for Smith."

" Yes," I agreed. " I suppose we are, since the other
two suppositions cannot be reasonably entertained.
But I could wish that it were a little more easy to accept.
It involves an uncomfortable amount of unproved
assumptions."

" So it does," he admitted. " But there it is. All
three hypotheses seem to be full of improbabilities.
But, as one of them must be the true one, since there
are no others, we have no choice but to adopt the one
that presents the smallest number of improbabilities
and the greatest number of probabilities. Still, as I
have said, our acceptance is only provisional. We may
have to revise our opinions when we have the evidence
of the witnesses at the inquest before us."

In the event, however, we did not. On the contrary, when, late in the evening, our very expert
stenographer delivered the copy of his notes—typed in
duplicate—the report of the witnesses' evidence tended
rather to confirm Thorndyke's conclusions. There was
nothing very definite, it is true ; but the few additional
facts all pointed in the same direction.

There was, for instance, the station-master's evidence. It seemed that, in the interval, he had thought
matters over, and his statements were now more
decided. He was able, moreover, to amplify his description of the suspected stranger. The latter he
described as a well-dressed man of about middle age,
carrying a good-sized hand-bag of brown leather, but no
stick or umbrella, and wearing a soft felt hat. The
man had a rather conspicuously red nose. He had
noticed that particularly—" thought the gentleman

looked as if he were in the habit of taking a drop."
And he was quite clear about the colour of the man's
hair. He noticed it as the stranger was getting into
the carriage and the sun shone on the back of his head.
It was distinctly red ; dark red or auburn—not bright
red, and certainly not sandy. Probably, in the sun-
light, it may have looked rather redder than it really
was. But it was definitely red hair.

" Do you think that you would recognise the man if
you were to see him ? " the coroner asked.

" I don't much think I should," was the cautious
reply. " At any rate, I shouldn't be able to swear to
him."

Here the coroner apparently produced the prison
form with the two photographs and handed it to the
witness.

" I want you to look at those two portraits," said he,
" and tell us whether you recognize them."

The witness examined them and replied that he did
not recognize them.

" Does the face that is shown in those photographs
seem to you to resemble the face of the red-haired
stranger ? "

" I don't see any resemblance," the witness replied.

" Do you mean," the coroner pursued, " that you
simply don't recognize the face, or that it seems to
you to be a different face ? "

" I should say that it is a different face. The man
I saw looked more like a gentleman."

" You are definitely of opinion that these photographs are not portraits of the man that you saw.
Is that so ? "

" Well, sir, I shouldn't like to be positive, but these
photos don't look to me like the man I saw on the
platform."

That was all that was to be got out of the station-master ; and, so far, it tended to support Thorndyke's view ; as also did the evidence of the ticket collector at Dartford, who was the next witness. He, like the station-master, seemed to have turned the matter over in his mind, though he was not able to give much more information. He did, however, remember collecting a first-class ticket, and recalled noticing that it was from Maidstone to London.

" That," said the coroner, " is a point of some significance. This passenger started from Maidstone with the intention of going to London, but at Dartford —the next station after Greenhithe—he suddenly changed his mind. It is a fact to be noted. Do you remember what this man was like ? "

" I can't say that I remember him very clearly," the witness answered. " You see, sir, I was looking at the tickets. But I do remember that he was carrying a largish brown hand-bag."

" Do you remember anything peculiar in his appearance ? You have heard the last witness's description of him. Can you say whether this passenger agreed with that description ? "

" I wouldn't like to say positively whether he did or whether he didn't. I can only say that I didn't notice that he had a particularly red nose, and I didn't notice the colour of his hair. As far as I remember him, he seemed an ordinary, gentlemanly sort of man ; the sort of man that you would expect to hand in a first-class ticket."

So much for the ticket collector. His evidence did not carry us very far. Nevertheless, such as it was, its tendency was to support Thorndyke's suggestion. There could be little doubt that the man who had given up the first-class ticket was the Strood man ; and the fact—though it was only a negative fact and of little weight at that—that the special peculiarities of nose and hair had not been observed, seemed to lend a faint support to Thorndyke's further suggestion that, as soon as the murder had been committed, those special peculiarities would be eliminated.

There was little else in the evidence that was of interest to us. The engine-driver's evidence had practically no bearing; for poor Badger's body was unquestionably on the line, and the details as to how long it could have been there did not affect our enquiry. As to the body itself, the fact that no injuries could be discovered other than those inflicted by the train now caused us no surprise, though, to the coroner, it was naturally rather puzzling. Indeed, the problem that had so exercised the mind of Superintendent Miller was the problem that the coroner discussed at the greatest length and with complete failure to find any plausible solution. I read his very just and reasonable comments with considerable sympathy, not without a twinge of compunction as I reflected on the way in which we had withheld from him the one conclusive and material fact.

" The greatest mystery in this strange case," he observed, " is the absence of any traces of injury. Here was a powerful, highly trained police-officer, flung out on the line by a man whom he had apparently intended to arrest. He had not been shot, or stabbed, or stunned by a blow on the head, or in any way disabled. He had been simply thrown out. It seemed incredible ; but there were the facts. But for the known presence in that carriage of another person, and that person a suspected criminal, the condition of the body would have pointed to an accident of a quite ordinary kind. But the presence of that other man, and especially the fact—which has been quite conclusively proved by the evidence of Chief Officer Cummings—that a certain document was taken from the pocket of the deceased, puts accident entirely out of the question.

" But it adds enormously to the difficulty of understanding how this crime could have been committed. For, obviously, deceased would not have allowed this document to be taken from him without very energetic resistance. The great mystery is how any ordinary man could have taken this document forcibly from this powerful, capable officer and then opened the door and thrown him out on to the line. I must confess that I cannot understand it at all.

" However, our failure to unravel the mystery of the actual method employed by the murderer does not leave us in any doubt as to how deceased met his death ; which is the subject of our inquiry. The presence of that unknown man, his immediate disappearance at the very first opportunity, and the theft of that document, are facts that are too significant to allow of any but one interpretation.

" The next question presents much more difficulty— the question as to the identity of that man. If we think that we can give him a name, it is our duty to do so. But it is not the concern of a coroner's inquest to prove the guilt of any particular person. That is the office of a court of criminal jurisdiction. Unlike such a court, we have the choice of returning an open verdict—open, that is to say, as regards the identity of the criminal. And, if we have any doubt as to his identity, that is our proper course. Now, you have heard the evidence relating to the identity of the man who shared the compartment with deceased. You cannot have failed to notice the conflicting nature of that evidence, nor can you have failed to be impressed by the unlikeliness of an escaped prisoner showing himself openly on the platform of Maidstone Station. Still, if you are satisfied with such proof of his identity as has been given, your finding must be to that effect ; but, if you have any doubts, you will be wiser to leave the investigation of that point to the police."

This eminently judicious advice the jury accepted, eventually returning a verdict of " Murder by some person unknown."

" Well," said Thorndyke, as I handed him back the copy of the notes, " has my learned friend any comments to make ? "

" Only," I replied, " that the evidence, such as it is, seems rather to justify your choice of the third hypothesis."

" Yes," he agreed. " There is not much that is new. But there is one point that I dare say you noticed. The Strood man was carrying a fair-sized hand-bag. That supports the ' make-up ' theory to this extent : that a hand-bag would be almost a necessity, seeing that a wig is a rather bulky article, and one that must not be too roughly treated, as it would be by being stuffed in the pocket. Then, the ticket collector's evidence, little as it was worth, leaned to our side. He did not notice that the passenger had either a red nose or red hair ; which might mean either that those characters were not there to notice, or simply that he took no note of the man's appearance. There isn't much in it either way.

" But there is one other point that emerges—a slightly speculative point, but very important in its bearing if we accept it, though rather obvious. If we assume that this man was made up to pass, at least in a printed description, as Frederick Smith, that points to some kind of connection between him and Smith. He must, as you very justly observed, have made his preparations in advance. That is to say, he had decided, at least a few days previously, and probably more, to adopt Smith's peculiarities to cover some unlawful proceedings of his own. Now, it is highly improbable that he would have selected a complete stranger as the model for his disguise ; and, as a stranger, he could not have known that Smith was under suspicion of being a member of the habitual criminal class. But it was this suspicion that gave the disguise its special value. The evident probability is that he had some rather intimate knowledge of Smith."

" That does seem to be so," I agreed. " But, if it is true, another interesting probability emerges. If he knew something about Smith, then there must have been something to know. That is to say, our friend Badger's suspicions of Smith were not without some real foundation. And, again, the connection that you suggest might account for the theft of the finger-print document. It might not suit the murderer to have the finger-prints of his under-study—or over-study—at Scotland Yard."

" I think you are right," said Thorndyke, " as to the probable facts, though I am doubtful about your view of the motive. The theft of the document threw the suspicion at once on Smith, since they were his finger-prints and description. That would appear to have been the object of the theft as it was the object of the disguise."

" If it was," said I, " it was a diabolical scheme."

" Very true," Thorndyke agreed ; " but murderers are not a peculiarly scrupulous class, and this specimen seems to have been even below the average in that respect. But, to revert to your suggestion that Badger's suspicions probably had some foundation, you notice that the fact of Smith's having taken the chance to escape tends to confirm your view. Taking his position at its face value, that escape was really not worth while. He was apparently innocent of the offence with which he was charged, and pretty secure of an acquittal. His escape merely complicated the position. But, if he was a regular criminal who ran the risk of being recognized by some visiting detective, it might well have appeared to him to be worth while to try the chance of getting away in the hope that he might keep away."

At this point our discussion was interrupted by the sound of a visitor approaching our landing. A moment later the identity of that visitor was disclosed by a characteristic knock at the door.

" I happened to be passing this way," said Miller, as I let him in, " so I thought I would just drop in and see if your shorthand notes were available. I have seen the newspaper reports of the inquest."

" Then you will have seen that the station-master did not recognise the prison photographs," said Thorndyke, as he handed the Superintendent his copy of the typed notes.

" Yes," growled Miller. " That's rather disappointing. But you can't expect an ordinary, unskilled person to spot a face after just one casual glance. Of course, Badger spotted him. But he was a genius in that way. It was a special gift."

" A rather dangerous one, as it turned out," I remarked.

" It was, under the circumstances," said Miller. " But what made it dangerous was poor Badger's secretiveness. He liked to hold the monopoly—to feel he was the only detective officer who could identify some man who was wanted but unknown. Even in cases that he was not really concerned in, he would keep a criminal's personal description up his sleeve, as it were. I remember, for instance, in that Hornby case—the Red Thumb Mark case, as they called it— how close he was."

" But he wasn't on that case, was he ? " I asked.

" No.   That was my case, and a pretty mess I made
of it.   But Badger was in court on another case, and it
seems that, for some reason, he kept an eye on that
man, Hornby—the one I had a warrant for, you know—
while the experts were giving their evidence.   Well, as
you remember, Hornby slipped off, and I went after
him and missed him ; and when it came to making out
a description of him, I had to apply to you for details.
I doubt if I could have spotted him if I had met him in
the street.   But long afterwards, Badger told me that
he had a perfectly clear mental picture of the man's face,
and that he was certain that he could spot him at a
glance if ever they should meet.   And he was like that
with quite a number of crooks of the more uncommon
kind.   He could recognize them when no one else could.
It was a valuable gift—to him.   Not so valuable to us.
And, as you say, it has its dangers.   If a really vicious
crook got to know what the position was, he might
show his teeth, as this man did in the train.   Badger
would have been wiser in several respects to have
shared his information with his brother officers."

" Yes," said Thorndyke, " it is not very safe to be
the sole repository of a secret that threatens another
man's life or liberty.   I have had reason to realize that
more than once.   By the way, have you had an
opportunity of getting that strange finger-print
examined—the one, I mean, that we found on the
cigar ? "

" Yes ; and drawn another blank.   I took it to the
Finger-print Bureau, but they haven't got it in any of
the files.   So your poison-monger is a ' person unknown ' at present.   What you might expect.   Probably
sits in the background and supplies his infernal wares
to crooks of a less subtle kind.   However, your photo
has been filed in the ' Scene of the Crime ' series of

single finger-prints. So we shall be able to place him, if we ever get him in custody. That will be quite a nice little surprise for him. But I mustn't stay here gossiping. I've got a lot to do before I knock off for the day. Among other things, I must go carefully through these notes that you have been so kind as to let me have, though I am afraid there is nothing very helpful in them."

As he retired down the stairs, Thorndyke stood looking after him with a faint smile.

"You observe," he remarked, "that our friend is still under the influence of the Smith obsession. I have never known Miller to be like this before. We have given him a piece of evidence of cardinal importance, and he treats it as something merely incidental. And that thumb-print, which is, almost beyond any doubt, the thumb-print of Badger's murderer, he files away as a thing that may possibly be of some slight interest on some unvisualized future occasion. It is an astonishing state of mind for an officer of his experience and real ability. We shall have to watch this case for his sake as well as our own. We must try to prevent him from making a false move; and we have got to find poor Badger's murderer, if any efforts of ours are equal to a task that looks so unpromising."

"It certainly looks unpromising enough," said I. "The man whom we have to find is a mere phantom, a disembodied finger-print, so to speak. We don't know his name; we don't even know what he is like, since the only description we have of him is the description of a disguise, not of a man. We can only assume that he has neither red hair nor a red nose. But that description applies to a good many other people."

Thorndyke smiled at my pessimism, but was fain to agree that I had not overstated the case. "Still," he continued, hopefully, " things might have been worse. After all, a finger-print is a tangible asset. We can identify the man if we are ever able to lay hands on him."

" No doubt," I agreed, less hopefully, " but the laying hands on him is the whole problem. And it seems to be a problem with no solution."

" Well," he rejoined, " what we have done before we can do again. We have had to deal with unknown quantities, and we have resolved them into known quantities. It is not the first time that we have been confronted with the uncompleted equation, ' $x = ?$ ' "

" No, indeed," said I. " You used that very formula, I remember, in the case of that man whom Miller was speaking of just now, Walter Hornby, and on the very occasion he referred to. I recall the incident very vividly. Don't you remember ? When you passed me that slip of paper with the scribbled note on it, ' $x =$ Walter Hornby ' ? "

" I remember it very well," he replied. " And I have quite good hopes that we shall complete the equation in this case, too, if we are patient and watchful."

" Knowing you as I do," said I, "and remembering those other cases, I, also, am not without hope. But I cannot imagine how you are going to get a start. At present there is absolutely nothing to go on."

" We shall have to wait for some new facts," he rejoined, " and remember that the force of evidence is cumulative. At present, as you say, the whole case is in the air. But I have a strong feeling that we have not heard the last of Mr. Frederick Smith. Now that his finger-prints and description are extant, I think we may look for him to make another appearance ; and when he does, I suspect that we shall make a step forward.''

At the moment, I did not quite perceive the bearing or significance of this statement ; but, later, as had so often happened, I looked back on this conversation and marvelled at my obtuseness.

THORNDYKE'S prediction was verified with a promptitude that neither of us expected, for little more than a fortnight had elapsed after our conversation on the subject when the elusive figure of Mr. Frederick Smith once more flitted across our field of vision. It was but a fleeting and spectral appearance and disappearance— at least that was what we gathered from the newspaper. Indeed, we might have missed it altogether had not Thorndyke's eye been attracted by the heading of the small and inconspicuous paragraph : " ESCAPED PRISONER BREAKS INTO HOUSE."

" What, already ! " he exclaimed ; and as I looked up enquiringly he proceeded to read out the brief account.

" ' A daring robbery—or rather, attempted robbery —was committed yesterday in broad daylight by a man who escaped a short time ago from Maidstone Gaol. The scene of the attempt was a detached house in Sudbury Park, N.W., which had been left unoccupied owing to the owners having gone out for a day's motoring. Apparently the man was disturbed, for he was seen making off hurriedly ; but, though he was immediately pursued, he disappeared and succeeded in making good his escape. However, he was seen distinctly by at least two persons, and the description that they were able to give to the police enabled the latter to identify him as the escaped prisoner.' "

As he laid down the paper, Thorndyke looked at me with a faint smile.

" Well," he said, "what does that announcement convey to my learned friend ? "

" Not very much," I replied, " excepting a red head with a red nose affixed to it. Obviously, the observers noted his trade-marks."

" Yes," he agreed. " And you observe that he elected to do this job in broad daylight. He must be a conceited fellow. He seems to be unduly proud of that nose and those auburn locks."

" Still," said I, " he had to enter the house when it was unoccupied, and that happened to be in the day-time, when the owners were out in their car. Only, what strikes me is that the identification is not very satisfactory, even allowing for the rarity of red hair in combination with a red nose."

" Wait until you have heard Miller's account of the affair," he rejoined. " I am prepared to hear that the identification was more complete than one would gather from the paper. But we shall see."

We did see, a few days later, and, as usual, Thorndyke was right. When, about eight o'clock at night, the Superintendent's well-known knock sounded on the door, I rose expectantly to admit him ; and, as he strode into the room, something of satisfaction and complacency in his manner suggested that he was the bearer of news that he was going to enjoy imparting to us. Accordingly, I hastened to dispose of the pre-liminaries—the whisky decanter, the siphon, and the inevitable box of cigars—and when he was comfortably settled in the arm-chair, I gave him the necessary " lead off."

" I am sorry to see that our friend, Freddy, has been naughty again."

He looked at me for a moment enquiringly, and then, as the vulgar phrase has it, he " rumbled " me.

" Ah," said he, " you mean Frederick Smith of Maidstone.   Saw the paragraph in the evening paper, I suppose ? "

" Yes.   And we thought it uncommonly smart of your people to spot Mr. Frederick Smith from the casual description of one or two persons who caught a glimpse of him as he was making off."

Miller evidently felt himself to be in a position to ignore the hardly veiled sarcasm, for, without noticing it, he replied :

" Ah, but it was a good deal more than that.   Of course, when we heard the description, we pricked up our ears.   But we soon got some clues that made us independent of the description.   I've come in to tell you about it, since you are really interested parties.

" I dare say you know this place, Sudbury Park. It is one of the queer old London survivals—a row of detached houses, each standing in its own grounds, with gardens backing on the Regent's Canal, and little lanes here and there running up from the tow-path between the gardens to the road on which the houses front.   The grounds that surround them are mostly pretty thickly wooded—sort of shrubberies—and they are enclosed by fairly high walls, the tops of which are guarded in the old-fashioned way by broken bottles and bits of glass set in cement.

" Now, it seems that our friend first drew attention to himself by breaking one of the back windows and making a good deal of noise in doing it.   Then a couple of women, attracted by the noise, saw him trying to get in at the window.   They were at a back window of one of the houses on the opposite side of the Canal.   Naturally, as soon as they saw what he was up to, they raised a philalloo and ran down to the garden to watch him

over the wall. Their squawking brought a party of
bargees along the tow-path, and when the bargees had
been 'put wise' about the house-breaker, off they
started, full gallop, towards a bridge that crosses the
Canal two or three hundred yards farther down.

"Meanwhile, our honest tradesman, hearing the
hullabaloo, concluded that the game was up, and came
tumbling out through the window like a harlequin, and
was in such a hurry that he left his cap inside, and so
displayed his beautiful auburn hair to the best advantage. He had been working in his shirt-sleeves, and,
when he started to run, the reason was obvious. He
wanted his coat—which he carried on his arm—to lay
on the broken bottles on the top of the wall so that he
could climb over without tearing his trousers. And
that is what he did. He laid the coat over the party
wall, and over he went into the next shrubbery. But,
unfortunately for him, as he dropped down on the
farther side, the coat slipped off the wall and dropped
down into the garden that he had left. For a moment,
he seemed disposed to go back for it. But by that time
the bargees were running across the bridge, bellowing
like bulls of Bashan. So our friend thought better of
it, and bolted away into the shrubbery and was lost
to sight."

"Was he not seen by the occupants of that house?"
Thorndyke asked.

"No—because there weren't any. It was an empty
house. So all he had to do was to slip up by the side
way and go out by the tradesmen's entrance. But it is
odd that no one saw him in the road. You would
think that a red-headed man in his shirt-sleeves, legging
it up a quiet road, would attract some attention. But,
apparently, no one saw him, so he got clear away—
for the present, at any rate.

"But we shall have him, sooner or later. Sooner, I

fancy. For, I tell you we mean to have him. And
the traces that he left will make him a valuable catch
when we do get him. A capture will mean a conviction
to a dead certainty."

"That is putting it rather strongly," I remarked.

"Not too strongly," he replied, confidently. "Let
me tell you what we found. First there was the broken
glass. We went through that carefully, and on one of
the pieces we found a most beautiful impression of Mr.
Frederick Smith's right thumb. And thereby hangs a
tale which I will tell you presently. Then there was
the coat. That looked hopeful. But what it actually
yielded was beyond our wildest hopes. Most of the
contents of the pockets were of no particular interest.
But there was one treasure of inestimable value—an
empty envelope that had apparently been used to carry
some hard object, for there were some sharp, rubbed
marks on it. But they did not interest us. What set
us all agog was the address—Mr. Charles Dobey,
103 Barnard's Buildings, Southwark.

"I need not tell you that we went off like record-
breaking lamplighters to Barnard's Buildings. There,
at the office, we learned that the tenant of number 103,
Mr. Dobey, was a gentleman with a red head and a
nose to match. So up we went to number 103. We
had provided ourselves with a search warrant, and the
officer who went with me took with him a little battery
of skeleton keys. So we soon had the door open."

"What kind of key opened it?" asked Thorndyke.

"Oh, just a common pipe key with the bit filed away.
The sort you generally use, I expect," Miller added with
a grin. "It was only a common builder's latch. Well,
when we got inside we had a look round, but at first
there didn't seem to be much to see. It was just a
common, squalid sort of room with hardly any furniture
in it. Looked as if it was not regularly lived in ; which

agreed with what the man in the office said—that he didn't very often see Mr. Dobey. However, presently we discovered, hidden under the bed, a good-sized oak box. It had a quite good lever lock which gave my colleague no end of trouble to open. But it was worth the trouble. When, at last, he got it open, we saw that we had struck it rich. It was a regular treasury of evidence.

" First there was a full outfit of good-class burglar's tools, and there were one or two little packets of jewellery which we have since been able to identify from our lists as part of the swag from a burglary at a jeweller's shop. Well, that was all to the good. But the real prize was at the bottom of the box. I wonder if you can guess what it was ? "

He looked a little anxiously at Thorndyke, and did not seem particularly gratified when the latter suggested :

" It did not chance to be a document ? "

" That is just what it did chance to be," Miller admitted, adding : " You are a devil at guessing, Doctor. But you are quite right. It was the paper that was taken from poor Badger's pocket in that infernal tunnel at Greenhithe. So now we have got conclusive evidence as to who murdered Badger. Of course, we shall have to look into the meaning of that cigar of yours. But we shan't want to produce it in evidence or rely on it in any way for the purposes of the prosecution ; which is as well, for it wouldn't have been particularly convincing to the jury. But there is one more point which makes this find extraordinarily complete. It is in connection with this finger-, or rather, thumb-print. You probably know that we started, some time ago, a special collection of finger-prints—mostly single impressions—known as the ' Scene of the Crime Series." They are either originals or photographs of prints that have been found at places where a crime has been committed, but where the criminal has got away without being recognized. Most of them are, naturally, the prints of known men. But there are a few prints that we cannot associate with any known criminal. We can't put a name to them.

"Now, in this collection we had three sets of prints which had been found on premises that had been broken into, evidently by a burglar of rather exceptional skill and ingenuity, who seemed to have worked alone, and whose technique we thought we recognized in several other jobs in which no finger-prints were found. For some reason, when we got Smith's finger-prints from Maidstone and found that they were not in the general collection, the officer in charge omitted to try them with the 'Scene of the Crime Series.' But, since then, he has made the comparison, and it turns out that those three sets of prints are undoubtedly Mr. Charles Dobey's. So, now, we are able to identify him as that peculiarly talented burglar."

"Is there any special advantage in being able to do so?" Thorndyke asked. "I take it that you will proceed on the murder charge."

"Certainly we shall," Miller replied. "But there is the question of identification. We have got to make it quite clear that the man who got into the train at Strood was this same Charles Dobey. And then there is the question of motive. Badger was the only officer who knew Dobey by sight. He went down to Maidstone that very day for the express purpose of identifying him."

"You are not forgetting that you cannot produce any evidence that he ever did identify him?"

"No, I am not forgetting that. But he went down, having judged from the description that Frederick Smith was the man who had committed those various burglaries. And it now turns out that he was right.

These finger-prints prove that Dobey was the man."

"It seems to me," said I, "that the fact that the stolen paper was found in his possession will be sufficient, unless it can be rebutted, to establish the case for the prosecution, without referring to the burglaries at all. You can't include them in the indictment— not in an indictment for murder—and if you attempt to introduce them, and if the court allows you to, you will have to prove them, which will complicate the issues."

The Superintendent admitted the truth of this, but persisted that he was not going to take any chances. "And, at any rate," he concluded, "you must agree that we have got a remarkably complete case."

Thorndyke did agree, and with so much emphasis that, once more, Miller looked at him with a shade of anxiety.

"I know what you are thinking, Doctor," said he. "You are thinking that it is too good to be true."

"Not at all," Thorndyke disclaimed with a smile, "though you must admit, Miller, that he has made things as easy for you as he could."

"He certainly behaved rather like a fool," Miller conceded; "that is often enough the way with crooks. You don't see any snags, do you?"

"No," replied Thorndyke. "It looks all perfectly plain sailing. All you have to do now is to catch your hare; and he doesn't seem to be a particularly easy hare to catch."

"I don't think we shall have very much difficulty about that," said Miller. "He is an easy man to describe, and we shall circulate his description all over the country; in fact, we have done so already."

"Yes," said Thorndyke, "that was what I meant. You had him placarded at all the police-stations throughout the land, and then you find him calmly engaged in breaking and entering in the very heart of London."

Yet again, Miller glanced with a trace of uneasiness at Thorndyke; but he made no comment on what sounded a little like a rather cryptic hint, and shortly afterwards rose and took his departure.

When he had gone, I was disposed to continue the discussion, but my colleague showed no enthusiasm. Yet I could see that he was reflecting profoundly on what the Superintendent had told us; which encouraged me to make a last effort.

"After all," I said, "we can't ignore plain facts. This story of Miller's is difficult to reconcile with what we know—with regard to that cigar, for instance— but it is a consistent body of evidence, each item of which can be proved beyond question. And the discovery of that paper in the man's possession seems as conclusive as it is possible for evidence to be. In spite of your very convincing argument, it does really appear as if the solution of your problem is, $x = $ Charles Dobey. Or is there some fallacy in Miller's case?"

"There is no obvious fallacy," Thorndyke replied. "The case presents, as you say, a perfectly consistent body of evidence. Taken at its face value, Miller's case is conclusive. The real question is whether the completeness and consistency are the results of un-aided chance or of an ingeniously devised plan. That question we are, at present, unable to decide. Perhaps, when Dobey is brought to trial, he may be able to produce some new facts that may help us to come to a conclusion."

As this seemed to close the discussion, I knocked out my pipe and glanced at my watch.

"Time for me to be moving on," said I, "if I am to get home within the permitted hours. I told Juliet that I should be home to-night. And, by the way, I have a message for you. I am instructed to remind you that it is quite a long time since you paid your last visit."

"So it is," he admitted. "But we have not had many spare afternoons lately. However, to-morrow afternoon is free. Do you think it would be convenient to Juliet if I were to call and pay my respects then ? "

"I happen to know that it will, as I took the precaution to ask what afternoons were unengaged. Then I will tell her to expect you, and you had better turn up as early as you can. She always looks for a long pow-wow when you come."

"Yes," he replied, "she is very patient of my garrulousness. Then I will come as early as possible, and prepare myself for a special conversational effort. But it is really very gracious of her to care for the friendship of an old curmudgeon like me."

"It is," I agreed. "Odd, too. I can't imagine why she does."

With this Parthian shot, and without waiting for a rejoinder, I took myself off *en route* for the Temple station.

Here, perhaps, since my records of Thorndyke's practice have contained so little reference to my own personal affairs, I should say a few words concerning my domestic habits. As the circumstances of our practice often made it desirable for me to stay late at our chambers, I had retained there the bedroom that I had occupied before my marriage ; and, as these circumstances could not always be foreseen, I had arranged with my wife the simple rule that the house closed at eleven o'clock. If I was unable to get home by that time, it was to be understood that I was staying at the Temple. It may sound like a rather undomestic arrangement, but it worked quite smoothly, and it was not without its advantages. For the brief absences gave to my homecomings a certain festive quality, and helped to keep alive the romantic element in my married life. It is possible for the most devoted husbands and wives to see too much of one another.

Thorndyke redeemed his promise handsomely on the following afternoon, for he arrived shortly after three o'clock, having, I suspect, taken an early lunch to that end ; for it presently transpired that he had come straight from Scotland Yard, where he had been conferring with the experts of the Finger-print Bureau.

" Was your pow-wow concerned with any particular case that we have in hand ? " I ventured to enquire.

" No," he replied. " I went there to get some further information respecting the new system of dealing with single finger-prints that was devised by Chief Inspector Battley. I have been studying his book on his method of classification and making a few tentative trials. But I wanted to make sure that my application of the method yielded the same results as were obtained by the experts. So I went to Scotland Yard and asked them to check my results."

" I suppose," my wife suggested, " you are still a good deal interested in finger-prints ? "

" Yes," he replied, " almost necessarily, since they so constantly crop up in evidence. But apart from that, they are curious and interesting things in a number of ways."

" Yes," she agreed ; " interesting and curious and rather horrible—at least that is how they appear to me. I never hear of a finger-print but my thoughts go back to that awful trial, with Reuben in the dock and poor Aunt Arabella in the witness-box giving evidence about the Thumbograph. What a dreadful time it was ! "

I am afraid I was disposed to grin at the recollection, for poor Mrs. Hornby had brought the proceedings as near to farce as is humanly possible in a criminal trial where an honourable gentleman stands indicted for a felony. But I controlled my features, and, as to Thorndyke, he was, as usual, gravely sympathetic.

"Yes," he agreed, "it was an anxious time. I was not at all confident as to how my evidence would be received by the judge and the jury; and, if they had failed to be properly impressed, Reuben would certainly have gone to penal servitude. By the way, we sent the Thumbograph back to Mrs. Hornby after the trial. Do you happen to know what she did with it?"

"She didn't do anything with it," Juliet replied, "because I annexed it."

"What for?" I asked, rather foolishly, perhaps.

"Can't you imagine?" she demanded, flushing slightly. "It was a little sentimental of me, I suppose, but I kept it as a souvenir. And why not? It had been a terrible experience, but it was over, and it had ended happily, for me, at any rate. I have something to thank the Thumbograph for."

"It is very nice of you to say that, Juliet," said I. "But why have you never shown it to me? I have at least as much to be thankful for, though, to tell the truth, I had overlooked the fact that it was the Thumbograph that introduced us to one another."

"Well," said Thorndyke, "suppose you produce this disreputable little matchmaker and let us revive our memories of those stirring times. I haven't seen a Thumbograph for years."

"I am not surprised," said Juliet. "The report of your evidence at the trial was enough to kill the demand for them for ever. But I will go and fetch it."

She went away and returned in a minute or two with

the souvenir, which she handed to Thorndyke ; a little
oblong volume, bound in red cloth with the name
" Thumbograph " stamped in gold on the cover. I
looked at it with a new interest as Thorndyke turned
over the leaves reminiscently while Juliet looked over
his shoulder.

" Doesn't it bring all those horrors back ? " said
she, " and especially poor Mrs. Hornby's evidence.
Here is Miss Colley's thumb-print, which Reuben was
supposed to have smeared, and here is Aunt Arabella's,
and here is mine, and there is that wretch Walter's."

" Characteristically, the best impression in the
book," said Thorndyke. " He was a remarkably
capable scoundrel. He did everything well."

" I wonder if we shall ever see him again ? " I
mused. " When he slipped away from the court, he
seemed to vanish into thin air."

" Yes," said Thorndyke ; " another instance of his
capability. It is not so very easy for a man who is
badly wanted by the police to disappear, once and
for all, as he did."

He turned over the leaves once more until he came
to the one which bore the print of Reuben Hornby's
thumb. Underneath it Reuben's name was written
in pencil and, below this, the signatures of the two
witnesses, " Arabella Hornby " and " Juliet Gibson."

" Do you remember," said Juliet, " the night Aunt
Arabella and I brought the Thumbograph to your
chambers ? It was a thrilling experience to me."

" And to Thorndyke too, I imagine," said I. " For
it was then that he knew for certain that the Red
Thumb Mark was a forgery. I saw him make the
discovery, though I did not know at the time what the
discovery was. Wasn't it so, Thorndyke ? "

" It was," he replied. " And what was even more
important, I thought I had found the means of con-

vincing the court. You are quite right, Juliet; it was a memorable occasion for me."

As he continued to turn over the leaves and scrutinize the various thumb-prints, I reverted to our previous conversation.

" I don't quite understand what you were doing at the Yard to-day," said I. " The classification of finger-prints is interesting enough in its way. But it doesn't specially concern us."

" It doesn't concern us at all," he agreed. " But identification does. And that is where Battley's method is valuable to us. The beauty of it is that, apart from classification for index purposes, it affords a means of rapid identification, and moreover makes it possible to express the distinctive characters of a given finger-print in a formula. Now this is an immense convenience. We often have occasion to identify a finger-print with an original or a photograph in our possession. But we can't always carry the print or photograph about with us. But if we can express the characters of the print in a formula, we can enter that formula in our note-books, and have it ready for reference at any moment."

" But," I objected, " a formula would hardly be sufficiently definite for a reliable identification."

" Not, perhaps, for a final identification to swear to in evidence," he replied, " though you would be surprised at the accuracy that is possible. But that is not the purpose aimed at. The use of the method at the Bureau is principally to enable the searchers to find a given finger-print quickly among the thousands in the collections of single finger-prints. Our use of it will be to form an opinion rapidly on the identity of a print in which we happen to be interested. Remember, we don't have to give evidence. Finger-print evidence, proper, is exclusively the province of the regular experts. We have only to form an opinion for our own guidance. Come," he continued, " I have the apparatus in my bag, which is in the hall, and here is the Thumbograph with a selection of prints to operate on. Why shouldn't we have a demonstration of the method? You will find it quite amusing."

" It does sound rather thrilling," said Juliet ; and, thus encouraged by the vote of the predominant partner, Thorndyke went out to find his bag.

" Let me first explain the general principle of the method," said he, when he returned with a small leather bag in his hand. " Like all really efficient methods, it is essentially simple though extremely ingenious. This is the sole apparatus that is necessary."

As he spoke, he opened the bag and took out a magnifying glass, which was mounted on three legs, the feet of which were fixed into a brass ring which enclosed a plate of glass.

" This circular glass plate," he explained, " is the essential part of the instrument. If you look through the lens, you will see that the glass plate has engraved on it and coloured red a central dot surrounded by seven concentric circles. The first circle is three millimetres from the dot ; the other circles are each two millimetres from the next. The central space is denoted by the letter A. The spaces between the other circles are denoted, successively, by the letters B, C, D, E, F, and G ; and the space outside the outermost circle is denoted by H. The letters are, of course, not marked on the glass ; but I have here a diagram which shows their position."

He laid on the table a card on which were described the seven circles, each marked with its appropriate letter, and then, taking up the Thumbograph, once more turned over the leaves.

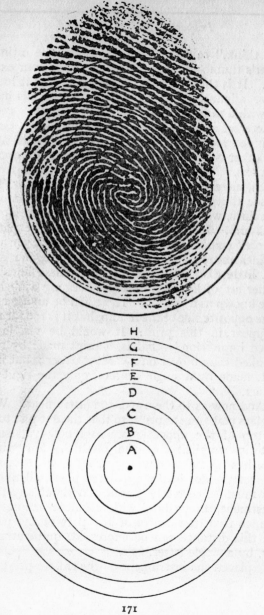

" I think," said he, " we will select the estimable
Walter's thumb-print as the *corpus vile* for our experiment. It is the best print in the book, and it has the
further advantage of being a peculiarly distinctive
type with a rather striking pattern. It has the general
character of a whorl with a tendency towards that of
a twinned loop—that is, a pair of loops folded into
each other with the convexities turned in opposite
directions. But we will call it a whorl, and treat it
as such, merely noting the alternative character. You
will see that the pattern is formed by a number of
black lines, which are the impressions of the ridges on
the thumb. In this print the centre of the pattern,
or ' core,' consists of a pair of little loops, from which
the lines meander away in a rather irregular spiral.
At a little distance from the core, these lines meet
another set of lines at an angle, forming a Y-shaped
figure known as a ' delta.' There will be another delta
on the opposite side of the thumb, but it is too far round
to appear in this print. It would be visible in a
' rolled impression '—that is, a print made by rolling
the inked thumb over on a card or paper ; but in this
print, made by a single contact, only the right delta
appears.

" And now as to the use of the instrument. We lay
the glass plate on the print, so that the dot just touches
the top of the upper loop. And now you see the
masterly simplicity of the method. For, since a
circle has no right or wrong way up, when once you
have set the dot in the appointed place, all the other
lines must be correctly placed. Without any further
adjustment, they show with absolute accuracy the
distance from the centre of any part of the pattern.
And this distance can be expressed, quite unmistakably, by a single letter."

He placed the instrument on the thumb-print in the

book, and, having carefully adjusted it, drew out his note-book and looked at my wife.

" Now, Juliet," said he, " just look through the lens and tell me the letter that indicates the position of the delta—which is actually the right delta, though it is the only one visible."

Juliet peered through the magnifying glass and studied the print for a while. At length, she looked up a little doubtfully and announced :

" It seems to me that the third line cuts right through it. So it lies half in the space C and half in D. Which of the two would you call it ? "

" The rule," he replied, " is that if a character is cut by a line, it is reckoned as lying in the space outside that line."

" Then this delta lies in the space D," she concluded.

" Quite right," said he. " We will mark it D ; and, as the other delta is not in the print, we must mark it simply with a query. And now we proceed to the rest of the examination, the ridge-tracing and ridge-counting. We will take the tracing first. What you would have to do if both the deltas were visible would be to follow the ridge that runs from the left delta towards the right. Obviously, it must take one of three courses : it may pass below, or outside, the right delta, or below, or inside, or it may meet, or nearly meet, the corresponding ridge from the right delta. Those are the three categories : outside, inside, or meeting, denoted by the initials, I, M, O."

" But," objected Juliet, " as the left delta is not visible, it is impossible to trace a ridge from it."

" That might be true in some cases," replied Thorndyke, " but it is not in this, for, if you look at the print, you will see that, wherever the left delta may have been, a ridge passing from it towards the right must have passed well outside the right delta."

Juliet examined the print again and agreed that it was so.

" Very well," said Thorndyke, " then we will mark it O, and proceed to the ridge-counting, which will complete the formula. You have to count the ridges between the centre of the core and the delta. Put aside the measuring glass and use my lens instead ; and I will give you a point to help you to count the ridges."

He handed her his pocket lens, and produced from his bag what looked suspiciously like a dentist's exca-vator, with the sharp point of which he indicated the ridges that were to be counted. Then he laid a visiting-card on the print to give a straight line from the centre to the delta, and she proceeded to count along its edge with the point of the excavator. Having gone over the ground twice, she announced the result.

" I make it twelve. But I am not quite sure, as some of the ridges fork, and might be counted as one or two. Will you count them ? "

Thorndyke took the excavator from her and rapidly checked her result.

" Yes," said he, " I agree with you. I think we may safely put it down as twelve, though the bifurcations do, as you say, create a slight ambiguity. If the other delta had been visible there would, of course, have been a second circle-reading and a second ridge-count, which would obviously have been an advantage for identification. Still, what we have done gives us the main distinctive characters of this print, and we can express them by a simple formula of a few letters and numbers. Thus, the type of pattern is a whorl, with something of the character of a twinned loop. Accord-ingly, we put down a W with T.L. in brackets. The core, or central character—the pair of little loops—lies entirely in the circle A. Now, there are five kinds of ' A ' cores : the plain eye—just a tiny circle—the eye enclosing some smaller character, the left-hand spiral, the right-hand spiral, and any other ' A ' form of an unclassifiable type. Now, in this print, the core is a left-hand, or anti-clockwise spiral, and accordingly belongs to the category A3. The delta, we agreed, lies in the space D. The ridge-tracing was outside—O— and the ridge-count twelve. We can express all these facts in a formula, thus :

"Walter Hornby. Right thumb. W (? T.L.), A 3, ?, O, D, ?, 12."

" That is concise enough," I remarked. " But, after all, it gives you only a skeleton of the pattern. It would not enable you to identify a print with any approach to certainty."

" It does not aim at certainty," he replied, " but merely at such a degree of probability as would justify action or further research. But I think you hardly appreciate the degree of probability that this formula expresses. It records five different positive characters and one negative. Now, taking the five only, if we accept the very modest chance of four to one against each of these characters being present in a print which is not Walter Hornby's, the cumulative effect of the five together yields a chance of over a thousand to one against the print being that of some person other than Walter Hornby.

" But, for our purposes, we are not obliged to stop at these five characters. We can add others ; and we can locate those others either by the use of Battley's circles or by ridge-counting with a direction-line. For instance, in this print, to the left of the core and a little downwards, the seventh ridge shows one of those little loops known as ' lakes,' the ninth bifurcates, and the

eleventh has another, larger lake. To the right of the
core the third ridge has a small lake, the fifth ridge
bifurcates, the eighth has a free end, and the tenth
bifurcates. There are seven additional characters
which we can add to our formula, giving us twelve
characters in all, the cumulative effect of which is a
probability of over sixteen millions to one against the
print being the thumb-print of any person other than
Walter Hornby ; and that is near enough to certainty
for our purpose. It would undoubtedly justify an
arrest ; and we could leave the final proof or disproof
to the experts."

He added the extra characters to the formula in his
note-book, and showed us the completed entry ; which
certainly afforded convincing testimony to the efficiency of the method. In fact, it impressed me—and my
wife, too—so profoundly that, in an access of enthusiasm, we fell upon the Thumbograph forthwith, and,
with the aid of Chief Inspector Battley's ingenious
instrument, proceeded to construct formulæ to
express the characters of the other thumb-prints in
the book, while Thorndyke smoked his pipe and
regarded our activities with benevolent interest,
seasoned by occasional advice and criticism of the
results.

" It is quite an amusing game," Juliet remarked.
" If only the inventors of the Thumbograph had known
of it and printed directions in the book, it might have
become a fashionable drawing-room pastime, and they
would have made a fortune."

" Perhaps it is as well that they did not," said I.
" The Thumbograph was a dangerous toy, as we discovered—or rather, as Thorndyke did."

" Yes," Thorndyke agreed, " it was a mischievous
plaything. But don't forget that it acted both ways.
If it supplied the false accusation, it also supplied the

conclusive answer. Walter Hornby had more reason than any of us to regret that he ever set eyes on the Thumbograph. And it may be that he has not yet come to the end of those reasons. He has evaded justice so far. But the debt is still outstanding."

BOOK III
THE MISSING COLLECTOR

INVENTORS are a much-misunderstood class. The common man, in his vanity and egotism, supposes that they exist to supply him with various commodities of which he dimly perceives the need. But this is an entirely mistaken view. The inventor produces his invention because, in the existing circumstances, it has become possible. It is true that he, himself, tends to confuse the issues by persuading himself optimistically that his invention has a real and important utility. His inventive mind goes so far as to create an imaginary consumer, so that he sees life in a somewhat false perspective. The genius who devised a family Bible which could be opened out to form a billiard table, no doubt envisaged a pious type of player who had need of some means of combining the canon of scripture with a cannon off the red ; while, to the inventor of a supermagic-lantern which could throw pictures on the clouds, the night sky was no more than a suitable background on which to declare the glory of Blunt's Milky Toffee.

But this is mere self-delusion. In reality, the inventor is concerned with his invention. Its use is but a side issue which hovers vaguely on the periphery of his mental field of vision. I emphasise the fact, because it has a bearing on the events which I am recording. For our invaluable laboratory assistant, Polton, was an inveterate inventor, and, being also an accomplished and versatile craftsman, was able to turn out his inventions in a completely realised form.

So it happened that a certain large cupboard in the laboratory was a veritable museum of the products of his inventive genius and manual skill ; examples of ingenuity—sometimes fantastically misguided—the utility of which he would expound to Thorndyke and me with pathetic earnestness and appeals to " give them a trial." There were spectacles which enabled the wearer to see behind him, there was a periscope walking-stick with which you could see round a corner, a large pedometer with movable dials for metres and yards and a micrometer adjustment of impracticable accuracy, and all sorts of clockwork devices and appliances for out-of-the-way photographic operations. But optical instruments were his special passion, whence it followed that most of his inventions took an optical turn.

I am afraid that I did not treat these children of Polton's imagination with the respect that they deserved. Thorndyke, on the other hand, made a point of always examining even the wildest flights of the inventor's fancy with appreciative attention, realizing—and pointing out to me—that their apparent oddity was really due to the absence of appropriate circumstances, and that those circumstances might arise at any moment and give an unexpected value to what seemed to be a mere toy. And that was what happened on the present occasion. One of Polton's most eccentric productions suddenly revealed itself as an invaluable instrument of research. But perhaps I am beginning the story at the wrong end. I had better turn back and take the incidents in their proper order.

It was rather late one afternoon when there arrived at our chambers a dapper, well-dressed gentleman of distinctly horsey appearance, who gave the name of Woodburn, and who, rather to my surprise, turned out to be a solicitor. He presented Mr. Brobribb's card, on which were scribbled a few words of introduction.

" I have come to see you," he explained, " on the advice of my friend Brodribb. I came up to Town expressly to confer with him on a rather queer case that has turned up in my practice. We talked over the legal issues without coming to any very definite conclusion, but Brodribb thought that there were certain points in the case that were more in your line than in either his or mine. And I am certainly inclined to agree with him to the extent that I am decidedly out of my depth."

" And what about Mr. Brodribb ? " Thorndyke asked. " He is a pretty acute lawyer."

" He is," Mr. Woodburn agreed, heartily. " But this is not altogether a question of law. There are some other points on which he thought you would be able to help us. I had better give you an outline of the case. But, first, I had better explain that I am a country practitioner, with my principal office at Packington in Kent, and that my clients are chiefly the farmers and country gentlemen of the surrounding district.

" Now, one of these clients is a gentleman named Mr. Didbury Toke. He is a sort of superior dealer in works of art and antiquities. He has an office in Town, but he resides at an ancient house called Hartsden Manor in the village of Hartsden and usually spends a good deal of his time there. But from time to time he has been in the habit of taking more or less prolonged trips to the Continent for the purpose of rooting about for antiques and works of art. On these occasions it has been his custom to shut up that part of the house in which his collection is lodged, and seal all the doors and windows in any way giving access to it.

" Well, about two months ago, he set forth on one of these expeditions, and, according to his usual custom, he locked up and sealed all the approaches to the rooms containing the collection and gave the keys into my custody."

" What happened to the seal ? " asked Thorndyke.

" That I can't tell you," replied Mr. Woodburn. " He didn't give it to me, but I have an impression that he deposited it at his bank in London. I know that he did on a previous occasion. Still, he may have carried it on his person. I happen to know that it is a large, clumsy, antique ring, which he was certainly not in the habit of wearing.

" Well, as I said, he handed the keys to me, but, at the same time, he gave me very definite instructions— in writing—that the rooms were not on any account to be entered or the seals tampered with in any way. You see that his instructions were quite explicit, and, in fact, decidedly emphatic."

" Apparently," said Thorndyke, " he allowed you no discretion and provided for no contingencies. Is that not so ? "

" That is so," replied Mr. Woodburn. " His instructions amounted to an absolute prohibition of any interference with the seals or any attempt to enter the enclosed rooms. That is the matter which I have been discussing with Mr. Brodribb, and which I want to discuss with you. Because this prohibition has become highly inconvenient. Circumstances have arisen which seem to make it very desirable to enter those enclosed rooms. But before I go into those circumstances, I had better tell you a little more about the arrangements of the house and those particular rooms.

" The main part of the closed premises consists of a very large room—about forty feet long—called the

great gallery; but adjoining this are three or four
smaller rooms, some of which are used to house part of
the collection, and some are kept as workrooms, in
which Mr. Toke does his mending and other odd jobs
connected with the collection. The great gallery and
the rooms attached to it occupy the whole of a wing
which runs at right angles to the rest of the house;
and, as there is only one door giving access to the
gallery and its annexed rooms, the whole group of
apartments is completely cut off and isolated.

"Now the circumstances to which I referred are
these. Mr. Toke's household ordinarily consists of his
housekeeper and her niece, who acts as housemaid; but,
when he is away from home, a nephew of the housekeeper usually comes to stay there, so that there may
be a man on the premises. He is there now; so there
are three persons living in the house; and those three
persons are agreed that, from time to time, they heve
heard sounds at night apparently coming from the
great gallery. It sounds incredible, and I must admit
that when they first reported the matter to me, I was
disposed to be sceptical. I am not entirely unsceptical
now. But they are extremely positive, and, as I said,
they are all agreed. So I thought it my duty to go
over to the manor house and make an inspection; and
the result of that inspection was only to make the whole
affair still more incomprehensible. For the seals were
all intact, and there was not a sign anywhere of anyone
having broken into the place."

"You examined the windows, of course?" said
Thorndyke.

"Yes. There are five large windows, and I examined
them all from outside by means of a ladder. They
certainly had not been opened, for I could see that the
catches were all in their places. But I may say that
the windows are all secured from inside with screws,

and those screws are sealed. Mr. Toke leaves nothing to chance."

" Could you see into the room ? " asked Thorndyke.

" No. The shutters were not closed, but the windows are covered by lace or net curtains, so that, although the gallery is quite light, it is impossible to see in from the outside."

" You have spoken of the collection," said Thorndyke. " Perhaps you had better tell us something about its nature and value."

" As to its value," said Mr. Woodburn, " I believe that is very considerable, but as it consists chiefly of pottery and porcelain, Bow and Chelsea figures, bronzes, and small statuary, it would be of no interest to a burglar—at least, that is what I understood from Mr. Toke."

" I am not sure that I agree with Mr. Toke," said Thorndyke. " Of course, since you cannot melt down porcelain figures into unrecognizable ingots, they are not suitable for the common type of burglar. The ordinary ' fence ' would not trade in them, and they could not be offered in the open market. But they are really valuable things and fairly portable, and they would not be so very difficult to dispose of. The ordinary collector is not always as scrupulous as he might be, but there is one kind of collector who is not scrupulous at all. One may take it that a millionaire who has made his millions by questionable transactions, may be prepared to spend them in a like manner. The point is of some importance ; for, whereas the repeated occurrence of these sounds—assuming them to have occurred—is not consistent with the idea of an ordinary burglary, it does suggest the bare possibility of some enterprising persons quietly removing the more valuable parts of the collection piecemeal."

"You do, then, really entertain the possibility that these sounds are not merely imaginary?"

"I have an entirely open mind," replied Thorndyke. "But I understood you to say that you had gone into the question of fact on the spot, and that you were satisfied that the reports were sufficiently convincing to justify serious enquiry."

"That is so," said Mr. Woodburn. "But I may say that Brodribb scouted the idea. He was incredulous as to the sounds having been heard at all, seeing that the closed rooms are so completely isolated and so distant from the rest of the house; and he suggested that if there had been any sounds, they were probably due to rats. I don't agree with him as to the rats. Of course, I enquired whether that could be the explanation, but I think it can be excluded. The noises that rats make are pretty characteristic, and they don't at all agree with the description of the sounds that these people gave. And they tell me that there are no rats in the house, which seems to settle the question; for, although rats will harbour in empty rooms, they don't stay there. They must come out for food. But Brodribb's other objection is more weighty. The great gallery is a good distance from the rest of the house. What do you really think of the probabilities?"

"Well," replied Thorndyke, "the answer to your question involves the statement of a rather bald truism. If there is no access to the closed rooms other than the door of which you spoke, and that door is still locked and the seal is still unbroken, evidently no one can possibly have entered those rooms. On the other hand, if sounds have been heard of such a nature as to make it certain that someone had entered those rooms, then it follows that there must be some means of access to those rooms other than those which are known to you. I apologize for the obviousness of the statement."

"You needn't," said Mr. Woodburn. "It puts the matter into a nutshell. I saw the dilemma myself. But what do you suggest?"

"In the first place," said Thorndyke, "may I ask if it is impossible to get into touch with Mr. Toke?"

"Ah," said Mr. Woodburn, "there you have raised another point. Apparently, it is impossible for me to get into touch with my client; and that is a matter that I am not entirely happy about. Mr. Toke is by no means a good correspondent. But, when he is travelling, as a rule, he sends me a short note now and again, just to give me the chance of communicating with him if the occasion should arise. And he has been in the habit of sending me parcels—purchases that he has made—to put in my strong room or to deposit at his bank. But this time, I have had not a single line from him since he went away. It is really rather strange, for Mr. Toke is a methodical, business-like man, and he must realize that it is most undesirable that his solicitor and man of business should have no means of communicating with him. It might be extremely awkward; even disastrous. It is extremely awkward now. If I could get into touch with him, he would pretty certainly authorize me to break the seals and see if his collection is all as it should be. As I can't, the question arises as to what I ought to do. Should I, for instance, take it that these exceptional circumstances absolve me from the obligation to abide literally by his instructions. Brodribb thought not. What is your view of the case?"

"I am disposed to agree with Brobribb. The difficulty seems to be that you have not established the exceptional circumstances. There is only a suspicion; and Mr. Toke might think, as Brobribb does, that the suspicion was not a reasonable one. You have said that Mr. Toke's instructions were very explicit and even emphatic. He was clearly most anxious that those rooms should not be entered or the seals broken. He has said so, and he has given quite definite instructions on the subject. This being so, we must assume that he had good and sufficient reasons for giving those instructions. We cannot judge what those reasons were, or how strong they were. But it is always safe to assume that a man means what he says, especially when he says it quite clearly and unmistakably.

" Suppose you ' interpret ' his instructions and proceed to break the seals and enter the rooms. Suppose you find everything normal, and, at the same time, find something that shows you that the rooms ought not to have been entered by anyone except Mr. Toke himself. That might create a very awkward situation."

Mr. Woodburn laughed. " You think it possible that Mr. Toke may have something hidden in those rooms that he wouldn't like anyone else to see ? Well, of course, it may be so. But I may mention that Mr. Didbury Toke is a most respectable gentleman."

" I am not suggesting the slightest reflection on Mr. Toke's moral character," said Thorndyke, laughing in his turn. " Probably, his motive was nothing more than extreme solicitude for his collection. Still, he may have things locked up in his gallery the existence of which, in that place, he might well wish to keep secret ; things, for instance, of great intrinsic value which might invite the attentions of burglars."

" Yes," said Woodburn, " I suppose you are right. He always swore that there was nothing there that a burglar would look at. But that may have been a mere precaution. Which brings us back to the question, What is to be done ? "

" I think the answer to that is fairly simple," said Thorndyke. " These statements certainly call for investigation. Two points require to be cleared up. First, is it certain that there is really no possibility of access to these rooms other than the door that you mentioned ? And, second, assuming the first to be true, is it certain that access has not been obtained by means of that door ? "

" But how could it have been ? " Mr. Woodburn exclaimed. " The door is sealed. I examined it myself most carefully, and I can assure you that the seals are undoubtedly intact."

" That is not absolutely conclusive," Thorndyke replied with a faint smile. " Seals are not very difficult to counterfeit. For instance, if, for any legitimate purpose you asked me to enter those rooms and replace the seals when I came out, I should find no difficulty in doing so."

" Really ! " exclaimed Mr. Woodburn. Then, subsiding into a grin, he added : " You are a rather dangerous sort of person, but I am not surprised that Brodribb has so much confidence in you. Perhaps you can suggest some way in which I might set about testing the correctness of these statements ; or, better still, perhaps you would be willing to undertake the investigation yourself ? I do feel that something ought to be done."

" So do I," said Thorndyke. " Incredible as the statements sound, what is stated is by no means impossible. And, if we should find that some persons either could have effected an entrance or had actually done so, the position would be entirely changed. You would then certainly be justified in breaking the seals and entering the rooms."

" And asking you to replace the seals afterwards, eh ? " suggested Woodburn, with a broad grin.

Apparently, Thorndyke's accomplishments had made a profound impression on him.

Thorndyke smilingly dismissed the suggestion and enquired :

" Is there no way, so far as you know, of getting a glimpse into the room from the outside ? "

" No way at all," was the reply. " I tried peering in at the windows, but it was impossible to see anything through the curtains. I even tried the keyhole. There is a monstrous great keyhole in the door. I should think the key must be quite a formidable weapon, though I have never seen it. The door is secured by a Chubb lock, of which I have the key. Well, I peered through that keyhole, but all I could see was a patch of wall on the side of the room opposite. Naturally ; because the door opens into the room at the extreme end of one side."

" Could you give me a description of the room, or, preferably, a sketch ? " Thorndyke asked.

" I have an architect's plan of the house in my bag," Woodburn replied. " I brought it up to show Brodribb, but he was not interested, as he did not believe the story. However, you are not so sceptical. I'll get it out."

He rummaged in his bag and presently produced a small roll of tracing-cloth, on which was a clearly drawn plan of the house and its immediate surroundings.

" The scale of the particular room," he remarked, " is not as large as we should like. But you can see the main features. This crooked corridor leads to the gallery wing, and you see that it ends in a turn at right angles. So, when the door is open, you look in across the end of the room. The door opens inwards, and here are three steps down to the floor level. You can see for yourself that a keyhole in that door is of no use for the purpose of inspection."

" Can you tell us anything about the furniture, or how the floor space is occupied ? " Thorndyke asked.

" With the exception of a few chairs and a large table across the farther end of the room, there is practically no furniture excepting the wall-cases. There is a range of them along each side wall between the windows and the two doors that open into the four small rooms at the side of the gallery."

" There seems to be no access to those rooms excepting through the doors from the gallery."

" No, there is not. Those rooms seem to have been originally a corridor, which has been divided up by partitions. They all open into one another—at least, each opens into the next. Two of them have cabinets full of pottery and porcelain, and the other two are work-rooms in which Mr. Toke does jobs such as mending and cleaning the pieces."

" What is there above and below the gallery ? " asked Thorndyke.

" Above, I suppose, are lofts. I don't know how you get to them, but I don't think they would help us. You couldn't see through the floor, and you couldn't bore holes in it, as the gallery has a fine seventeenth-century plaster ceiling. Under the gallery is a range of cellars, but they are not accessible, as they are all secured with good padlocks, and both the padlocks and the doors are sealed."

" Mr. Toke was certainly pretty thorough in his methods," Thorndyke remarked. " It would be a serious responsibility to break into his Bluebeard chambers."

" Yes, confound him," Woodburn agreed. " I wish to goodness it was possible to communicate with him and let him take the responsibility. I wonder why the deuce he has never sent me a line. I hope nothing has happened to him abroad. You can never be sure in these days of motors and sudden death."

" When did you say he went away ? " Thorndyke asked.

" On the ninth of August," replied Woodburn, " at least that is the date he gave me. He came to my office on the eighth to give me the keys and his final instructions, and he then said that he intended to start for Paris on the following night."

" Do you know if he did actually start then ? "

" Well, yes—indirectly. I happen to use the same garage to put up my car, when I come to town, as Mr. Toke uses. He recommended it to me, as a matter of fact. There I ascertained that he deposited his car on the morning of the ninth of August. But, oddly enough, he took it out again in the evening, and it was not returned until some time in the small hours of the following morning."

" Then," I said, " he couldn't have caught his train."

" I think he did. He did not return the car himself. It was brought in by a stranger, whom the night watchman described, picturesquely, as a ' ginger Lushington,' and this person reported that Mr Toke had caught his train, and that the lateness of the delivery of the car was due to some fault of his own."

" I wonder what the watchman meant by a ' ginger Lushington ' ? " said I.

" Yes," said Woodburn, " it is a quaint expression. I asked him what it meant in common English. Apparently, it was a term of inference. The word ' ginger ' referred to the colour of the man's hair, and, as his nose was tinted to match, the watchman inferred the habitual use of stimulants. But apparently Toke caught his train all right."

As Mr. Woodburn interpreted the watchman's description, I caught Thorndyke's eyes for a single

7

instant, and I saw that he had noted the significance of
that description. It was probably the merest coinci
dence, but I knew that it would not pass without close
scrutiny. And I could not but perceive that thereafter
his interest in Mr. Woodburn's affairs became appre
ciably more acute.

"Do I understand," he asked, "that you feel any
actual uneasiness about your client?"

"Well," was the reply, "I must admit that I am by
no means happy about him. You see, this prolonged
silence is a complete departure from his usual habits.
And time is running on. This is the eleventh of
October, and he has made no sign. All sorts of things
may happen to a man who is in a strange country and
out of all touch with his friends. I don't like it at all.
However, it was not about Mr. Toke that I came to
consult you, though I may have to ask for your assistance later. It is about these queer happenings at the
Manor House. Now, what do you suggest? I should
like you, as an expert, to take up the inquiry yourself.
Do you care to do that?"

"I am quite willing to make a preliminary investiga
tion," Thorndyke replied. "That would involve
personally interrogating the servants and making a
careful survey of the premises. If it seems to be a
mare's nest, we can let it drop. But if we discover
some hitherto unsuspected means of access to the
gallery, or find evidence that some persons have, in
fact, entered the premises, we can consider what action
is to be taken. Would that meet your views?"

"Perfectly," replied Woodburn. "When could you
come down and take a look at the place?"

"I suggest the day after to-morrow, early in the
afternoon, if that will suit you."

"It will do quite well," said Woodburn. "There is
a good train from Charing Cross at two-thirty. If you

can catch that, I will meet you at the station with my car and take you straight on to the house."

Thorndyke made a note of this arrangement, and Mr. Woodburn then took his leave, evidently very well pleased at having transferred some of his anxieties to more capable shoulders.

When he returned from the landing, having seen his visitor safely launched down the stairs, Thorndyke picked up the plan, which Mr. Woodburn had left on the table, and, glancing at it, turned to me with a smile.

" A queer affair, Jervis," said he. " I wonder if there is anything in it ? "

" Personally," I replied, " I should be disposed to suspect a mare's nest. There is something a little creepy about a big, old house, especially if a part of it is shut up and sealed. Those servants may easily have got a trifle jumpy and imagined that they heard sounds in the dead of the night."

" That is quite possible," he agreed. " But then we must not overlook the fact that the thing alleged is also quite possible. And it is not so very improbable. Precautions of the kind that Mr. Toke has taken may have a certain boomerang quality. The place is locked, bolted, barred, and sealed. That is all well enough so long as the precautions take their expected effect. But if they fail, they fail with a most horrid completeness. Here, for instance, is a collection of really valuable things. It is all nonsense to say that they are of no interest to burglars. It depends on the burglar. Fine pieces of porcelain and high-class bronzes are easily negotiable in the right markets. The burglar's real difficulty is in getting them away. Silver and gold can be carried away regardless of injury, as they are to be melted down ; but these things are fragile, and their value depends on their being uninjured. Now, if it is only possible for a burglar to obtain access to Mr. Toke's gallery, everything else is made easy for him.   He can work at his leisure and take these things away one or two at a time in the most suitable manner.   I think the affair is worth looking into, even on its own merits.

" But you notice that there is another aspect of the case that deserves attention.   Woodburn is obviously anxious about Mr. Toke.   And not without some reason.   In a legal sense, Mr. Toke has disappeared. His whereabouts are unknown to the very man to whom they should be known.   Now, suppose that some mishap has befallen him, and suppose that circumstance to be known to some person—some unscrupulous person— who also knows about the collection.   That is a bare possibility that has to be considered.   And then we have to note the fact that the only evidence that Toke did really catch his train is the statement of an unknown stranger."

" Who happens to have had red hair and a red nose," I remarked.

Thorndyke chuckled.   " True, " he admitted.   " But we mustn't allow ourselves, like Miller, to be obsessed by a mere matter of complexion.   Still, we will bear even that fact in mind.   And there is one other fact, with a possible inference.   Toke's instructions to Woodburn suggest something more than mere caution. They have a suggestion of secrecy.   So much so that one asks oneself if it is possible that he may have some property concealed in the gallery of a different kind from the ostensible collection.   I find it quite an attractive case, though, as you say, it may easily turn out to be a mare's nest."

" What do you propose to do when you go down to Hartsden ? " I asked.

" I have no definite programme," he replied, " beyond making the best possible use of my eyes and ears.

The obviously desirable thing would be to get a look at the interior of the gallery, and see if there are any signs of disturbance—whether, for instance, the cases have or have not been emptied."

" Yes," I agreed, " I realize that ; but I don't see how you are going to manage it, as, apparently, it is impossible to see in either by the windows or the door."

" It doesn't sound promising, I must admit," said he. " But we shall see when we get there. Perhaps Polton may be able to help us."

" Polton ! " I exclaimed. " How do you suppose that he may be able to help ? "

" Don't be so scornful," he protested. " Is an inventor and mechanical genius nothing worth ? I shall certainly put the problem to him as soon as I am clear about it myself."

In spite of the rather ambiguous phraseology, I suspected that Thorndyke had something quite definite in his mind. But I asked for no particulars ; long experience had taught me that he preferred to present his ideas in a mature and complete form rather than in that of a preliminary sketch. And, to tell the bald truth, my curiosity was not painfully acute. So I could wait patiently for enlightenment to come in due course.

As the train moved out of the station, Thorndyke lifted his invaluable green canvas research case from the seat to the rack, and then, with the tenderest care, disposed similarly of a walking-stick of the most surpassing hideousness.

"That," I remarked, eyeing it with profound disfavour, "looks like one of Polton's contraptions."

"It is," he replied, "if the word 'contraption' can be accepted as the proper designation of an extremely efficient and ingenious optical instrument. He made it many years ago ; but an instrument of virtually identical construction was produced during the war under the name of 'trench periscope.' It is really a modern version of the ancient device of parallel inclined mirrors, which you may see in any old book on physics ; only the mirrors are replaced by total-reflection prisms."

"Have you ever used it before ? " I asked.

"Yes, on one or two occasions, and found it to answer its purpose perfectly. I have brought it to-day on the chance that we may find some chink or hole through which we can poke it to get a view of the inside of the gallery."

"You won't get it through that keyhole that Woodburn spoke of, large as it is," said I.

"No," he agreed. "But, as to that, we are not at the end of our resources—or rather Polton's. He has devised an instrument for the express purpose of looking through awkwardly placed keyholes. I have it in my case."

He lifted the case down, and, having opened it, produced from it a small cylindrical wooden case with a screw cap. The latter being removed, he was able to draw out what looked like a brass pencil holder.

"This," he explained, "is a little Galilean telescope, magnifying about one and a half diameters. In front of the object glass is fixed a small, oblong mirror, which is pivoted so that it can be set at any angle by turning this milled ring at the eyepiece end. Of course, it has to be parallel to the tube when the instrument is passed into the keyhole."

He handed it to me, and I put it to my eye, after setting the mirror at a suitable angle.

"It doesn't seem a very efficient affair," I remarked. "It has such a wretchedly small field."

"Yes," he admitted, "that is the trouble with keyholes. But this is only an experimental form. If it seems suitable in principle, we can easily devise something more efficient. What we have to ascertain first of all is whether we can see through the keyhole at all. Looking at the plan, there seems to be nothing structural in the way ; but there may be some piece of furniture that will cut off the view of the room. If there is, the keyhole will be of no use to us."

I handed the little toy back to him with a shade of impatience.

"But why," I asked, "all this fuss ? Why go about a perfectly simple inquiry in this complicated, roundabout way ? If there is good reason to believe that someone has entered the room, why not just walk in and investigate in a reasonable, straightforward manner ? It seems to me that you and Brodribb are standing on rather pedantic legal scruples."

He shook his head. "I don't think so, Jervis," said he. "When you get clear instructions, you ought to assume that the instructor means what he says. But there is another matter, which I could only hint at to Woodburn. This man, Toke, is extraordinarily secretive. He has not only fastened up every opening with locks and bolts and screws, and put seals on the fastenings, but he has forbidden his solicitor, in the most emphatic way, to enter those rooms. Now, seals furnish no security against burglars. Their security is against his own trusted man of business. You or I or any reasonable person would have left the seal with Woodburn and asked him to inspect the place from time to time to see that all was well. Why has he shut out Woodburn in this secretive fashion ? We must assume that he has his reasons. But what can they be ? It may be mere crankiness, or it may not. Mr. Toke may be, and probably is, a most respectable gentleman. But supposing he is not ? Supposing that his activities as a dealer in works of art cover some other activities of a less reputable kind ? And supposing that the products of those other activities should happen to be hidden in those sealed rooms ? It is not impossible. But if Woodburn—or we, as his agents—should enter, in the face of explicit instructions to the contrary, and discover something illicit, the position would be extremely awkward. Professional secrecy does not cover that kind of thing."

" Still," I objected, " you are prepared to enter if you find evidence that someone else has."

" Certainly," he replied. " We should have to enter or inform the police. But we should then have no choice, whereas we have at present. And that raises another question. If we break in and find traces of unlawful visitors, we shall probably spoil our chances of making a capture. We are not ready now, and our entry would almost certainly leave some traces that would warn them not to reappear. Whereas, if we should discover evidences of visitors before we make our own entry, we should be able to make arrangements to catch them when they make their next visit."

I agreed without much enthusiasm, for it seemed to me that Thorndyke was taking a mere rumour much more seriously than the circumstances justified. In fact, I ventured a hint to that effect.

"That is quite true, Jervis," he admitted. "It is a mere report, at present. Yet I shall be a little surprised if we find a mare's nest. There is something distinctly abnormal about the whole affair. But we shall be better able to judge when we have got a statement from the servants."

"We have heard what they have to say," I replied, still extremely sceptical of the whole affair. "But, possibly, cross-examination may elicit something more definite. As you say, we shall see."

With this the discussion dropped, and we smoked our pipes in silence as we watched, from the window, the gradual transition from the grey and rather dreary suburbs to the fresh green of the country. At Hartsden Junction, Mr. Woodburn was waiting on the platform, looking more like a smart livery stable keeper than a lawyer, and evidently keenly interested in our arrival.

"I am glad to see you," he said, as we walked out to the approach, "for, the more I think about this affair, the more do I suspect that there is something amiss. And I have been reflecting on what you said about the seals. I had no idea that it was possible to forge a seal."

"I don't think," said Thorndyke, "that you need attach much weight to the forgery question. It is merely a possibility that has to be borne in mind. In the present case, it is highly improbable, as an intruder would have to pass through the house to reach the sealed door."

"Still," objected Mr. Woodburn, "that door seems

7*

to be the only way in.   Otherwise, why should Mr.
Toke have sealed it ? ''

There was a fairly obvious reply to this, but Thorndyke made no rejoinder ; and by this time we had
reached the car, into which Mr. Woodburn ushered us,
and then took his place at the steering-wheel, looking as
unsuitable for his post as if he had been at the tiller of
a fishing smack.

As the car was of the saloon type, we saw little of our
surroundings and nothing of the house until, entering
through an open gate, we passed up a shady drive and
stopped opposite a handsome stone porch.   The door
stood open and framed the figure of a pleasant-looking
middle-aged woman.

'' This,'' said Mr. Woodburn, introducing us, '' is
Mr. Toke's housekeeper, Mrs. Gibbins.   I have told her
about you, and she is as much interested in you as I am.''

Mrs. Gibbins confirmed this by a smile and a curtsy.

'' I am sure, gentlemen,'' said she, '' we shall all be
very grateful to you if you can find out what these
mysterious sounds are, and put a stop to them.   It is
very uncomfortable to feel that strangers—and dis-
honest strangers, too—are creeping about the house
in the dead of the night.''

'' It must be,'' Thorndyke agreed, warmly.   '' But,
before we start to find out what those sounds are, we
want to be quite sure that they really exist.''

'' There is no doubt about their existing,'' Mrs.
Gibbins rejoined, with intense conviction.   '' We have
all heard them.   And they certainly come from the
gallery wing, for my nephew, Edward, got out of bed
on two occasions and went part of the way down the
corridor and listened ; and he was quite sure that the
sounds came from the gallery or the rooms that open
out of it.   And it wasn't rats.   Everybody knows the
kind of sound that rats make, scampering about an

empty room. It wasn't like that, at all. It was like someone moving about quietly and, now and again, moving things. But there is another thing that can't be explained away. This house is supplied with water from an Artesian well. The water is pumped up by a windmill into a tank, which is on the level of the top floor, and it runs from the tank into the pipes that supply the house. The tank being so high up, the pressure of the water is quite considerable, and whenever a tap is running in any part of the house, you can hear a distinct hum in the main pipe. Of course, you can hear it much more distinctly at night when everything else is quiet.

" Now, I am a rather light sleeper, especially towards morning, and, on several occasions—over and over again—I have heard the water humming in the pipe when all the household were in bed and asleep. And always about the same time—just before it begins to get light."

" That is very remarkable, Mrs. Gibbins," said Woodburn. " You did not tell me about the water. It is a most striking fact. Don't you think so, Doctor ? "

" I do," replied Thorndyke, " especially when taken with the other sounds. I take it, Mrs. Gibbins, that there is water laid on in the gallery wing ? "

" Yes, sir. There is a lavatory with a fixed basin and a cold-water tap over it, and there is also a peculiar sort of sink—Mr. Toke calls it a chemical sink, I believe —in the work-room."

" And you say that the sound of running water occurs always at the same time ? Do you never hear it at other times ? "

" Oh, yes," she replied, " we hear it occasionally at other times. Not very often, though. But it seems to occur always when we have heard the other sounds.

It is just as if the person had been doing some job and had a wash before he went away."

Mr. Woodburn laughed cheerfully. " Tidy fellow, this," said he. " I wonder what he does in there. It's a quaint situation. He'll be ringing for his breakfast next."

" Can you form any idea," Thorndyke asked, " how often these sounds occur ? "

" I should say," replied Mrs. Gibbins, " that they happen pretty regularly twice a week—generally on Wednesdays and Fridays."

Mr. Woodburn laughed heartily. Thorndyke's appearance on the scene had evidently acted favourably on his spirits.

" Quite a methodical chap," he chuckled. " Keeps regular hours, and has a wash and brush up before he goes home."

" We mustn't take him too much for granted," Thorndyke reminded him. " We have got to establish his existence as a matter of undoubted fact, though I must admit that Mrs. Gibbins's account is extremely circumstantial and convincing. It establishes a case for a very thorough investigation and I think we had better begin by having a look at the door of the gallery. What will be about the height of that keyhole that you spoke of ? "

Mr. Woodburn indicated the height by reference to a point on his own waistcoat. " But I am afraid the keyhole won't help you much," he added. " As I think I told you, I couldn't see anything through it, excepting a patch of the opposite wall."

" Perhaps we can manage to get a better view," said Thorndyke ; " that is, if there is nothing in the way. Probably, Mrs. Gibbins can tell us about that. How was the furniture arranged when you were in there last ? "

" There is very little furniture in there, at all," the housekeeper replied, " unless you call the wall-cases furniture. There is a large table across the end of the room, and there are three chairs, one arm-chair and two ordinary dining-room chairs. The arm-chair is behind the table, nearly in the middle, and the other two are at the ends of the table."

" You say they ' are,' " Thorndyke remarked. " Do you mean that that is how they were placed when you were last in the room ? "

" Yes, sir. But I think they must be like that still, because the last time I was in there was on the day when Mr. Toke went away. I helped him to shut up the room and seal the door. They couldn't very well have been moved after that."

" Apparently not," Thorndyke admitted. " Then, in that case, we may as well go and have a look at the door and see if it is possible to get a glimpse of the inside of the room. And perhaps we had better take a chair with us, as the keyhole is at a rather inconvenient height."

Mr. Woodburn picked up a chair and led the way out of the morning room in which we had been holding our conversation, across the hall and into a narrow passage, which became almost dark as a sharp turn cut off the light from the doorway by which we had entered.

" Queer old place," he remarked as the corridor took another turn. " All holes and corners. I am wondering how you are going to see into that room. I couldn't ; but I suppose a man who can produce another man's seal out of a top hat won't make any difficulty about seeing round a corner."

" We have only undertaken to try," Thorndyke reminded him. " Don't let us take credit prematurely."

The disclaimer was not entirely unnecessary ; for, when the corridor took yet another abrupt turn and brought us to a blind end in which was a massive door, it became clear to me, from the manner both of Mrs. Gibbins and Mr. Woodburn, that there was an expectation of some sort of display of occult powers on Thorndyke's part. So much so that, for the first time, I felt quite grateful to Polton.

"There you are," said Mr. Woodburn, placing the chair in position, and standing back expectantly to watch the proceedings, as if he had some hopes of seeing Thorndyke put his head through the keyhole. "Let us see how you do it."

My colleague seated himself with a deprecating smile, and, laying the research case on the floor, unfastened the catch and raised the lid ; whereupon Mr. Woodburn and Mrs. Gibbins craned forward to peer in. Having taken a preliminary peep through the keyhole, Thorndyke produced the little wooden case and drew out Polton's diminutive spy-glass, which he inserted easily enough into the roomy opening. As he applied his eye to the tiny eyepiece and turned the milled ring to adjust the mirror, the two observers watched him with bated breath ; as, indeed, did I, and with no small anxiety. For, apart from the importance of the result, a complete failure would have been a shocking anti-climax. Great, therefore, was my relief when Thorndyke announced :

"Well, at any rate, there is no obstruction to the view, such as it is. But it is not easy to make out the arrangement and relative positions of things with such a very restricted field of vision. However, as far as I can see, there are no signs of any appreciable disturbance. I can see the wall-cases at the end of the room, and their shelves are filled with what look like Bow and Chelsea figures. So there has been no robbery there. The cases at the sides of the room are not so easy to see, but I think I can make out the contents, and they appear to contain their full complement. Evidently, so far as the collection is concerned, there has been no robbery on any considerable scale.

"Then the position of the furniture corresponds generally with Mrs. Gibbins's description. There is an arm-chair behind the table and an ordinary dining-chair at each end. I can also see what looks like a shallow box or case of some kind on the table."

"A box on the table?" exclaimed Mrs. Gibbins. "That is curious. I don't remember any box, or anything else, on the table."

"Perhaps Mr. Toke put it there after you left," suggested Mr. Woodburn.

"But he couldn't," Mrs. Gibbins objected. "I went out with him and helped him to seal up the door. He couldn't have gone back after that."

"No. That is obvious," Woodburn admitted. "So it looks as if someone had been in the room, after all."

"Do you say, positively, Mrs. Gibbins, that there was nothing on the table when you left the room with Mr. Toke?" Thorndyke asked.

"Well, sir," the housekeeper replied, "one doesn't like to be too positive, but I certainly thought that there was nothing on the table. In fact, I feel sure that there wasn't."

"That seems pretty conclusive," said Woodburn. "What do you think, Doctor?"

"It is conclusive enough to us," Thorndyke replied, diplomatically. "But, as a lawyer, you will realize the difficulty of coming to a definite decision on negative evidence. To justify you in acting in direct opposition to your client's instructions, you ought to have undeniable positive evidence. We are not considering our own beliefs, but the legal position."

"Yes, that is true," Mr. Woodburn conceded, evidently interpreting Thorndyke's polite hint that ladies are sometimes apt to confuse the subjective with the objective aspects of certainty. " Do you see anything else ? "

" No. I think that is the sum of my observations. But remember that the room is strange to me. Perhaps if you, who know the room, were to take a look through the instrument, you might detect some change that would not be apparent to me."

To say that Woodburn jumped at the offer would be to understate the case. In his eagerness to occupy the seat of observation, he nearly sat on Thorndyke's lap. But, apparently, Polton's " contraption " did not come up to his expectations, for, after peering in at the eyepiece for some seconds, he said in a tone of slight disappointment :

" I don't seem to make much of it. I can only see a tiny bit at a time, and everything looks in its wrong place. The table seems to be right opposite this door instead of where I know it to be."

" You must disregard the positions of things," Thorndyke explained. " Remember that you are looking into a mirror."

" Oh, I hadn't realized that," said Woodburn, hastily. " Of course, that explains the odd appearance of the room."

He reapplied his eye to the instrument, and now was able to manage it better, for he presently reported :

" I think the cases look all right and everything else appears as usual. As to that box, of course, I can say nothing. I have never seen it before, and I can't quite make out what sort of box it is. It looks like metal."

" That was what I thought," said Thorndyke. " Perhaps Mrs. Gibbins may recognize it."

The suggestion was evidently acceptable, for the housekeeper " outed " Mr. Woodburn with great promptness, and, having seated herself, applied her eye to the instrument. But she was even less successful than her predecessor, for, after a prolonged stare through the eyepiece, she announced that she could see nothing but the carpet, which appeared, unreasonably, to have affixed itself to the opposite wall. However, Thorndyke came to her aid, and eventually enabled her to see the mysterious box on the table ; concerning which she again asserted with deep conviction that, not only was she quite sure that it had not been there when she and Mr. Toke had vacated the room, but that she was equally certain that she had never seen the box before at all.

When she had finished her observations (which seemed to concern themselves principally with the floor and the ceiling), I came into the reversion of the chair, by way, ostensibly, of confirming the previous observations. And, when I came to look through the little instrument in the conditions for which it was designed, I was disposed to be apologetic to Polton. The field of view was, indeed, extremely small, but the little circular picture at which one looked was beautifully clear and bright ; and the fine adjustment for moving the mirror enabled one to shift the field of vision gradually and preserve a continuity in the things seen that had, to some extent, the effect of a larger field.

" Well," said Woodburn, as I rose from the chair, " what have we arrived at ? Or haven't we arrived at any conclusion ? "

" I think," said Thorndyke, " that we must conclude that our observations tend to confirm the suspicion that someone had obtained access to this room. But I do not think that we have enough evidence to justify us in disregarding Mr. Toke's very definite instructions."

" Then," said Woodburn, " what do you suggest that we ought to do ? "

" I suggest that we make a careful survey of the house

to see if we can find any means of access to this room that the seals do not cover ; and if, as I expect, we fail to find any such means, then we must make some more exact and continuous observations from this door."

" You don't suggest that we post someone at this keyhole to keep watch continuously, do you ? " exclaimed Woodburn.

" No," replied Thorndyke. " That would be impracticable. But I think we could achieve the same result in another way. At any rate, I will take the preliminary measures before we go away from here, in case they may be needed."

He withdrew the " spy-glass " from the keyhole, and, having put it away in the research case, produced from the latter a small cardboard box which, when the lid was removed, was seen to contain a number of little cylinders of hardwood about six inches long and of varying diameters, from a quarter of an inch up to five-eighths.

" These," he explained, " are gauges that my assistant has made to obtain the exact dimensions of the keyhole, so that he can make a more efficient instrument."

" The instrument that you have got is efficient enough," said Woodburn. " The trouble will be to get someone to stay here to use it."

" Perhaps we can produce an instrument that will do its work without an attendant," replied Thorndyke. " But we will talk about that when we have made our survey. Now, I will just take these measurements."

He seated himself once more and proceeded to pass the larger cylinders one by one through the keyhole. All of them passed through fairly easily excepting the two largest, which were returned to the box.

" The internal diameter of the keyhole," said Thorndyke, " is nearly nine-sixteenths of an inch. Probably

it has been a little enlarged by wear, but even so the
key must have been an out-size. I shall call it half an
inch."

He marked, with a pencil, the approved cylinder,
and, having returned it to the box, announced that he
was ready to proceed to the next item in the programme.

" Perhaps," he suggested, " we had better take a
glance at the lofts which are over the gallery."

Mr. Woodburn looked interrogatively at the housekeeper, who volunteered the information that the
entrance to them was at the top of the back staircase,
and that the key was on her bunch.

" The entrance to the lofts is not sealed, then ? "
Thorndyke remarked.

" Apparently not," said Woodburn ; " which suggests that we are not likely to find anything of interest
in them. Still, we may as well have a look at them
and satisfy ourselves."

We followed the housekeeper through a surprising
labyrinth of passages and rooms, which seemed to be
on all sorts of levels, with steps up and down, which
made it necessary to approach all doors with caution
to avoid being tripped up or stepping into empty air.
Eventually, we came to an unlocked door which gave
entrance to the back staircase, up which Mrs. Gibbins
preceded us in a dim twilight. At each landing, open
doors gave glimpses into dark and mysterious corridors
which apparently burrowed among the bedrooms, and
the top landing showed us, in addition, a locked door
with an enormous keyhole, into which the housekeeper
inserted a ponderous key. The door creaked open, and
revealed a flight of narrow, ladder-like stairs, up which
we crawled painfully and cautiously, Thorndyke
bringing up the rear, encumbered with his research
case and the Poltonic walking-stick.

There was no door at the top of the stairs (which

seemed a lost opportunity on the part of the architect), and only a pretence of a landing outside the narrow doorway which gave entrance to the lofts. Here we stood for a few moments, looking into the long range of well-lighted lofts that stretched away on either side. There was something a little weird and impressive in the aspect of those great, wide attics with their rough oaken floors, littered with the cast-off household gods of forgotten generations, stretching away into the distance among the massive and almost unhewn timber of the great roof. Each of the two ranges—for we stood at the angle of the body and the wing of the house—was lighted by a pair of dormer windows on each side, filled with little panes of greenish glass set in leaded casements, so that we were able to see the whole extent with the exception of a few dark corners at the extreme ends.

" Well," said Woodburn, looking a little distastefully at the littered floor, covered, as it seemed, with the dust of centuries, " is it worth while to go in ? Looks a bit dusty," he added, with a glance at his brilliantly polished boots.

" I think I will just walk down the lofts," said Thorndyke, " as a matter of form, though it is pretty clear that there have been no recent visitors. But there is no need for you to come."

That it was but a mere formality became evident as soon as we had started ; for, glancing back, I could see that we had left plain and conspicuous footprints in the impalpable dust that lay in an even coating on the bumpy floor. Evidently, we were the first visitors who had trodden that floor for, at least, some years.

" Still," said Thorndyke, when I made a remark to this effect, " we had to establish the fact. If there is some secret way into the gallery, our only chance of discovering it will be by excluding, one by one, all the places in which it is not to be found. This is evidently one of them."

" Well," said Woodburn, as we emerged ; " we can write off the lofts, I think. Dust has its uses, after all. What are we going to explore next ? "

" I suppose," Thorndyke replied, " we had better examine the outside of the premises."

" Yes," Woodburn agreed, " that seems to be the reasonable thing to do, seeing that, if there have been any visitors, that is where they must have come from. But there is mighty little to see. I can tell you that much, for I have made a thorough inspection, myself."

Mr. Woodburn was right. There was very little indeed to see. The gallery stood above a range of what were now cellars, but had formerly been rooms, as we gathered from the windows, some entirely bricked up, while others were reduced to small openings, glazed with ground glass and protected by stout iron bars. The only approach to them was from within the house, by a massive door at the bottom of a flight of stone steps ; and that door was not only sealed, but also secured by a heavy padlock of the Yale type, of which the minute key-slit was covered by a sealed label.

From outside the house, there was no entrance of any kind to the gallery wing. The windows of the gallery, itself, looked on the garden at the back of the house ; but an inspection of them by means of the ladder, which had been put there for our convenience, only served to confirm Woodburn's account of them. They were obviously untouched ; and the lace curtains on the inside made it impossible to get the faintest glimpse into the room. The windows of the rooms which communicated with the gallery were equally impossible as a means of access. We examined them with the aid of the ladder from the narrow strip of garden that separated the side of the wing from the high wall that

enclosed the whole domain.   They, also, were evidently
intact, and were guarded internally by massive shutters
that effectually excluded the possibility of seeing in.

" That seems to be the lot," said Woodburn, as we
put the ladder back where we had found it, " unless
there is anything else that you would like to see."

Thorndyke looked up at the house, inquisitively, and
then glanced along the wall down the garden. " I
think," said he, " I understood you to say that there
was a churchyard on the other side of that wall."

" Yes.   Do you want to see it ?   I don't know why
you should."

" We may as well take a look at it," was the reply.
" Any visitors, entering the house at night, would
probably come over that wall rather than through the
front grounds, particularly if there is a churchyard to
take off from.   A country churchyard is pretty secluded
at night.   It would even be possible to use a portable
ladder."

" So it would," agreed Woodburn.   " And this is a
disused churchyard.   They have built a new church
at the other end of the village, the Lord knows why.
They had better have restored the old church.   But
any visitors to the old churchyard would have the
place to themselves at night."

" Then let us go and inspect it," said Thorndyke.
" If there have been repeated visits, there ought to be
some traces of the visitors."

We went back through the house and out by way of
the drive and the front gate.   Turning to the right, we
walked along the front of the Manor House grounds to
the end of the enclosing wall where it was joined by the
lower wall of the churchyard.   Presently, we came to
a dilapidated wooden gate which yawned wide open on
its rickety hinges.   Passing in through this, we took
our way along an overgrown path, past a tall head-

stone and a decayed altar tomb, enclosed by rusty, ivy-grown railings. In front of us, a great yew tree cast a deep shadow across the path; and beyond, a smallish, ancient-looking church, with gaping windows from which the tracery had disappeared, huddled under a dense mantle of ivy, looking the very picture of desolation and decay.

As we walked, Thorndyke looked about him critically, keeping an attentive eye on the ground beside the path, the high, neglected grass which everywhere sprang up between the graves being obviously favourable to a search for " traces." So we advanced until we entered the gloomy shadow of the great yew tree. Here Thorndyke halted to look about him.

"Somewhere in this neighbourhood," said he, " would be the most probable place for a nocturnal operator to make his arrangements. That is the Manor House wall in front of us. I can see the roof of the gallery wing through the trees. That big sarcophagus tomb will be nearly opposite the end of the wing."

" Yes," I said. " It seems to mark the position that would be most convenient for negotiating the wall ; and, if you notice the grass, there seems to be a faint, rather wide track, as if it had been walked over by someone who had been careful not to tread it down all in one place."

" I think you are right," said Woodburn. " Now you mention it, I think I can make out the track quite plainly. It seems to lead towards that tomb."

" The grass has certainly been walked over, " Thorndyke agreed, " and I see no signs of its having been trodden anywhere else. But don't let us confuse matters by walking over it ourselves. Let us strike across the graves and approach along the wall."

We followed this course, keeping close to the wall as we approached the great tomb. The latter stood about ten feet from the wall, and, as we drew near, I was surprised to notice that the grass between the tomb and the wall appeared quite untrodden. Thorndyke had also noticed this rather unexpected circumstance, and, when we were within a yard or two of the tomb, he halted and looked curiously along the ground at the foot of the wall.

" There is certainly no sign of the use of any ladder," he remarked. " In fact, there is no indication of any-one having approached close to the wall. The track, if it really is one, doesn't appear to go beyond the tomb."

" That is what it looks like to me," agreed Woodburn, " though I am hanged if I can see any reason why it should. They couldn't have jumped from the top of the tomb over the wall."

" It looks," I suggested, " as if this place had been used rather as a post of observation, or a lurking-place where the sportsman could keep out of sight until the coast was clear."

We approached the tomb from the direction of the wall and sauntered round it, idly reading the inscriptions, which recorded briefly the life-histories of a whole dynasty of Greenlees, " late of Hartsden Manor in this Parish," beginning with one John Greenlees who died in 1611.

" They were a turbulent family, these Greenlees," said Woodburn. " Always in hot water. Bigoted Papists in the early days, and, of course, Jacobites after the Revolution. From what I have heard, Hartsden Manor House must have seen some stirring times."

While he was speaking, I was glancing through the inscriptions on the back of the tomb. Happening to look down, I noticed a match in the grass at my feet, and stooped to pick it up. As I did so, I observed another ; on which I made a search and ultimately salved no less than six.

" What have you found, Jervis ? " Thorndyke asked, as I rose.

I held out my hand with the six matches in it. " All from the same place at the back of the tomb," said I. " What do you make of that ? "

" It might mean five failures on a windy day or night," he replied, " or six separate cigarettes ; and the operator may have come here to get a ' lee side,' or he may have got behind the tomb so that the light should not be seen from the road. But we must not let our imaginations run away with us. There is nothing to show that the person or persons who came to this tomb have any connection with our problem. We are looking for some means of access to the gallery, and, up to the present, we have not found any. The fact, if it were one, that some persons had been lurking about here, waiting for a chance to enter, wouldn't help us. It would not tell us how they got in ; which is what we want to know."

Nevertheless, he continued, for some time, to browse round the tomb, dividing his attention between the inscriptions and the grass that bordered the low plinth.

At length he turned away and began to retrace his steps down the path towards the gate.

" Well," said Woodburn, " we seem to have exhausted the possibilities, unless there is anything else that you want to see."

" No," replied Thorndyke, " I don't think it is of any use to prolong our search. I suspect that there is some way into the house ; but, if there is, it is too well hidden to be discoverable without some guiding hint, which we haven't got. So the answer to our first question is negative, and we must concentrate on the second—does anyone, in fact, effect an entrance to the gallery ? "

" And how do you propose to solve that problem ? "
enquired Woodburn.

" I propose to install an automatic recorder which
will give us a series of photographs of the interior of the
room."

" And catch 'em on the hop, eh ? " said Woodburn.
" But it doesn't seem possible.   Why, you would have
to take a photograph every few minutes ; and then you
wouldn't bring it off, because the beggars seem to come
only at night."

" I am not expecting to get photographs of the
visitors themselves," Thorndyke explained.   " My
idea is that, if any persons do frequent those rooms,
they will almost certainly leave some traces of their
visits.   Even the moving of a chair would be conclusive evidence, if it could be proved, as it could be
by the comparison of two photographs which showed it
in different positions.   I shall send my assistant, Mr.
Polton, down to set up the apparatus, and perhaps you
will give Mrs. Gibbins instructions to give him all
necessary facilities, including the means of locking up
the corridor when he has fixed the apparatus and set it
going."

To this Mr. Woodburn agreed, gleefully, and, as a
train was due in a quarter of an hour, we embarked in
his car without re-entering the house.

FROM Charing Cross we walked home to the Temple, entering it by way of Pump Court and the Cloisters. As we were about to cross King's Bench Walk, I glanced up at the laboratory window, and caught a momentary glimpse of Polton's head, which, however, vanished even as I looked ; and, when we arrived at our landing, the door of our chambers was open, and he was visible within, making a hypocritical pretence of laying the dinner-table, which had obviously been laid hours previously. But his pretended occupation did not conceal the fact that he was in a twitter of anxiety and impatience, which Thorndyke proceeded at once humanely to allay.

" It had to be a cold dinner, as I didn't know what time you would be home," Polton explained ; but Thorndyke cut short his explanations and came to the essential matter.

" Never mind the dinner, Polton," said he. " The important point is that your automatic watcher will be wanted, and as soon as you can get it ready."

Polton beamed delightedly on his employer as he replied :

" It is ready now, sir, all except the objective. You see, the clock and the camera were really made already. They only wanted a little adaptation. And I have made an experimental objective, and done some trial exposures with it. So I am ready to go ahead as soon as I have the dimensions of the keyhole."

" I can give you those at once," said Thorndyke,

opening the research case and taking out the wooden cylinders. " The keyhole will take a half-inch tube fairly easily."

Polton slapped his thigh joyfully. " There's a stroke of luck ! " he exclaimed. " You said it would be about half an inch, so I used a half-inch tube for my experimental objective. But I never dared to hope that it would be the exact size. As it is, all I have got to do is to fix it on to the camera. I can do that to-night and give it a final trial. Then it will be ready to set up in place to-morrow. Perhaps, sir, you will come up presently and see if you think it will do. I shall have got it fixed by the time you have finished dinner."

With this, having taken a last glance at the table, he retired in triumph, with the box of cylinders in his hand.

" What is this ' automatic watcher ' ? " I asked, as we sat down to our meal. " I assume that it is some sort of automatic camera. But what is its special peculiarity ? "

" In its original form," replied Thorndyke, " it consisted of a clock of the kind known as an English Dial, with a magazine camera fixed inside it. There was a simplified striking movement which released the shutter at any intervals previously arranged. It also had an arrangement for recording the time at which each exposure was made. It was quite a valuable appliance for keeping a watch on any particular place. It could be set up, for instance, opposite the door of a strong room or in any similar position."

" But suppose the thief made his visit in the interval between two exposures ? "

" That was provided for by a special attachment whereby the opening of the door was made to break an electric circuit and release the shutter. So that whenever the door was opened an exposure was made and the time recorded. But, for our present purpose, although we have retained the principle, we have had to modify the details considerably. For instance, we have separated the clock from the camera, so that it can be fixed far enough away from the door to prevent its tick from being heard in the gallery. The releasing mechanism of the clock is connected with an electro-magnet in the camera which actuates the shutter and the film roller. The lens is in a tube five inches long, with a reflecting prism at the farther end, which will, of course, be passed through the keyhole, and the camera screwed on to the door. That is a rough sketch of the apparatus. You will see the details of it when we go up to make our inspection."

" And how often do you propose to make an ex-posure ? " I asked.

" One exposure every twenty-four hours would do for us," he replied, " as we merely want a daily record of the positions of the various objects in the room. But that does not satisfy Polton. He would like an ex-posure every hour. So we have arrived at a com-promise. There will be an exposure every six hours. Of course, those made at night will show nothing, and both of those made in daylight, when the room will be unoccupied, will, presumably, be alike. But I can see that Polton will not be happy if there is not a good string of exposures."

"Supposing the exposures are all alike?" I suggested.

Thorndyke laughed grimly. " Don't be a wet blanket, Jervis," said he. " But I must admit that it would be something of an anticlimax and distinctly disappointing, though not entirely unexpected. For, if there are really visitors, it is quite possible that they do not go to the gallery at all. Their business, what-ever it may be, is, quite conceivably, carried on in one of the rooms that open out of the gallery. So a negative result with the camera would not prove that no one had entered the gallery wing."

It was my turn to smile, and I did so. " It is my belief, Thorndyke," said I, " that you don't mean anything to disprove it. You are not approaching this investigation with an open mind."

" Not very open," he admitted. " The housekeeper's statement, together with all the other circumstances of the case, make a very strong suggestion of something abnormal, so strong that, as you say, I am not prepared to be easily satisfied with a negative result. And now, if we have finished, we had better go up to the laboratory and have a look at Polton's masterpiece."

We rose, and were just moving towards the door when a firm tread became audible on the landing, and was followed by a familiar knock on the brass knocker of the inner door.

" Miller, by Jove ! " I exclaimed. " How unfortunate ! But I can entertain him while you go up to Polton."

" Let us hear what he has to say, first," replied Thorndyke ; and he proceeded to throw open the door.

As the Superintendent entered, I was impressed by a certain curious mixture of jauntiness and anxiety in his manner. But the former predominated, especially as he made his triumphant announcement.

" Well, gentlemen, I thought you would be interested to hear that we have got our man."

" Dobey ? " asked Thorndyke.

" Dobey it is," replied Miller. " We've got him, we've charged him, and he is committed for trial."

" Come and sit down," said Thorndyke, " and tell us all about it."

He deposited the Superintendent in a comfortable arm-chair, placed on the little table at his elbow the whisky decanter, the siphon, and the box of the specially favoured cigars, and while the tumbler was being charged and the cigar lighted, he filled his pipe and regarded his visitor with a slightly speculative eye.

" Where did you catch him ? " he asked, when the preliminary formalities were disposed of.

Miller removed the cigar from his mouth in order the more conveniently to smile.

" It was a quaint affair," he chuckled. " We caught him in the act of picking the lock of his own front door. Rum position, wasn't it ? Of course, the key was at the police station at Maidstone. We had been keeping a watch on the flat, but it happened that day that one of our sergeants was going there with a search warrant to have another look over the premises in case anything should have been missed at the first search. When he got up to the landing, there was my nabs, angling at the keyhole with a piece of wire. He was mightily surprised when the sergeant introduced himself, and still more so when he was told what he was charged with."

" Was he charged with the murder or the house-breaking ? "

" Both. Of course, the usual caution was administered, but, Lord, you might as well have cautioned an oyster."

" Did he say nothing at all ? "

" Oh, the usual thing. Expressed astonishment— that was real enough, beyond a doubt. Said he didn't know what we were talking about, but was perfectly sure that he didn't want to make any statement."

" I suppose he pleaded ' not guilty ' at the police court ? "

" Yes. But he wouldn't say anything in his defence, excepting that he knew nothing about the murder and had never heard of Inspector Badger, until he had got legal advice. So the magistrate adjourned the hearing for a couple of days, and Dobey got a lawyer to defend him—a chappie named Morris Coleman."

" Of Kennington Lane ? "

" That's the man. Solicitor and advocate. Hebrew, of course. Downy bird, too, but quite a good lawyer."

" Yes," said Thorndyke, " I have seen him in court. A cut above the ordinary police-court advocate. And what did he have to say ? "

" Reserved his defence, of course. They always do if the case is going for trial. That's the worst of these police-court solicitors. But it usually means that they haven't got any defence, and of course that is what it means now, so it doesn't matter. But it is a time-wasting plan when they have got a defence, and the judge usually has something to say about it. Still, you can't cure them. They think they get an advantage by springing a defence on the court that nobody expected."

" You say you are proceeding on both the charges. Why are you bringing in the house-breaking ? "

" Well, of course," replied Miller, " it is the murder that he will actually be tried for. But we shall have to prove the facts of the house-breaking to explain how the stolen paper came to be found."

As he gave this explanation, the Superintendent stole a slightly furtive glance at Thorndyke, which I understood when the latter remarked, dryly :

" True. And the evidence of the witnesses to the house-breaking may serve to supply the deficiencies of the station-master at Strood. I take it that they will be able to identify Dobey."

" They have. Picked him out instantly from a crowd of thirty other men. And as to that station-master, it's just a silly excess of caution and over-conscientiousness. He didn't look at the man particularly, and so he won't swear to him. But, as his description of the man agrees with that of the witnesses to the house-breaking, and they are ready to swear to Dobey, it will, as you say, help matters a bit. But, of course, the finding of the paper in his possession is the really crucial piece of evidence."

" It is more than that," said Thorndyke. " It is the whole of the evidence in regard to the murder. Without it your bill would never get past the Grand Jury. And, as to the house-breaking, as it can't be included in the indictment, I doubt whether the court will allow any reference to it. That, however, remains to be seen."

" Well," rejoined Miller, " it doesn't matter a great deal. The paper fixes the crime on him."

With this, he dipped his nose into his glass and resumed his cigar with the air of having disposed of the subject ; and I took the opportunity to raise another point.

" Did you say that Dobey was found picking his lock with a piece of wire ? " I asked.

" Yes," he answered with a chuckle. " Quaint situation, wasn't it ? "

" It strikes me as more than quaint," I replied. " It is most extraordinary that he should not have provided himself with a key of some sort."

" It is," Miller agreed. " But it was a simple latch, and I expect he was pretty handy with the wire. And I don't suppose he often went to the flat. Still, as you say, he must have been a fool not to get a key."

" He must," said I. " It is a striking example of the criminal mentality."

" Yes," agreed Miller, " they are not a very bright lot." He paused reflectively for a few moments, puffing at his cigar reflectively, and then resumed in a meditative tone : " And yet it doesn't do to rate them

8

too low. We say to ourselves that they are all fools. So they are, or they wouldn't be crooks. Crime is never a really sound economic proposition. But there is one thing that we must bear in mind : there are two kinds of crooks—those that get caught, and those that don't. And a crook that doesn't get caught may never come into sight at all. If he manages well enough, his existence may never be even suspected. I have just heard of a case in which the existence of a man of this class has been disclosed by a mere chance. But we don't know who he is, and we are not very likely to find out. I'll tell you about the case. It's a queer affair.

" Just recently, one of our men who specializes in note forgeries and knows a good deal about money of all kinds, had to spend a week or two on the Continent. When he was about to return, he changed his foreign money into English and got one or two sovereigns. Now, when he got home and had a look at those sovereigns, he thought there seemed to be something queer about one of them. So he got a chemist to weigh it, but the weight was apparently all right—it was only an ordinary shop scale, you know, but it weighed within a fraction of a grain. Then he measured it ; but all the dimensions seemed to be correct. But, still, to his expert eye, it didn't look right ; and it didn't sound right when he rang it. So he took it to an assayist whom he knew, and the assayist tried its specific gravity and tested it so far as was possible without damaging the coin, and he reported that it was undoubtedly gold of about the correct fineness. But still our man wasn't satisfied. So he took it to the Mint, and showed it to one of the chief officials. And then the murder was out. It wasn't a milled coin at all. It was a casting. An uncommonly good casting and very neatly finished off at the edge, but an undoubted casting to the skilled eye. So they passed it on to the assay department and made a regular assay of it. The result was very quaint. It was gold right enough, and just about 22 carat ; but it was not exactly the composition of a sovereign. There was a slight difference in the alloy. That was all. There was no fraud. The proper amount of gold was there. Yet it was a counterfeit coin. Now, what do you make of that ? "

" Nothing," I answered, " unless it was a practical joke."

" Well, it wasn't. The Mint people asked us to look into the matter, and we did. The result was that we found one or two more specimens of this queer, un-official money—you couldn't call it base coin—in France, Belgium, and Holland. Evidently, there is a regular manufacture."

" But what on earth can be the meaning of it ? " I demanded.

Miller chuckled. " We can only guess," said he, " but we can take it that the sportsman who makes those sovereigns doesn't do it for fun. And, if he makes a profit on them, he doesn't buy his gold from the bullion dealers, and he doesn't pay the market price for it. On the other hand, he probably sells it for export at con-siderably above its nominal value, now that gold is so difficult to get. So, if he steals his gold, or gets it cheap from the thieves, and sells it at a premium, he doesn't do so badly. And he will be mighty hard to catch. For the coins are genuine golden sovereigns, and only a fairly expert person would be able to spot them. And experts are pretty rare, nowadays. Once, every little shopkeeper was an expert ; but now there are plenty of people who have never seen a sovereign."

" It is a clever dodge," I remarked, " if the gold is really stolen."

" Clever ! " repeated Miller, enthusiastically. " It's

a stroke of genius. You see, it avoids all the crook's ordinary difficulties. He can get rid of the stones pretty easily, as they can't be identified separately. But the gold is less easy to dispose of at a decent price. For, if a bullion dealer is willing to buy it—which he probably isn't, if he is a respectable man—the transaction is known, and the vendor has left dangerous tracks ; and the ordinary fence will only give a knockdown price. He must make a big profit to set off the risk that he takes.

" But there is another case that has just come to light—probably the same man. You know that, for some time past, the Mint has been calling in all real silver money. Now, since this sovereign incident, it occurred to the people there to look over the silver coins that came in ; and, at the first cast, they came on a half-crown that turned out to be a casting. But it was silver. Further search brought one or two more to light. Someone was making silver half-crowns.

" Now, here was a paradoxical situation ! The coiner was making good silver coin while the Mint was issuing base money. Of course, coining is illegal. But this coiner could not be charged with uttering base coin. It would be hard to prove to a jury that it was counterfeit.

" Here you see the difference between the stupid crook and the clever crook. The fool tries to grab the whole—and doesn't do it. He makes his coin of pewter and probably steals that. They generally used to. If he got half a crown for his pewter snide, it would be all profit. But he doesn't, because it is a duffer. So he has to sell it cheap to the snide man. And he gets caught. But this sportsman puts, say, a shilling'sworth of silver into his half-crown, and he doesn't have to pay the snide man. He can pass it quite safely himself. And he doesn't get caught."

" He runs the risk of getting caught if he passes it himself," I objected.

"Not at all," said Miller. " How should he ? What you're overlooking is that the coins are good coins. They pass freely, and they will bear assay. Only an expert can spot them, and then only after close examination. But he must make a big profit. He could easily get rid of a hundred a day. There's seven pounds ten shillings profit, even if he buys the silver at the market price, which he probably does not. That silver is most likely burglars' loot—silver tea-pots and candlesticks melted down ; stuff that he would have to sell to a fence at about the price of brass. I tell you, Dr. Jervis, that coiner is a brainy customer. He'll want a lot of salt sprinkled on his tail before he'll get caught."

" I think you are rather over-estimating his profits," said I. " He has not only to pass the coins ; he has got to make them. Good workmanship like that means time and labour. And there is the gold. Most trade jewellery is made of a lower-grade gold than 22 carat. He would either have to buy fine gold from the bullion dealers to bring his low-grade gold up to standard or to do a good deal of conversion himself."

While Miller was considering this difficulty, the door opened, and Polton's head became visible, his eyes riveted on the Superintendent's back with an expression of consternation. I think he would have withdrawn, but that Miller, in some occult manner, became aware of his presence and addressed him.

" Good evening, Mr. Polton. We were just discussing a little problem that is rather in your line. Perhaps you would give us your opinion on it."

On this, Polton advanced with a slightly suspicious eye on the Superintendent, and Miller proceeded to put his case.

" The problem is, how to make sovereigns—castings, you know—out of jewellery composed of low-grade gold. Supposing you had got a lot of rings, for instance, of 18-carat gold. Now, how would you go about turning them into 22-carat sovereigns ? "

Polton crinkled at him reproachfully. " I am surprised at you, Mr. Miller—an officer of the law, too—suggesting such a thing. Of course, I wouldn't do anything of the sort."

" No, no," chuckled Miller, " we know that. It's just a question of method that we want explained. Because somebody has done it, and we would like to know how he managed it."

" Well, sir," said Polton, " there is no particular difficulty about it. He would weigh up the 18-carat gold and take part of it, say a little more than half, flatten it out on the stake or in a rolling mill, if he had one, break it up quite small, and boil it up in nitric acid. That would dissolve out the alloy—the copper and silver—and leave him pure gold. Then he would melt that down with the proper proportion of the 18-carat stuff, and that would give him 22-carat gold."

" And as to making the coins ? Would that be much of a job ? How many do you think he could make in a day ? "

" A man who knew his job," said Polton, " wouldn't make any trouble about it. He would make his mould in a casting flask that would cast, say, twenty at a time, and he would use a matrix that would dry hard and give a good many repeats. There would be a bit of finishing work to do on each coin—cutting off the sprue, where the metal ran in, and making good the edge. But that is not a big job. They make a special edge tool for the purpose."

" Oh, do they ? " said Miller, with a sly grin. " You seem to know a good deal about it, Mr. Polton."

" Of course I do," was the indignant response, " seeing that I have been dealing with tool-makers in he metal trade since I was a boy. Not that the respectable makers in Clerkenwell have anything to do with burglars' and coiners' tools. But, naturally, they get to know what is made."

" Yes, I know," said Miller. " Our people get some useful tips from them, now and again. And I shall know where to send them if they want some more, eh, Mr. Polton ? Technical tips, I mean, of course."

Polton crinkled indulgently at the Superintendent, and when the latter, having glanced at his watch, suddenly emptied his glass and rose, his expression became positively affectionate.

" I am afraid I have wasted a lot of your time with my gossip," said Miller, apologetically, as he drew on his gloves, " but I thought you would like to have the news. Probably you will look in at the Old Bailey and see how the case goes. The sessions are just beginning now, and I expect the case will come on in the course of a few days."

" We shall certainly drop in if we can," said Thorndyke, " and see what comes of your efforts. Won't you throw away that stump and take a fresh cigar ? " he added, holding out the box as the Superintendent essayed to strike a match.

" Seems a waste," replied Miller, turning a thrifty eye on the stump. But he succumbed, nevertheless ; and when he had selected a fresh cigar and amputated its point with anxious care, he lit it (with a match that Polton had struck in readiness), shook hands, and took his leave.

As the door closed on the sound of his retiring footsteps, Polton fell to, in his noiseless, dexterous fashion, on the dismantling of the dinner-table ; and, as he prepared a tray for transport to the upper regions, he announced :

" The camera is finished, sir, and all ready for inspection, if you have time to come up and have a look at it."

" Then let us go up at once," said Thorndyke ; " and perhaps we can take some of the debris with us and save another journey."

He loaded a second tray and followed Polton up the stairs, while I brought up the rear with an empty claret jug and a couple of dish covers.

The " automatic watcher," which its creator exhibited with justifiable complacency, was a singularly ingenious appliance. The clock was enclosed in a small box, on the front of which was a miniature dial ; and the almost inaudible tick was further muffled by a pad of felt between its back and the wall. The camera, to which it was connected by an insulated wire, was another small box, fitted with mirror plates to fasten it to the door. From its front projected a brass tube, five inches long, and half an inch thick, at the end of which was an enclosed prism with a circular opening facing at right angles to the axis of the tube.

" There are two film holders," Polton explained, " each taking six yards of kinematograph film, and each enclosed in a light-tight case with a dark-slide, so that it can be taken out and another put in its place. So I can go down and bring away one film for development and leave the other to carry on. I have set the clock to make an exposure every six hours, beginning at twelve o'clock, noon."

" And what about the shutter ? " asked Thorndyke. " Does it make much of a click ? "

" It doesn't make any sound at all," replied Polton, " because it moves quite slowly. It is just a disc with a hole in it. When the clock makes the circuit, the disc moves so that the hole is opposite the lens ; and stays there until the circuit is broken. Then it moves round and closes the lens, and, at the same time, the roller makes a turn and winds on a fresh piece of film. I'll make an exposure now."

He turned the hand of the clock until it came to six, while Thorndyke and I listened with our heads close to the camera. But no sound could be heard ; and it was only by repeating the proceeding with our ears actually applied to the camera that it was possible to detect faint sounds of movement as the shutter-disc revolved.

" I suppose," said Thorndyke, " you focus on the film ? "

" Yes," replied Polton ; " there's plenty to spare, so I use a piece as a focusing screen and waste it. And the barrel of the lens can be turned so as to get the prism pointing at the right spot. I think it will do, sir."

" I am sure it will," Thorndyke agreed, heartily ; " and I only hope that all your trouble and ingenuity and skill will not have been expended in vain."

" That can hardly be, sir," was the cheerful response. " The photographs are bound to show something, though it may not be exactly what you want. At any rate, it's ready ; and, with your permission, I will pop down with it to-morrow, as soon as I have finished with the breakfasts."

" Excellent ! " said Thorndyke. " Then, if Mrs. Gibbins's belief is well founded, the ' watcher ' will be installed in time for the Wednesday-night visit."

DURING the next day or two, I was sensible of a certain tension and unrest that seemed to affect the atmosphere of our chambers in King's Bench Walk. Polton, having successfully installed his apparatus in the corridor at Hartsden Manor House, was in a fever of impatience to harvest the results. I believe that he would have liked to sit down beside his camera and change the film after each exposure. As it was, he had fixed it on Tuesday morning, and, as no result could be expected until Thursday, at the earliest, circumstances condemned him to two whole days of suspense.

But Polton was not the only sufferer. My long association with Thorndyke enabled me to detect changes in his emotional states that were hidden from the eye of the casual observer by his habitually calm and impassive exterior; and, in these days, a certain gravity and preoccupation in his manner conveyed to me the impression that something was weighing on his mind. At first, I was disposed to connect his preoccupation with the affairs of Hartsden Manor; but I soon dismissed this idea. For in those affairs there was nothing that could reasonably cause him any anxiety. And Thorndyke was by no means addicted to fussing unnecessarily.

The explanation came on the Wednesday evening, when we had finished dinner and taken our armchairs, and were preparing the post-prandial pipes.

" I suppose," said he, pushing the tobacco jar to my

side of the little table, " you will turn up at the Old
Bailey to hear how Dobey fares ? "

" When is the trial ? " I asked.

" To-morrow," he replied. " I thought you knew."

" No," said I. " Miller didn't mention any date,
and I have heard nothing since. I think it would be
interesting to hear the evidence, though we know
pretty well what it will be."

" Yes, we know the case for the prosecution. But we
don't know what Dobey may have to say in reply. That
is what interests me. I am not at all happy about the
case. I don't much like the attitude of the prosecution—if Miller has represented it fairly—particularly
the dragging in of the house-breaking affair."

" No," I agreed, " that seems quite irrelevant."

" It is," said he. " And it is a flagrant instance of
the old forensic dodge of proving the wrong conclusion. The identification of Dobey by these women is
evidently expected to convey to the jury in a vague
sort of way that the station-master's refusal to
swear to the identity of the Strood man is of no
consequence."

" It is quite possible that the judge may refuse to
allow the house-breaking affair to be introduced at all."

" Quite," he agreed, " especially if the defence
objects. But, still, I am not happy about the case.
The intention of the prosecution to introduce this
irrelevant matter to prejudice the jury and their
suppression of the evidence regarding the poisoned
cigar—which really is highly relevant—suggests a very
determined effort to obtain a conviction."

" I take it that you do not entertain the possibility
that Dobey may have committed the murder ? "

" No, I don't think I do. As you say, we know the
case for the prosecution, and we know that it is a bad
case. There is a total lack of positive evidence. But,

still, there is the chance that they may get a conviction.
That would be a disaster ; and it would, at once, raise
the question as to what we should have to do. Obviously, we couldn't let an innocent man go to the gal-
lows.   But it would be a very difficult position."

" What are the chances of a conviction, so far as you
can see ? "

" That depends on what Dobey has to say.   The
case for the prosecution rests on the finding of the
stolen document in his flat.   There is no denying that
that is a highly incriminating circumstance, and, if he
can produce nothing more than a mere denial of having
taken it, the chances will be decidedly against him."

" It is difficult to see what answer he can give," said
I.   " The document was certainly taken from Badger,
before or after his death ;   it was certainly found in
Dobey's flat ;   and, apparently, Dobey was the sole
occupant of that flat.   I don't see how he is going to
escape from those facts."

" Neither do I," said Thorndyke.   " But we shall
hear what he has to say to-morrow ; and if he is found
guilty, we shall have to consider very seriously what our
next move is to be."

With this, the subject dropped.   But, at intervals
during the evening, my thoughts went back to it, and I
found myself wondering whether Thorndyke had not
perhaps allowed himself to undervalue the evidence
against Dobey.   The finding of that document in his
rooms would take a great deal of explaining.

My intention to hear the case from the beginning
was frustrated by a troublesome solicitor, who first
failed to keep an appointment, and then detained me
inordinately, so that when, at last, I arrived at the
Central Criminal Court and, having hurriedly donned
my wig and gown, slipped into the counsels' seats
beside Thorndyke, the case for the prosecution was

nearly concluded.   But by the fact that the finger-print
expert was then giving evidence, I knew that the
prosecution had succeeded in introducing the house-
breaking incident.   As I listened to the evidence, I
looked quickly round the court to identify the various
dramatis personæ ; and, naturally, looked first at the
dock, where the prisoner stood " on his deliverance,"
listening with stolid calm to the apparently indestruc-
tible evidence of the expert.

As I looked him over critically, I was not surprised at
the eagerness with which the police had fastened on
his salient peculiarities.   He was quite a striking figure.
Dull and commonplace enough in face and feature, the
combination of a rather untidy mop of dark-red hair
with a noticeably red nose set in a large pale face made
him an ideal subject for identification.   From the
prisoner I turned to his defending solicitor, Mr. Coleman,
who sat at the solicitors' table, listening with sphinx-
like impassiveness to the expert's authoritative pro-
nouncements.   Equally unmoved was the prisoner's
counsel, a good-looking Jew named Lyon, who special-
ized in criminal practice.   The counsel for the prosecution, a Mr. Barnes, K.C., was on his feet at the
moment, and his junior, Mr. Callow, was industriously
taking notes of the evidence.

" Have the defence objected to this evidence ? " I
asked Thorndyke in a whisper, as the leader for the
Crown put what seemed to be his final question.

" No," was the reply.   " The judge questioned the
relevance of it ; but, as the defence did not seem
interested, he gave no ruling."

It seemed to me that Mr. Dobey's case was being
rather mismanaged ; and I was confirmed in this
opinion when his counsel rose to cross-examine.

" You have stated that the marks on this window-
glass are the prints of the prisoner's fingers.   Are you

quite certain that those marks were not made by the fingers of some other person ? "

" The chances against their having been made by the fingers of any person other than the prisoner are several thousand millions."

" But is it not possible that you may have made some mistake in the comparison ? You don't, I suppose, claim to be infallible ? "

" I claim that the method employed at the Bureau is infallible. It does not depend on personal judgment, but on comparison, detail by detail, of the questioned finger-print with the one which is known. I have made the comparison with the greatest care, and I am certain that I have made no mistake."

" And do you swear, positively, of your certain knowledge, that the marks on this window-glass were made by the fingers of the prisoner ? "

" I do," was the reply ; whereupon, having thus unnecessarily piled up the evidence against his client, Mr. Lyon sat down with an air of calm satisfaction.

I was astonished at the apparent stupidity of the proceeding. It is seldom worth while to cross-examine finger-print experts at all closely, for the more they are pressed, the more do they affirm their absolute certainty. And I noticed that my surprise seemed to be shared by the judge, who glanced with a sort of impatient perplexity from the counsel to the sphinx-like solicitor who was instructing him. It must be an exasperating experience for a judge—who knows all the ropes—to have to watch a counsel making a hopeless muddle of a case.

The next witness was a middle-aged woman who gave the name of Martha Bunsbury, and who was examined by Mr. Barnes in the plain, straightforward fashion proper to a prosecuting counsel.

" Kindly look at the prisoner and tell us whether you recognize him."

The witness bestowed a disdainful stare on the prisoner, and replied, promptly : " Yes. I picked him out of a whole crowd at Brixton Prison."

" Where and when had you seen him before that ? "

" I saw him on the second of August, breaking into a house in Sudbury Park. I happened to be at the window at the back of my house when I heard the sound of glass being broken. So I looked out, and then I saw the prisoner getting into the back window of the house in Sudbury Park that is just opposite mine. So I opened the window and called out. Then I ran down to the garden and gave the alarm to two men who were coming along the towing-path of the canal."

" And what happened next ? "

" The lady next door to me came out into her garden and she began to call out too. Then the two men started to run along the tow-path towards the bridge, but the prisoner, who had heard us giving the alarm, backed out of the window and ran across the garden with his coat on his arm. When he came to the wall, he laid the coat on the top of it, because the wall has broken glass all along the top, and climbed over. But, as he dropped down outside, the coat dropped down inside. He turned round, and was going to climb back to get it, but, by that time, the two men were running over the bridge. So he left the coat and made off up a side lane between two houses. And that is the last I saw of him."

" Yes. A very excellent description," said Mr. Barnes. " But now I want you to be extremely careful. Look again at the prisoner, and see if you are quite certain that he is really the man whom you saw in the garden of that house. It is most important that there should be no possibility of a mistake."

" There isn't," was the immediate and confident reply. " I am perfectly certain that he is the man."

On this, Mr. Barnes sat down and Mr. Lyon rose to cross-examine.

" You have said that you saw the housebreaker from the back window of your house, breaking a back window of a house opposite. How far would that window be from yours ? "

" I really couldn't say. A fair distance. Not so very far."

" You spoke of a canal. Is the opposite house on the same side of the canal as your house ? "

" No, of course it isn't. How could it be ? It is on the opposite side."

" And how long is your garden ? "

" Oh, a moderate length. You know what London gardens are."

" Should I be right in saying that, at the time that you saw this man, you were separated from him by the length of two gardens and the width of the canal ? "

" Yes. That is what I said."

" And you say that, having seen this total stranger at that very considerable distance, you are quite certain that you are able to recognize and remember him ? "

" Yes, I am quite certain."

" Can you tell us how you are able to identify him with such certainty ? "

" Well," said the witness, " there's his nose, you see. I could see that."

" Quite so. You looked upon the nose when it was red."

" I should think it is always red," said Mrs. Bunsbury. " At any rate, it was red then, and it is red now. And then there is his hair."

" Very true. There is his hair. But he is not the only man in the world with a red nose and red hair."

" I don't know anything about that," replied the witness, doggedly. " But I do know that he is the man. I'd swear to him among ten thousand."

This apparently finished Mr. Lyon, for, having again prejudiced his client's case to the best of his ability, he sat down with unimpaired complacency.

The next witness, Miss Doris Gray, gave evidence to the same effect, though with somewhat less emphasis ; and, when she had been cross-examined and finally vacated the witness-box, Mr. Barnes rose and announced that "that was his case." As soon as he sat down, Mr. Lyon rose and made his announcement.

" I call witnesses, my lord."

" Now," Thorndyke said to me in a low tone, " we are going to see whether there is really a case for the defence."

" They haven't made much of it up to the present," I remarked.

" Exactly," he replied. " That is what makes me a little hopeful. They have certainly given the prosecution plenty of rope."

I should have liked to have this observation elucidated somewhat—and so, probably, would Superintendent Miller, who, at this moment, came forth from some inconspicuous corner and took his place at the solicitors' table ; for there was more than a shade of anxiety on his face as he looked expectantly at the witness-box. But there was no opportunity for explanations. Even as Miller took his seat, the first witness for the defence was called, and appeared in the person of a pleasant-looking middle-aged lady wearing the uniform of a trained nurse, and bearing, it transpired, the name of Helen Royden. In reply to a question from Mr. Lyon, she deposed that she was the matron of the cottage hospital at Hook Green, near Biddenden in Kent.

" Will you kindly look at the prisoner and tell us if you recognize him ? "

The witness turned her head and cast a smiling glance at the accused (whereupon Mr. Dobey's rather saturnine countenance relaxed into a friendly grin).

" Yes," she replied, " I recognize him as Mr. Charles Dobey, lately a patient at my hospital."

" When did you last see him ? "

" On the first of October, when he was discharged from hospital."

" What were the date and the circumstances of his admission ? "

" He was brought to the hospital on the thirtieth of July by Dr. Wale, the medical officer of the hospital, suffering from a compound fracture of the left tibia. I understand that the doctor found him lying in the road."

" Do you remember the exact time at which he was brought in ? "

" It was a little before eleven in the forenoon."

As the dates were mentioned, I observed the judge and the two prosecuting counsel hurriedly turn over their notes with an expression of astonishment and incredulity, and the jury very visibly " sat up and took notice."

" Did you communicate with any of the patient's relatives ? "

" Yes. At the patient's request, I wrote to his wife, who lives at East Malling in Kent, informing her of his admission, and inviting her to come and see him."

" And did she come ? "

" Yes. She came the next day, and I allowed her to

stay the night at the hospital. After that, she came to see him usually twice a week."

" Have you any doubt that the prisoner is the man whom you have described as your patient, Charles Dobey ? "

" No. I couldn't very well be mistaken. He was in the hospital just over two months, and I saw him several times every day, and often had quite long talks with him. Ours is a small hospital, and the patients are rather like a family."

" Did you learn what his occupation was ? "

" Yes. He described himself as a plumber and gas-fitter."

" Had you any reason to doubt that that was his real occupation ? "

" None whatever. In fact, we had evidence that it was ; for, when he was convalescent and able to get about, he repaired all the taps in the hospital, and did a number of odd jobs. He seemed to be quite a clever workman."

" Do you keep a record of admissions and discharges ? "

" Yes. I have brought the register with me."

Here she produced from a business-like hand-bag a rather chubby quarto volume which she opened at a marked place and handed to the usher, who conveyed it to the counsel. When the latter had examined it and verified the dates, he passed it up to the judge, who scanned it curiously and compared it with his notes. Finally, it was handed to the prosecuting counsel, who appeared to gaze on it with stupefaction, and returned it to Mr. Lyon, who handed it back to the usher for transmission to the witness.

This concluded the examination-in-chief, and Mr. Lyon accordingly thanked the witness and sat down. I waited curiously for the cross-examination, but neither of the Crown counsel made any sign. The judge glanced at them enquiringly, and, after a short pause, the witness was dismissed and her place taken by her successor.

The new witness was a shrewd-looking, clean-shaved man, in whom I seemed to recognize a professional brother. And a doctor he turned out to be; one Egbert Wale by name, and the medical officer of the Hook Green Cottage Hospital. Having given the usual particulars, and been asked the inevitable question, he deposed as follows:

"On the thirtieth of last July, at about twenty minutes to eleven in the forenoon, I was driving down a by-road between Headcorn and Biddenden when I saw a man lying in the road. I stopped my car and got out to examine him, when I found that he had sustained a compound fracture of the left leg below the knee. I accordingly dressed the wound, put on a temporary splint, lifted him into my car, and drove him to the Hook Green Cottage Hospital, of which I am visiting medical officer. He gave the name of Charles Dobey, and explained that he had broken his leg in dropping from a motor-lorry on which he had taken a free lift without the knowledge of the driver. I identify the prisoner as the man of whom I am speaking. I detained him in the hospital for two months, and discharged him as convalescent on the first of October."

"What is meant by a compound fracture? Is it a very serious injury?"

"A compound fracture is a break in a bone accompanied by a wound of the flesh and skin which communicates with the broken part of the bone and exposes it to the air. It is always a serious injury, even under modern surgical conditions, because the wound and the fracture have both to be treated, and each may interfere with the treatment of the other."

" Did Dobey make a good recovery ? "

" Yes, excellent. When he left the hospital, the wound was quite healed, and the broken bone firmly united, but there was a large knob of callus, or new bone, which, I hope, will disappear in time."

" Would you recognize the wound if you were to examine it ? "

" Certainly I should. I saw it last only about three weeks ago."

" Then, if his lordship will grant his permission, I will ask you to make the examination."

His lordship—bearing in mind, no doubt, the evidence of the finger-print experts—gave his permission readily ; whereupon the doctor came out of the witness-box and went over to the dock. There he proceeded dexterously to unwind a length of bandage from the prisoner's leg—which had been exposed by its owner in readiness for the inspection—and examine the member by sight and touch. Then he replaced the bandage and returned to the witness-box.

" What is the result of your examination ? " Mr. Lyon asked.

" I find the wound and the fracture in much the same condition as when I saw it last about three weeks ago."

" You have no doubt that it is the same injury ? "

" Not the slightest. I recognize every detail of it."

" And you have no doubt that the prisoner is the person whom you treated at the hospital ? "

" I am quite certain that he is the same person."

On receiving this answer, Mr. Lyon sat down, and the witness looked expectantly at the counsel for the prosecution. But, as before, they made no sign, and, accordingly, the witness was dismissed. As he retired, the foreman of the jury rose and announced that he and his colleagues did not want to hear any more evidence. "The jury are of opinion," he added, "that this is a case of mistaken identity."

"It is difficult to avoid that conclusion," the judge admitted. Then, turning to the prisoner's counsel, he enquired what further evidence he had proposed to offer.

"I had proposed to call the prisoner's wife, my lord, and then to put the prisoner in the box."

The judge reflected for a few moments and then, addressing the foreman, said :

"I think, in fairness to the prisoner, we should hear the rest of the evidence. You will note that the question of the document has not been cleared up. That document was found, you will remember, on premises belonging to the prisoner. We had better hear the evidence, though it may not be necessary for the learned counsel for the defence to address you."

The jury having agreed to this eminently sensible suggestion, the prisoner's wife, Elizabeth Dobey, was called and took her place in the witness-box.

"Is the address at East Malling that you have given your permanent address ? Is that your home ?" Mr. Lyon asked, when the preliminaries had been disposed of, and the witness had described herself as the wife of Charles Dobey, the prisoner.

"Yes. We rent a cottage with a nice bit of garden. My husband is very fond of gardening."

"With regard to the flat in London, 103 Barnard's Buildings ? Do you spend much of your time there ?"

"Me ? I have never been there at all. It isn't a flat. It's just a place where my husband can sleep and cook a meal when he is in Town, looking for a job."

"Do you remember when the prisoner first went up

to Barnard's Buildings after he came home from the hospital ? "

" He only went up once. That was when the police took him. It was about a week after he came home— on the eighth of October."

" Did he send anyone else up to the flat, before he went himself ? "

" No. There wasn't anyone to send, and there wasn't any reason to send them."

This concluded the examination-in-chief. But, this time, as Mr. Lyon resumed his seat, Mr. Barnes rose with remarkable promptitude.

" You have said that your husband kept this flat in London to sleep in when he was looking for a job. What kind of jobs would he be looking for ? "

" He is a plumber and gas-fitter by trade. He would be looking for jobs in his own line, of course."

" You have heard the police witnesses state that they found in that flat a number of burglars' tools, a quantity of stolen jewellery, and a stolen document. Do those tools and that stolen property suggest anything to you as to the kind of jobs that your husband went to London to look for ? "

" No, they have got nothing to do with his trade."

" Can you account for the presence of burglars' tools and stolen property in the rooms of a plumber and gas-fitter ? "

" Yes, I can," Mrs. Dobey replied, viciously, " after all the false swearing that there has been in this court to-day. If you ask me, I should say that the police put them there."

At this rather unexpected reply a low rumble of laughter filled the court, including the jury box ; and a faint, appreciative smile stole over the judge's face, and was even reflected on the countenance of Mr. Barnes himself.

" I am afraid," he said, good-humouredly, " that you are taking a prejudiced view. But with regard to this flat ; have you ever taken any measures to ascertain what your husband does at those rooms ? "

" No," she replied. " I don't go spying on my husband. It isn't necessary. I can trust him, if other people can't."

Here it apparently dawned upon Mr. Barnes that he was not going to do his case any good with this witness. Accordingly, he thanked her, and resumed his seat ; and, as Mr. Lyon was not disposed to re-examine, Mrs. Dobey retired in triumph, and her husband was conducted from the dock to the witness-box.

When he had been sworn and had given the usual particulars, his counsel directed him to describe his movements after his escape from the prison, which he did with picturesque conciseness.

" As soon as I was clear of the prison, I scooted round a corner into a by-street, and there I saw a motor wagon piled up with empty baskets. The driver was cranking up the engine, and, as there was nobody in sight, I climbed up behind and laid down on the floor among the baskets. Then the driver got up and off she went. When we got out somewhere between Headcorn and Biddenden the wagon turned down a by-lane, and as I thought that we might be getting near the farm that we seemed to be bound for, I decided to hop off. So I did. But she was going faster than I thought, and I came down a cropper and broke my leg. I laid there in the road for about a quarter of an hour, and then the doctor came along and picked me up, and took me off to the hospital. And there I stayed until I was discharged on the first of October."

" When did you first go up to your London flat ? "

" I only went once. That was when I had been at

home just over a week—on the eighth of October. The detectives came and collared me just as I was picking the lock to let myself in."

" Why did you have to pick the lock ? "

" Because I hadn't got my key. They took all the things out of my pockets at Maidstone police-station. But I had forgotten that I hadn't got my key until I was close to the Buildings, so I had to pop into an ironmonger's shop and get a piece of wire. And I was picking the lock with that piece of wire when the cops nabbed me."

" You have heard about the burglars' tools and the stolen property that the police found in your room. Can you tell us anything about them ? "

" No, I don't know anything about them. They were not mine, and I didn't put them there. Somebody must have got into the rooms and planted them there while I was in the hospital."

" Have you any idea who might have planted those things, and for what purpose ? "

" I should think anyone could see what they were planted for. It was to put this murder on to me. But, as to who planted them, if the police didn't—and I suppose they didn't, though they do seem to have been working the oracle a bit—it must have been the person who did the murder, seeing that he had got the paper that was taken from the murdered man."

" Do you swear that you never went to the flat after leaving the hospital until the eighth of October ? "

" I do. I shouldn't have gone there a second time with a bit of wire to let myself in. I should have got a key."

This was Mr. Lyon's final question, and, as he sat down, Mr. Barnes rose to cross-examine, but with no great show of enthusiasm. He began by pressing the witness for a clearer explanation of the purpose for

which he kept the rooms in London.   But at this point
the foreman of the jury again intervened with a protest
that the jury were not interested in the prisoner's
occupation, and that they did not want to hear any
more evidence ; whereupon Mr. Barnes sat down with
no appearance of reluctance, and the judge enquired of
Mr. Lyon if he desired to address the jury.

" If the gentlemen of the jury have come to a decision," was the reply, " it would be useless for me to
occupy the time of the court with an address."

Accordingly, the prisoner was led back to the dock,
and the judge proceeded to make a few observations.

" I do not pretend to understand this case," said he.
" We have been told that it is an impossibility for two
different persons to have identically similar finger-
prints.   Yet, here, the impossible seems to have happened.   Finger-prints which have been identified as
those of the prisoner were made in a house in London
on the second of August ; at which time the prisoner
appears to have been lying, with a broken leg, in a
hospital some forty miles away.   It would seem that
there is some person whose finger-prints are identical
with those of the prisoner ; and, unfortunately for the
prisoner, that person appears to be a house-breaker.
However, there is no use in trying to resolve this
puzzle, for, after all, the question is not relevant to the
issue that you are trying.   What you have to decide is
whether you are prepared to accept as true the evidence
of the matron of the hospital and Dr. Wale.   If their
evidence is true, it is physically impossible that the
prisoner could have committed the murder with which
he is charged.   That is for you to decide, and I do not
think that I need say anything more."

When the judge had finished speaking, the grey-
wigged clerk of the court rose and put the formal
question :

" Are you all agreed upon your verdict, gentlemen ? "

To which the foreman replied, promptly : " We are."

" What do you say, gentlemen ? Is the prisoner guilty or not guilty ? "

" Not guilty," was the reply, delivered with noticeable emphasis.

The judge briefly expressed his entire concurrence, and then proceeded :

" I understand that the prisoner, having escaped from prison while awaiting his trial, is still in custody, on the original charge. Have you any instructions on the subject ? "

" Yes, my lord," replied Mr. Barnes. " It appears that the bill was presented to the Grand Jury at Maidstone on the day on which the prisoner absconded. There would seem to have been some error in presenting the bill ; but, at any rate, the Grand Jury threw it out."

" I am glad to hear that," said the judge. Then, addressing the prisoner, he continued : " Charles Dobey, you have been tried for the crime on which you were indicted, and have been found not guilty—very properly, as I think—and, as the bill in respect of the original offence has been thrown out by the Grand Jury at Maidstone, there is now no charge against you, and you are accordingly discharged."

He accompanied the rather dry statement with a smile and a kindly nod, which Dobey acknowledged with a low bow, and, as the gate of the dock was now thrown open, he descended to meet, with a somewhat stolid grin, the effusive greetings of his wife and the congratulations of his friends from the hospital.

" Well," I said, as we rose to depart, " I hope you find the result of the trial satisfactory."

" I do," Thorndyke replied, " but I don't think

Miller does. He looks most uncommonly glum. But I do not feel sympathetic. The police—if they instructed the prosecution—have been hoist with their own petard. They insisted on dragging in these finger-prints and those two women, whose evidence was quite irrelevant and was intended merely to discredit the prisoner, and behold the result. From this time forward, Dobey is practically immune from finger-print evidence and evidence of personal identification. He can prove, from the records of this trial, that there is some person, who is engaged in the practice of house-breaking, who is in appearance his exact double, and whose finger-prints are identically similar to his. He can actually quote the judge to that effect."

"Yes," I agreed. "Dobey need not trouble to wear gloves now, if he really is a cracksman, as I have no doubt he is. One cannot help admiring the masterly strategy of the defence in egging on the prosecution to play their trump cards and prove those very facts. But, even now, I don't see how you came to be so certain of Dobey's innocence. You knew nothing about the alibi. And, apart from that, there was a case against him. Yet, apparently, you never entertained the possibility of his being guilty."

"I don't think I did," he admitted; "and, if you will reconsider the case in general terms and in detail, I think you will see why. Let me recommend you to do this now, as the completion of the case devolves on us. I must stay and have a few words with Miller; and I suggest that you go on ahead and spend half an hour in going over the case with an open mind. You know where to find our notes of the case. Get them out and look them through. Note all the facts that are known to us, consider them separately and as a whole, and see if there does not emerge a perfectly coherent theory of the crime. The evidence that you have heard to-day, inasmuch as it is in agreement with that theory, ought be be helpful to you."

" When you speak of a theory of the crime," said I, " do you mean a general theory, or one capable of a particular application ? "

" Our function," he replied, " is to discover the identity of the person who murdered Inspector Badger ; and the theory that I refer to is one which is capable of leading us to that discovery."

With this he stepped out into the body of the court to go in search of the Superintendent, and I made my way to the robing-room to divest myself of wig and gown before issuing forth into places of public resort.

ON my way westward from the Old Bailey to the
Temple, I turned over in my mind Thorndyke's last
statement. Its exact meaning was not perfectly clear
to me ; but what I did gather was that he had enough
knowledge of the circumstances surrounding Badger's
death to make the belief in Dobey's guilt untenable.
That implied some positive knowledge pointing to the
guilt of some other person ; but as to whether that
other person was an actual individual to whom a name
could be given, or a mere abstraction whom we had
yet to convert into a reality, I was unable to decide.
What did, however, emerge clearly from his statement
was that whatever facts were known to him were also
known to me. My problem, therefore, was to examine
the facts that I already knew, and try to extract their
significance, which I had apparently missed up to the
present.

When I arrived at our chambers, I became aware,
by certain familiar signs, that Polton had returned from
his expedition to Hartsden, and was engaged in some
kind of photographic work in the laboratory. Presumably, he was developing the films from the " automatic
watcher," and I was tempted to go up and see what
luck he had had. But I restrained my curiosity, and,
having drawn a chair up to the table and procured a
note-block and pencil, I went to the cabinet in which
the portfolios of current cases were kept and unlocked
it. The one labelled " Inspector Badger, deceased,"
was uppermost, with the finger-print measuring-glass

lying on its cover. I lifted them out together, and, laying the glass on the table, opened the portfolio and began to glance through its contents, laying the papers out in their order as to the dates.

The first that I picked up I put aside, as it did not appear to belong to the series. It was a rough copy of the entry that Thorndyke had made in his note-book when we were experimenting on the Thumbograph, and had apparently been put in the portfolio out of the way—though it was extremely unlike Thorndyke to put anything in its wrong place. Then I began to go through the various notes, *seriatim*, trying to refresh my memory as to the order of the events and the way in which the case had developed. But as I turned over the notes, I was aware of a growing sense of disappointment. There was nothing new; nothing that I did not remember quite clearly without their aid. I glanced through the brief notes of our expedition to Greenhithe. It was all fresh in my memory. The description of the body, the examination of the tunnel, the finding of the cigar; then the analysis of the cigar, the report of the inquest, and the evidence of the witnesses. I knew it all, and it conveyed nothing to me but a mysterious crime of which we held not a single clue to guide us to the identity of the perpetrator. There was a brief summary of Miller's account of the house-breaking incident, which did now, after the event, point pretty definitely to a personation and the making of false finger-prints. But there was no suggestion as to the identity of the personator. To me, the whole case remained in the air.

At the end of the portfolio was a separate folder labelled "finger-prints," which I took out, doggedly, but with a sense of deep discouragement. Nothing could be much less illuminating than a collection of unidentified finger-prints. Nevertheless, I opened the folder and began to look through the collection. There were Badger's prints, devoid of any meaning to me, and the photograph of Dobey's, taken from the official paper that Miller had shown us, which told me nothing at all. Then I opened a smaller folder, labelled " Prints from cigar." There were two sets of photographs, one the natural size and the other enlarged to about four diameters. Discarding the smaller photographs, I examined the enlargements, and read the inscriptions written below them, with as much attention as I could muster ; for, little as they conveyed to me, I realized that they constituted evidence of the highest importance, if only the opportunity should ever come to apply it.

The first was Inspector Badger's left thumb, remarkably clear for a developed print. But, though it was, in effect, an indictment of murder, it gave me no help, since I knew already that poor Badger had been murdered. I laid it down and took up the next. " Right thumb of person unknown." Having read the inscription, I glanced at the print. This one, too, was admirably clear and distinct. The experts should have no difficulty in identifying it if they could get a known print with which to compare it. Not only was the general pattern—a very distinctive one—perfectly plain, but all the minor " characteristics " were easily legible.

I sat with the print in my hand and my eyes fixed on it musingly, reflecting on all that it meant and all that it did not mean. This thumb-print had been made by the man who had given the poisoned cigar to poor Badger—who had almost certainly murdered him ; who had personated Dobey at the sham house-breaking, and who had entered Dobey's flat and there planted the stolen document. It was capable of giving infallible proof of that villain's identity ; and yet it offered not the faintest hint as to what manner of man that villain might be. In spite of our possession of this infallible touchstone we might pass this murderer in the street a hundred times without the faintest glimmer of suspicion as to who he was. A finger-print is a poor instrument with which to start the search for an unknown criminal.

As I sat thus, with my eyes fixed only half-consciously on the print, I became aware of a dim sense of familiarity. A finger-print is, to an accustomed eye, much more easy to remember than might be supposed; and, as my eye rested on this print, I began to have the feeling that I had seen it before. At first the feeling was not more than vaguely reminiscent; but yet it was enough to arouse my attention. I looked, now, with a critical and purposeful scrutiny and a definite effort of memory. And then, suddenly, in a flash, the revelation came and left me gazing open-mouthed.

It was amazing, incredible; so incredible that I sought instantly for corroboration or disproof. Snatching up the measuring-glass, and picking out the natural-sized print, I placed the central dot of the scale of circles on the summit of the central character of the core and wrote down on the note-block the measurements shown. The pattern was intermediate between a whorl and a twinned loop; but, remembering Thorndyke's rule, I treated it as a whorl. Then, as it was a left-handed, or anti-clockwise, whorl, and as the " core-character " lay entirely within the centre circle (" Space A "), the whorl was of the type A3. I wrote this down, and then measured the distance to the right delta. The latter was intersected by the circle, C, and therefore, by the rule, lay in the space, D. The ridge-tracing was clearly outside the delta, and I therefore wrote down O. The left delta was outside the print, and therefore could not be located. The number of

9

ridges between the centre of the core and the right delta
was twelve, while the left ridge-count—since the left
delta was outside the print—was unascertainable.

When I had finished, I set out my results in the
regular formula, so far as I remembered the method,
thus :

Right thumb—Unknown.
W (? T.L.).   Core, A3, ?, O, D, ?, 12.

Then I turned back through the portfolio until I found
the slip of paper on which Thorndyke had copied the
entry in his note-book. The first eager glance at it
showed me that my memory had not deceived me.
The entry ran :

Walter Hornby.   Right thumb.
W (? T.L.).   Core, A3, ?, O, D, ?, 12.

In addition to the formula, Thorndyke had written
down a few of the " ridge characteristics " with their
ridge-counts from the centre of the core, and a direction-
arrow to show their position, thus :

$\longrightarrow$ 3, Lake, 5, Bif., 8, End, 10, Bif.
$\longleftarrow$ 7, Lake, 9, Bif., 11, Lake.

With intense excitement, I proceeded to verify these
characters, not a little surprised at the ease with which
they could be recognized and located. Taking first
the right direction-arrow, and counting the ridges from
the centre of the core, I found in the third ridge one
of those little loops, or eyes, known, technically, as
" lakes." The fifth ridge divided into a fork, or
bifurcation ; the eighth ridge terminated abruptly in
a free end, and the tenth showed another bifurcation.
Then, following the left direction-arrow, the seventh
ridge showed a small lake, the ninth a bifurcation, and

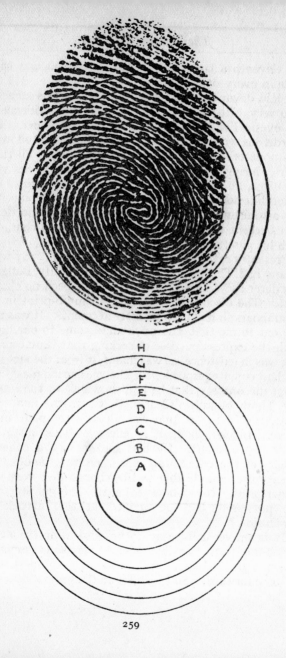

the eleventh a larger lake. The agreement was complete in every detail.

I laid down the print and reflected on this amazing discovery, still hardly able to credit the evidence of my eyes. For the thing seemed beyond belief. The murderous wretch whose tracks we had been following was none other than Walter Hornby. After all these years, during which I had almost forgotten his very existence, he had suddenly swum into the field of our vision like some strange and horrible apparition. Yet my astonishment was hardly justified; for no detail of his recent villainy was in any way out of character with his past, as it was known to me.

Presently my thoughts took another turn. By what means had Thorndyke been able to identify Badger's murderer as Walter Hornby? It had been no chance shot. The discovery of Hornby's thumb-print in the Thumbograph had been no mere accident. It was now evident to me that Thorndyke had come to our house with the express purpose of seeking that thumb-print, if it was in existence, as was manifest from the fact that he had come equipped with the measuring-glass, and from the anxiety that he had shown as to the fate of the Thumbograph. Clearly, that was the final verification of a theory that was already complete in his mind. Indeed, he had, in effect, said as much this very day in court. He had spoken of "a coherent theory of the crime," an expression that would have been quite inapplicable to the chance discovery of a finger-print. Now, how, from the information that we possessed, had he arrived at this astonishing conclusion?

It is proverbially easy to be wise after the event. "Jobbing back," as this mental exercise is named on the Stock Exchange, is considerably simpler than jobbing forward. So I found it on the present occasion.

Now that the conclusion was known to me, I was in a favourable position to consider the processes of reasoning which had led to it. And when I did so, and when I recalled the hints that Thorndyke had dropped from time to time, I was surprised that no inkling of the truth had ever dawned on me. For what Thorndyke had said was perfectly true. When all the facts were considered, separately and as a whole, a consistent theory of the crime emerged, and inevitably brought the figure of Walter Hornby into the picture.

Taking the facts separately, there were those that related to technique and method and those that related to motive. The technique in the present crime included the use of a poisoned cigar and of counterfeit finger-prints. But this was the technique employed, years ago, by Walter Hornby ; and it was not only a peculiar and distinctive technique ; it was absolutely unique. No other criminal, so far as I had ever heard, had employed it. Then the method of employing it was the same in both cases. In the Hornby case—the case of the Red Thumb Mark—an original finger-print (in the Thumbograph) had been obtained from the victim, Reuben Hornby, from which to make, by photo-mechanical process, the stamps for the counterfeits. In the Badger case, a sheet of finger-prints had been stolen, evidently for the same purpose. Again, in both cases, the forged finger-prints had been "planted" at the scene of the crime. In short, the technique and method in the Badger case repeated, in the main, those of the Red Thumb Mark case.

Then the motive showed a like similarity in the two cases. When Walter Hornby had tried to murder Thorndyke (by means of a poisoned cigar) his motive was to get rid of the only person who suspected him. As to the motive for the murder of Badger, Miller was almost certainly right, although he had guessed wrong

as to the identity of the murderer. Badger's uncanny
memory for faces had made him a dangerous enemy.
And we had Miller's statement that Badger was the
only officer who was able to identify Walter Hornby.

Finally, taking the whole set of facts together, the
similarity of the two cases was very striking. In each
crime, the criminal act had been preceded by a careful
preparation to incriminate an innocent person. There
had been a systematic scheme of false evidence, thought
out and arranged in advance with remarkable completeness and ingenuity, before the criminal had committed himself. Thus, as a whole and in detail, the
murder of Inspector Badger virtually repeated a crime
which was known to me, and which was utterly unlike
any other crime of which I had ever heard. Reluctantly,
I had to admit that I had been distinctly " slow in the
uptake."

I had just reached this rather unsatisfactory conclusion when I heard a latchkey inserted in the outer
door. A moment later, Thorndyke entered, and, as
his eye lighted on the open portfolio, he greeted me
with the enquiry :

" Well, what says my learned friend ? Has he
reached any conclusion ? "

By way of answer, I wrote on a scrap of paper :
" X=Walter Hornby," and pushed it along the table
towards him.

" Yes," he said, when he had glanced at it, " history
repeats itself. We had this equation once before,
you remember."

" I remember," said I, " and I ought to have remembered sooner. But, tell me, Thorndyke, when
did you first suspect Hornby in this case ? "

" The word ' suspect,' " he replied, " is a little
indefinite. But I may say that when we established
the fact of a poisoned cigar, the name of Walter Hornby

inevitably floated into my mind, especially as the cigar
was associated with a stolen sheet of finger-prints, which
were pretty evidently not those of the person who stole
them. In fact, I adopted, provisionally, the hypothesis that the murderer was Walter Hornby, but only
as a mere possibility which had to be borne in mind
while further developments were being watched for. I
argued that if the hypothesis was correct, certain events
might be confidently expected to follow. There
would be some crime, probably committed in daylight
by a man with red hair and a red nose, who would
leave Frederick Smith's finger-prints at the scene of the
crime ; and the stolen paper would be found in some
place connected with Frederick Smith.

" As you know, these events occurred exactly
according to plan. Thereupon, the mere hypothesis
became a very weighty probability. But the *experi-
mentum crucis* was made possible by Juliet. When the
Thumbograph had spoken, the hypothesis passed into
the domain of established fact."

" Yes," I said ; " you have established the murderer's identity beyond any reasonable doubt. The
next thing is to ascertain his whereabouts. At present
he is no more than a name."

" That," he replied, " is Miller's problem. The
police have all the facilities for finding a wanted man.
We have none. By the way, have you seen Polton ? "

" No," I replied, " but I expect you will see him
before long. He always knows, in some occult way,
when you come in. In fact, I think I hear him approaching at this moment."

Almost as I spoke, the door opened and Polton
entered, bearing a large vulcanite dish and a long strip
of kinematograph film. There was no need to ask for
his news, for his face was one large and incredibly
crinkly smile of triumph and satisfaction.

" We've brought it off, sir," he announced, gleefully, " first shot. I went down to the Manor House this morning, and I waited by the camera until I heard the twelve-o'clock exposure go off. Then I took out the roll-holder and put in a fresh one. But I don't think you will want it. I have developed the strip—nine exposures, altogether, but only two of them matter, and those two I have enlarged to half-plate. They are those made at twelve o'clock on Tuesday and twelve o'clock to-day."

He laid the dish on the table, and watched Thorndyke ecstatically as the latter stooped over it to examine the enlargements.

" The top one is the Tuesday exposure," he explained. " Shows the room just as you saw it, with the box on the table. The bottom one is to-day's. You see there's no box there, and the arm-chair has been moved about a couple of inches, as you can see by the sash of the case behind it."

" Yes," Thorndyke agreed, " it is a true bill, Polton. The box is gone from the table ; and boxes don't fly away of themselves. By the way, Polton, what do you make of that box ? "

" Well, sir," was the reply, " if it didn't seem so unlikely, I should have said that it looked like a casting-box ; one of those biggish flasks that silversmiths use for casting the blanks of things like spoons. It is certainly a metal box, and those things at the side look very much like pin-lugs."

" So I thought," said Thorndyke ; " but we shall probably know all about it, before long. At any rate, Polton, you have solved our problem for us, and now we can go ahead with confidence. I shall send Mr. Woodburn a letter and a telegram. He will probably get the letter to-morrow morning, but the telegram will make it safer."

" There's the telephone, sir," Polton suggested.

" Yes, I know," said Thorndyke ; " but when I whisper secrets, I like to know whose ear they are going into."

" What are you going to say to him ? " I asked.

" I shall ask him to meet us to-morrow morning and bring the key of the gallery door. That is what we arranged."

" Then you are going to break the seals and explore the rooms ? "

" Certainly. There is now no doubt that someone visits those rooms ; and as the next visit seems to be due to-morrow night, we may as well be there to give the visitor a hospitable reception."

" Shall you want me to come with you, sir ? " Polton enquired, anxiously.

My impression was that Thorndyke did not particularly want him. But the wistfulness of the little man's face proved irresistible.

" I think you had better come, Polton," he said, " and bring a few tools with you. But it would be as well if you went on ahead of us, so that we don't make too large a party. We mustn't be too noticeable."

" No, sir," Polton agreed, undisguisedly jubilant at being included in the expeditionary party; " I will go down by the early train. Are there any tools in particular that you wish me to bring ? "

" Well, Polton," Thorndyke replied, " you know what our problem is. Someone has got into these rooms by some means other than an ordinary door. We may have to pick one or two locks, and they may be rather unusual locks. I would not suggest burglars' tools, because, of course, you haven't any. If you had, they might be useful."

Polton crinkled knowingly as he protested : " There is nothing improper about burglars' tools in themselves.

9*

It is the use that is made of them. The tools are quite innocent if they are used for a lawful purpose."

Having delivered himself of this slightly questionable legal dictum, he departed, leaving the photographs for us to examine at our leisure.

Very curious productions they were. I took up the strip of film and examined the tiny negatives through my pocket lens. Small as they were—barely an inch and a half square—they were full of minute detail, and the enlargements, magnified about four diameters, were as clear as if they had been taken with a full-sized camera. The " Automatic Watcher " had turned out, in respect of its efficiency, far beyond my expectations.

" Yes," said Thorndyke, in reply to my admiring comments, " with first-class lenses, you can get surprising results ; in fact, the only limit to enlargement is the grain of the film. But we had better put the photographs away for the present, as I am expecting Miller to drop in at any moment. He is dreadfully disgruntled at the result of the trial, though the fiasco is very largely of his own producing. Still, we shall have to try to comfort him, and it had occurred to me that we might take him into this Hartsden adventure. What do you think ? We really ought to have a police officer with us."

" Yes, I think it is rather necessary," I agreed. " We don't want a search warrant, as we are acting with Woodburn's authority, but, as we may have to make an arrest, it would be more regular to have a police officer to direct that part of the business. Besides, we don't know how many we may have to deal with. It looks like a one-man job, but we don't know. It may turn out to be a gang. Let us have Miller's beef and experience, by all means."

On this, Thorndyke took the photographs and retired to the laboratory to write and dispatch his letter

and telegram. When he returned, he brought in with
him the Superintendent, whom he had encountered on
the landing.

" Well," growled Miller, as I placed an arm-chair
for him, with the usual creature comforts, " we've
brought our pigs to a pretty fine market."

Thorndyke chuckled, but refrained from pointing
out that the market was of his own choosing.

" What I can't understand," the Superintendent
continued, " is why that fool couldn't have trotted out
his infernal alibi when we charged him. Then there
needn't have been any trial."

Again we refrained from the obvious answer to this
question. Instead, Thorndyke proceeded at once to
the " comforting " operation.

" Well, Miller," said he, " now that we have cleared
Dobey off the stage, we can give our attention to
realities. I suppose you will now agree with me that
the man who gave Badger that poisoned cigar is the
man who murdered him."

" Yes," Miller admitted, " I'll agree to that much.
But it doesn't get us a great deal forrarder. The
fellow is a mere abstraction. He isn't even a name.
He is just a finger-print that we haven't got on our
files."

" Not at all," said Thorndyke. " We can tell you
who he is. It will then be for you to find out where
he is."

The Superintendent laid down a match that he had
just struck, and stared at Thorndyke, open-mouthed.

" You can tell me who he is ! " he exclaimed.
" Do you mean that you can give him a name ? "

" I do," replied Thorndyke. " His name is Walter
Hornby."

The Superintendent was thunderstruck. " Walter
Hornby ! " he gasped in amazement. Then, suddenly,

he brought his large hand down heavily on the little table, causing it to rock visibly, to the imminent peril of the whisky decanter. " Now," he exclaimed, " I understand how it happened. Badger told me, himself, that he thought he had seen Walter Hornby, and he was mighty pleased with himself for having spotted him. I gathered that Hornby was either very much changed or else disguised, though Badger didn't actually say so. But I have no doubt that poor old Badger, in his secretive way, kept an eye on him, and probably shadowed him a bit too openly. Then Hornby got alarmed and, in his turn, shadowed Badger, and finally enticed him into that first-class carriage with the cigar all ready in his pocket. But, if you knew, Doctor, why on earth didn't you tell me ? "

" My dear Miller," protested Thorndyke, " of course I didn't know in time to prevent the prosecution. I have only just completed the case."

" By the way, Doctor," said Miller, " I suppose I can take it that there is no mistake this time ? You are quite sure of your man ? "

" I am prepared to sign a sworn information," Thorndyke replied, " and I will undertake to present a convincing case for the prosecution. Naturally, I cannot promise a conviction."

" Of course you can't," said Miller. " But a sworn information from you is good enough for me, to start with. We can go into the evidence another time. But I am hanged if I know how to go about looking for the beggar. I suppose you have no idea what he looks like nowadays ? "

" I can only guess," replied Thorndyke. " We can safely assume that he has *not* red hair or a red nose. Probably he has shaved off his beard and moustache, and, judging from what Badger told you and from the fact that he has certainly worn a wig when personating

Dobey, it is likely that he habitually wears a wig of a colour different from the lightish brown of his own hair. But I must admit that those assumptions are not very helpful. Still, you have the finger-prints that I handed to you, so, if you make an arrest on suspicion you will know, at once, whether you have or have not got the right man. And now let us dismiss this case, and have a few words about another one that we want you to help us to work at."

Here Thorndyke gave the Superintendent a brief outline of the mystery of Hartsden Manor House, dwelling principally on the testimony of the servants and, characteristically, keeping his own counsel about the " Automatic Watcher." Consequently, Miller, though deeply interested, was a little disposed to be sceptical.

" It sounds a tall story," he remarked, " though it is by no means impossible. At any rate, it is worth looking into. Of course, if a party of crooks have managed to get in there, they have got ideal premises for some kinds of jobs. Just think of a bank-note forger, for instance, getting the use of a set of sealed rooms where he could work in perfect safety, and leave all his incriminating stuff about with the certainty that no one would stumble on it by chance ! Or a maker of bombs, or any other kind of illicit artisan. Yes, I certainly think it is worth looking into. And you think the sportsmen are likely to turn up to-morrow night ? "

" That is merely a matter of probability," said Thorndyke. " Apparently, the visitor or visitors keep to regular days for their calls, and Friday is one of those days. So we shall take the chance and spend the night there. I think you had better come, Miller," he added, persuasively. " Even if nobody turns up, it will be worth your while to look over the premises.

You may be able to spot something that we might miss."

"I don't think you are likely to miss much, Doctor," said Miller, with a faint grin. "However, I'd like to come with you ; in fact, the more I think of the job, the more it takes my fancy. There are all sorts of possibilities in it. But, if you don't mind, I think I will bring a couple of spare men, or let them come on later. You see, we may want to post them in some cover outside, in case our sportsmen should happen to spot us first and nip off. They would know the place better than we should, and they might easily get away while we were trying to find the way out. In that case it would be very handy to have a couple of men outside who could hear the alarm and pounce on them as they came out."

We both agreed heartily to this excellent arrangement ; and, when we had discussed a few further details and settled the time for starting in the morning, Miller lighted a fresh cigar and took his departure quite revived in spirits by the prospect of the morrow's adventure.

DURING our journey down to Hartsden on the following morning, Superintendent Miller's state of mind seemed to alternate between a rather extravagant optimism and a haunting fear of an anticlimax that might expose him to the derision of his subordinates. And such was his condition when we introduced him to Mr. Woodburn at Hartsden Station.

" Well, sir," said he, " this is a very remarkable affair—if it isn't a mare's nest. I hope it isn't."

" I rather hope it is," replied Woodburn, " though that is not my expectation. But we shall soon know."

He held open the door of the car, and, when we had taken our places, he drove off at a smart pace and soon covered the short distance between the station and the Manor House. There, at the open door, we found Mrs. Gibbins awaiting us, supported by Polton, who seemed to have established himself as the master of ceremonies, and who conveyed to Thorndyke, in a conspiratorial whisper, that the " Automatic Watcher " had been removed and put out of sight. Evidently, he did not intend that his patent should be infringed by the official investigators.

" We may as well go straight to the gallery," said Woodburn. " I've got the key. Shall I show the way ? "

Without waiting for an answer, he passed through the narrow doorway that led into the corridor and the rest of the party followed, with the exception of the housekeeper, whose good manners were even greater than her curiosity, and who contented herself with a wistful observation of our departure, following us with her eyes until we were lost in the darkness of the corridor.

"Now," said Woodburn, as we drew up before the massive door of the gallery, "we are going to clear up the mystery, if there is one. And, if there isn't, we are going to catch it from Mr. Toke. At any rate, here goes."

He opened his pocket knife and deliberately cut the stout tape that connected the two seals. Then he inserted the little flat key into the modern lock, grasped the handle of the door, and turned them both together. The door moved slightly, far enough to disengage both the latches, but no farther. He gave one or two vigorous pushes and then looked round at us with a somewhat mystified expression.

"This is very odd," said he. "The door is free of the latches, but it won't open. There seems to be something inside preventing it."

The Superintendent laid his large hand on the door and gave a hearty shove. But still the door refused to move more than half an inch.

"Rum," said he. "Doesn't feel like a solid obstruction. There's a distinct give in it. Shall I throw my weight against the door?"

"Better not," said Woodburn. "There's a flight of steps on the inside."

Here Polton's voice was heard enquiring meekly if it wouldn't be better to lever the door open.

"Certainly it would," replied Miller, "if you know where to find a lever."

"I happen to have a case-opener in my pocket," said Polton, in the matter-of-fact tone of one announcing the possession of a lead pencil or a fountain pen. "I think it would answer the purpose."

" I expect it would," Miller agreed, casting an inquisitive glance at our versatile artificer. " At any rate, you may as well try."

Thus encouraged, Polton advanced to the door and unblushingly produced from a long inside pocket a powerful telescopic jemmy of the most undeniably felonious aspect. Quite unmoved by the Superintendent's stare of astonishment, he first felt the door critically to locate the point of resistance, and then, skilfully insinuating the beak of the jemmy into the rebate of the door-jamb, gave a firm wrench at the long handle of the lever. Immediately, there came a bursting sound from within, and the door swung open, disclosing a short flight of steps leading down to the gallery floor.

The Superintendent tripped down the steps and turned to look for the obstruction.

" Well, I'm jiggered ! " he exclaimed. " Your Mr. Toke is a cautious man with a vengeance ! He isn't taking any risks. Just look at that."

He pointed to the door-post, on which was a large seal, and, depending from it, a length of strong tape with a mass of sealing-wax adhering to its free end. We came down the steps and stood gazing at this singular phenomenon, while Miller swung the door round and exhibited, near its edge, the broken seal from which the tape had torn out.

" Now, why the deuce," demanded Miller, " should he have wanted to seal the door on the inside ? And when he had done it, how the devil did he get out ? "

" Exactly," said Thorndyke, " that is what interests us. This inside seal gives a conclusive answer to our principal question. He couldn't have got out by this door, so there must be some other way out. And a way out is a way in."

" M'yes," Miller agreed in a reflective tone. " That

is so. But it seems to raise another question. Is it quite certain that Mr. Toke has really gone abroad ? Is it certain, for instance, that he is not just keeping out of sight for some private reasons ? "

" Of course," Woodburn replied, a trifle stiffly, " there is no absolute proof that he has gone abroad. But he said that he was going abroad ; he locked and sealed his premises, and was seen thereafter to go away from his house. He put his car into storage, and he has not since been seen in any of his usual places of resort. I may say further that he is a gentleman of the highest character and repute, and that I can imagine no reasons that should induce him to keep out of sight."

" Then," said Miller, apologetic—but unconvinced, as I suspected—" that settles it. You must excuse me, Mr. Woodburn, but I did not know Mr. Toke. We shall have to look for some other explanation. Probably we shall find it when we have made our examination of the premises ; when we have ascertained, for instance, whether there is anything missing. Shall we take a look round and check the property ? I suppose you know roughly what there was in these rooms when Mr. Toke went away ? "

" Yes," replied Woodburn ; " I think I should know if anything of value had been taken away."

With this, Miller and the solicitor proceeded to make a systematic tour of inspection, passing along the range of wall-cases and rapidly glancing at the objects on the shelves and apparently finding the collection intact.

" It's rather queer, you know," said Miller, when they had made the round, " that none of these things should have been taken. I imagine that they are pretty valuable pieces."

" They are," replied Woodburn, " but they wouldn't be much use to a thief, seeing that they could be so easily identified ; at least, that was Mr. Toke's opinion.

He always considered the collection quite safe, so far as burglars were concerned."

"To a certain extent he was right," said Miller. "This stuff would be no use to an ordinary burglar if there was a hue and cry and a description of the stolen property. But that doesn't apply to the present conditions. If someone has been entering these rooms, he might have taken the whole boiling away and have offered it quite safely at a common auction, in small lots at a time. Because, you see, nobody would have known that it had been taken. And there's plenty of demand for this sort of stuff. What is in this room?" he added, as their peregrinations brought them to a door near the entrance.

"That is where the collection of bronzes is kept," replied Woodburn. "We may as well see if they are all right, too."

Thereupon, he opened the door and entered the room with the Superintendent.

Meanwhile, Thorndyke had been devoting his attention to the seals on the gallery door, making a minute comparison of the outside seal with that on the inside door-post. As Miller and the solicitor disappeared into the adjoining room (closely attended by Polton, who was apparently determined that the Superintendent should not steal a march on his employer), Thorndyke handed me his lens, remarking:

"The seals appear to be identical. I should say that they were both made with the same matrix."

"Is there any reason why they should not be?" I asked in some surprise.

"No," he replied, "I don't think there is."

I made a somewhat perfunctory comparison—for Thorndyke's opinion was good enough for me—and then remarked:

"I am in the same case as Miller. I can't imagine

what object Toke can have had in sealing the inside of the door. Do you understand it ?"

"Not if the seals were affixed by Toke," he replied ; "seeing that Toke had access to the whole of the house and could examine the sealed door from the outside to satisfy himself that the seals were intact. But it would be quite understandable if the inside seals were fixed by someone who had not access to the house, but who would wish to be assured that the outside seals had not been broken. Supposing, for instance, there had been no inside seals, and supposing that we made our inspection without disturbing anything and went away, locking the door behind us. There would be no trace of our visit, nor any evidence that the rooms had been entered. But now, if we should go away and our friends should return to-night, they would see at a glance that someone had been here, and, no doubt, they would discreetly clear off and abandon their tenancy."

"Yes," said I. "That seems to be the explanation. It had not occurred to me, nor, apparently to Miller. But there is another point. If the visitors sealed the door on the inside, they must be in possession of the seal."

"Obviously," he agreed. "That is the important point. If it is a fact, it is an extremely significant fact, especially when it is considered in connection with a certain ' Ginger Lushington.' "

At this critical stage, our conversation was interrupted by the Superintendent's voice, hailing us from an adjoining room. At once we hurried into the room which we had seen him enter, but, finding it empty, passed through into a second room, with which it communicated, and so, by another communicating doorway, into a third. This also was empty, save for a company of bronze statuettes on its shelves, but, through the farther doorway, we could see into a fourth, larger room, and thither we made our way.

As we entered, I looked round me with no little surprise. The three small rooms through which we had passed, with their glazed wall-cases and rare and curious contents, had the trim, well-kept aspect of an art museum. This fourth room presented a startling contrast. Considerably larger than the others, it had the appearance of a goldsmith's or metal-worker's workshop. In one corner was a large, rectangular chemical sink, and, adjoining it a fixed wash-hand basin. At one side was a massive crucible-furnace, arranged to burn charcoal and fitted with a foot-bellows. Close by was a massive post, fitted with a flat stake and a jeweller's "sparrowhawk." There were one or two cupboards and enclosed nests of drawers, and a strong bench provided with a service-able vice. These details my eye took in rapidly, but there was no time for a complete survey, for my atten-tion was instantly riveted on an object on the bench round which our three friends were gathered in a mighty ferment of excitement.

"Here's a discovery, if you like, Doctor!" the Superintendent exclaimed, gleefully. "You remember my telling you about those bogus sovereigns? Well, we've struck the sovereign factory! Just look at this!"

He indicated the object on the bench—which I now recognized as the box that I had seen through the key-hole periscope, resting on the gallery table, and that had been shown in the "Tuesday" photograph.

Polton's diagnosis had been correct. It was a casting box, or "flask,"—an iron frame in two halves, held together in position by pins and eyes at the sides. The upper, or pin, half had now been lifted off, and the mould which filled the interior was displayed. And a very remarkable mould it was, and very illuminating

as to the kind of industry that was being carried on in
this room.   In the smooth, flat surface of the matrix
were twenty sunk impressions of sovereigns, each
beautifully clear and shiny with graphite.   The
impressions were connected with one another, and with
the " pour " or inlet of the mould, by a deep groove,
which was one-half of the channel along which the
molten metal was conducted to the impressions.

"Quite a workmanlike outfit," chuckled the de-
lighted Superintendent.   "Don't you think so, Mr.
Polton ? "

Polton crinkled approvingly.   " Yes, sir," he replied ;
" and he knows how to use it.   He's no amateur.
That is a wonderfully good matrix; hard enough to stand
brushing with graphite, and to be used over and over
again.   I should like to know what it is.   There's bone-
ash in it, but there's something else on the surface."

" Well," said Miller, " that's more interesting to you
than to me.   Let us have a look at that other flask."

He indicated a second, similar flask that had been
pushed to the back of the bench.   Reaching out, he
drew it forward and passed it to Polton, who tenderly
lifted off the top half and turned it over, laying it
beside the lower half and thus exhibiting the two halves
of the mould.   As he laid it down, he bestowed a crinkly
leer on the Superintendent.

" Well, I'm jiggered ! " the latter exclaimed.
" Half-crowns, too ! But I always suspected that the
half-crowns and the sovereigns were made by the same
man.   It was the same idea in both cases.   But now
we have got to find out where the stuff came from—
where he kept his bullion, I mean.   We had better
go through these cupboards and drawers."

He gave a lead by throwing open a deep cupboard,
and, as the door swung out, he uttered the single word,
" Moses ! "   The relevancy of the exclamation was not

obvious, but the cause was extremely so. For the deep shelves were occupied by an assemblage of silver articles—candle-sticks, tea-pots, spoons, and the like, mostly a good deal battered, and many of them reduced to small fragments, apparently by means of shears. A second cupboard made a similar sinister display, though the quantity was smaller. But of gold there was no trace.

" He must have kept his gold in the drawers," said Miller. " He couldn't have brought it with him."

" He brought some of it with him, sir," said Polton, who had been pulling out the drawers of a nest and peering in with a school-boy's delight in a treasure-hunt. " Here is a piece of fine gold plate—twenty-four carats—which certainly came from a bullion dealer's."

At this report, Thorndyke, who had hitherto maintained the attitude of a mildly interested observer, suddenly woke up. Taking a pair of pliers from the bench, he went to the drawer which Polton was holding open and carefully lifted out the piece of plate. Having scrutinized it closely on both sides, he held it out for Miller's inspection.

" You had better secure this," said he. " There are some fairly clear finger-prints on it which may be helpful later on, if our friend should fail to keep his appointment to-night."

The Superintendent took the pliers from him, and examined the gold plate, but with less enthusiasm than I should have expected. However, he laid it carefully on a shelf of the cupboard, and then returned to the quest in which he appeared to be specially interested. By this time Polton had made some further discoveries that seemed more relevant, one of which he announced by pulling a drawer out bodily and placing it on the bench.

" Sovereigns, by gosh ! " exclaimed Miller, as he looked into the drawer. " Now, I wonder whether these are some of the castings, or the originals that he worked from. What do you think, Doctor ? "

Thorndyke picked out one of the coins and examined its edge through his lens, turning it round and inspecting the whole circumference.

" I should say that this is certainly genuine," he reported. " There is no trace of the edge tool. The milling is quite perfect, and it seems to show slight traces of wear. Moreover, the number—there are about two dozen in the drawer—is not more than would be required as models to avoid repetition of a particular coin."

" Yes, I expect you are right," said Miller, " but they will know at the Mint, in any case. Ah ! " he exclaimed, as Polton laid another drawer on the bench. " This looks more interesting. No bullion dealer's stuff this time, I fancy."

The drawer contained about a dozen small ingots of gold, each marked by means of a punch with a number—presumably the carats of " fineness." One of these Miller took up and held out for Polton's inspection.

" No, sir," said the latter, " that did not come from a dealer. It was cast in that ingot mould on the shelf, there."

As he spoke, he took the mould down from the shelf and slipped the ingot into it, when it was seen to fit with quite convincing accuracy.

The Superintendent regarded it with profound attention for some moments. Suddenly he turned to Polton and asked impressively :

" I want you to tell me, Mr. Polton, which of these things might have been brought here by an outsider and which must have been put here by Mr. Toke.

There is this gold plate. That must have been brought
here. But what was it brought for ? "

" To melt down with these ingots," replied Polton,
" to bring the gold up to 22 carats. The ingots are all
18 carats or less."

" But why couldn't he have used that acid process
that you spoke of ? "

" Because he would have had to cut up the ingots
and hammer the pieces out thin on the stake. But, if
he had done that at night, they'd have heard him all
over the house. Besides, the fine gold plate would be
quicker and less trouble, and it would come to the
same thing. He would get his money back. As to
what you were asking, I should say that the whole outfit of this place must have been put here by Mr. Toke.
The furnace certainly was, and the crucibles and ingot
moulds seem to belong to it ; in fact, it is a regular
metal-worker's shop."

" And what do you make of those ingots ? "

Polton crinkled knowingly. " I think, sir," he
answered, " they are more in your line than mine.
They are not trade ingots, but they are about the fineness of good-class jewellery."

At this point, Thorndyke, who had been listening
with rather detached interest to this discussion,
sauntered out into the gallery, leaving Polton and
Miller to their devices.

" I think," said he, as I followed him out, " we had
better get on with our own job. This coining business
is no concern of ours."

With this, he went along to the entrance door, on
the steps of which he had left his research case, and,
picking it up, carried it back to the table and deposited
it thereon.

" We may as well begin with the most obvious
probabilities," said he, as he opened the case and ran

his eye over the contents. " I suppose you noticed this end of the room, as it showed in the photograph ? "

I had to admit that I had not taken especial note of it, nor did I now perceive anything particularly striking in its appearance. The end wall was decorated pleasantly enough, by a low elliptical arch of simply moulded oak supported by a pair of oaken pilasters, the surfaces of which were enriched with shallow strap carving in the form of a guilloche with small rosettes in the spaces. There was nothing remarkable about it ; and, to tell the truth, I was not quite clear as to what I was expected to see. And Thorndyke's proceedings enlightened me not at all.

" The police methods are good enough for our present purpose," he remarked, as he took out a wide-mouthed bottle and a large camel-hair brush. " The good old *Hyd. cum Creta.*"

Removing the stopper from the bottle, he picked up the latter and the brush, and walked across to the pilaster nearest the window. Dipping the brush into the bottle of powder, he began to paint it lightly over the carved surface. I watched him with slightly bewildered curiosity ; and, looking through the doorway into the workshop, where I noticed Woodburn listening with an anxious and rather disapproving expression to the comments of our assistant and the Superintendent, I perceived that the two latter had developed a sudden interest in my colleague's activities. Presently Miller came out for a closer inspection.

" I thought you always used a powder-spray," he remarked. " And you needn't worry about fingerprints. Those on the gold plate will tell us all we want to know. And," he added in a lower tone, " let me give you a hint. Your nocturnal stranger is a myth. The name of the chappie who runs the sovereign factory is Toke. Mustn't say so before Woodburn, but it's a

fact. It stares you in the face. Mr. Toke is a fence.
Dam' clever fence, too. Buys the scrap from the
jewel-robbers, sells the stones, and melts down the
settings into sovereigns. I take my hat off to him, and
I only hope he'll turn up to-night and let me have the
pleasure of making his acquaintance."

Thorndyke nodded, but continued to brush the grey
powder on to the woodwork in a broad band from near
the floor to a little above the eye level. The Superintendent watched him with a slightly anxious expression, and presently resumed : " I don't see why you
are so keen on finger-prints, all of a sudden, or why
you should expect to find them in this particular, and
rather unlikely, place. At any rate, there don seem
to be any."

" No," said Thorndyke, " we seem to have drawn a
blank. Let us try the other side."

He crossed the room and began operations on the
second pilaster, watched, not only by Miller, but also
by Polton and Woodburn. But this time he did not
draw a blank, for, at the first sweep of the brush, the
pale-grey tint of the powder was interrupted by a number of oval shapes, forming an irregular, crowded
group close to one side of the pilaster about four feet
above the floor. Thorndyke blew away the super-
fluous powder and examined the group of finger-prints
closely. It seemed to be divided into two subgroups,
one on the extreme edge of the pilaster and extending
round to the side, and the other in the space of one
member of the guilloche, around and over the enclosed
rosette. After another close inspection, Thorndyke
grasped the marked rosette between his fingers and
thumb, and tried if it were possible to rotate it.
Apparently it turned quite easily ; but, beyond the
rotation, no result followed. After a moment's reflection, Thorndyke took a fresh hold, and gave it another

turn in the same direction. Suddenly, from within, came a soft click; and then the whole shaft of the pilaster, from the capital to the plinth, swung out a couple of inches like an absurdly tall and narrow door. Thorndyke grasped it by the edge and drew it fully open, when there came into view a small triangular space of floor and a low, narrow opening at the side, with the beginning of a flight of ladder-like steps, the remainder of which was lost to view in the impenetrable darkness of a passage which seemed to burrow into the substance of the wall.

"Well, I'm jiggered!" exclaimed Miller. "Now, I wonder how you guessed that door was there, Doctor?"

"I only guessed that it might be there," said Thorndyke. "Hence the search for finger-prints. Without them, we might have spent hours trying to find the secret door, and especially the fastening, which was so cleverly concealed. However, we have solved the most difficult part of our problem. The outside opening of this passage is probably as cleverly hidden as the inside one. But it will be hidden from without, whereas we shall approach it from within, where there is probably no concealment."

"I suppose it is worth while to explore that passage," said Miller, looking a little distastefully at the narrow, black chink, "though, really, we want to know who the man is, not how he got in."

"Perhaps," replied Thorndyke, "an exploration of the passage may answer both questions. At any rate, Mr. Woodburn will want to know how the house was entered from the outside."

"Certainly," Woodburn agreed. "That was, in fact, what we came to find out."

As Thorndyke produced from his case a couple of powerful electric inspection lamps, one of which he handed to me, I reflected on his slightly cryptic answer

to the Superintendent's question ; as also did Miller
himself.   At least, so I judged from the inquisitive look
that he cast at Thorndyke.   But he made no remark ;
and, when he had provided himself with an electric
lantern from his bag, he announced that he was ready
for the exploration.

Thereupon, Thorndyke turned on his lamp, and,
squeezing through the narrow opening, began to de-
scend the steps, followed, at due intervals, by the rest of
the expeditionary party.

IN the course of my descent of that interminable stairway, I found myself speculating curiously on the physical characteristics of the dead and gone Greenlees. They must, I decided, have been a thin family ; for, surely, no corpulent person, no matter how hard pressed or how deeply embroiled in political machinations, could ever have got down those steps. Vainly did I seek to avoid contact with those slimy, fungus-encrusted walls. They pressed in on me from either side as if I had been sliding down a tube. Not, indeed, that this close contact was without its compensations, for, since there was no hand-rail, and the steps were incredibly steep and narrow, and, like the walls, slippery with slime and fungus, it gave some slight feeling of security.

But it was a hideous experience. Soon the faint glimmer of daylight from the doorway above faded out and gave place to the ghostly light of the electric lamps, which glanced off the shiny, unsavoury walls and ceiling in fitful gleams that dazzled rather than illuminated. Moreover, the air, which at first had seemed only musty and close, grew more and more foul, and pervaded by a strange, cadaverous odour unlike the usual earthiness of underground cellars and passages.

At length, the sudden eclipse of Thorndyke's lamp, followed by that of Miller's, and a faint reflection on the wall, told me that they had turned into some other passage. Then I, bringing up the rear, reached the bottom of that apparently endless flight, and found myself on a small paved space from which opened a low tunnel along which my predecessors were creeping in postures more suited to chimpanzees than to representatives of the law. I lowered my head and shoulders and followed, concentrating my attention on avoiding contact with the unclean ceiling. Presently Miller's voice came rumbling unnaturally along the tube-like passage.

" What does your compass say, Doctor ? Which way are we travelling ? "

" Due west," was the reply. " Towards the church."

I had hardly time to consider the significance of this piece of information when the Superintendent's voice again rang out, this time in a slightly startled tone :

" Why, this is a vault ! "

A few moments more, and I was able to confirm the statement. The tunnel ended in a narrow, oblong chamber, barely three feet wide, but more than a dozen feet long, and of a height that, at least, allowed one to stand upright. I availed myself of this advantage, and looked around me with some curiosity and a strong desire to find the way out. For, if the air had been foul on the stairs and in the tunnel, it was here suffocatingly fetid.

The light of the three powerful lamps made it easily possible to see all the details of structure and arrangement. And a strange and gruesome place it looked in that lurid illumination ; a long, passage-like chamber, as I have said, paved with stone and enclosed with walls of damp and slimy brick. At the ends, the walls were solid, excepting the arched opening of the tunnel, but the long side walls were each interrupted by a widish arch which opened into a side chamber. Both chambers were fitted with massive stone shelves, something like the bins of a wine-cellar, and on these could be seen the ends of the coffins containing, presumably, mature specimens of the Greenlees vintage. Above, at a height of about ten feet, the long walls supported what looked like a bottomless brickwork box about eight feet long, the rest of the chamber being roofed in with stone slabs. Under the box, towards one end, a thick iron bar—or what would nowadays be called a girder—crossed the chamber and supported at its middle an upright iron post that seemed to be fixed into the top of the box.

But the feature that interested me most was a flight of steep and narrow, but perfectly practicable, brick steps, which started from the mouth of the tunnel and passed up the left-hand wall above the arch to the base of the box near the end opposite to that which was crossed by the iron bar.

" I don't quite understand that contraption up there," said Miller, throwing the light of his lantern on the under-side of the box, " but there's a flight of steps, so I suppose there's a way out ; and I propose that we try it without delay. The atmosphere of this place is enough to stifle a pole-cat."

" We mustn't be precipitate, Miller," said Thorndyke. " We want to find the way out, but we don't want to publish it to the world at large. Before we go out, we must send someone up to see that the coast is clear."

" I suppose we shall be able to get out," said Woodburn, " though I don't see very clearly how we are going to do it. But I expect you do, as you nosed out that doorway so readily."

" I think it is pretty obvious," replied Thorndyke. " That coffer-like structure up there I take to be the Greenlees tomb in the churchyard. The top slab seems to rotate on that iron pivot and those curved runners that cross on the under-side. But I will run up and make sure of it before we send out our scouts."

He climbed cautiously up the brick steps, and having reached the top, threw the light of his lamp on the under-side of the slab and examined the simple mechanism.

" Yes," he reported, " I think it is all plain sailing. The runners are clean and smooth, and both they and the pivot have been kept well oiled. It won't do to try it, in case there should be anyone in the churchyard. Now, who is going up as scout ? I suggest that you go, Woodburn, as you know the tomb ; and the Superintendent had better go with you to learn the lie of the land. Take a stick with you, and, if it is all clear, give five distinct taps on the side of the tomb ; and be careful not to leave any more tracks than you can help."

Neither of the scouts showed any reluctance. On the contrary, they both assented with a readiness that I attributed to the influence of the deceased Greenlees. At any rate, they waited for no further instructions, but dived forthwith into the tunnel, whence presently came the echoes of their footsteps as they scrambled up the steps towards the fresh air and the light of day.

As they disappeared, Thorndyke began a systematic exploration of the vault, throwing the light of the lamp into all the darker corners and finally extending his researches into the side chambers.

" Isn't it rather odd," said I, " that the air of this place should be so extraordinarily foul ? I take it that there have been no recent burials here."

" If the inscriptions are to be accepted," he replied, ' the last burial took place more than sixty years ago. I agree with you that the physical conditions do not seem to be quite consistent with the inscriptions. Perhaps we may find some explanation."

10

He walked slowly round the first chamber that he had entered, throwing the light on the shelves and examining the latter with minute and suspicious scrutiny, reading each of the coffin-plates, and inspecting each coffin critically as to its condition. Having made his round of the first chamber, he crossed to the second, followed by me and Polton—who had developed a profound and ghoulish interest in the investigation. He had passed along nearly the whole length of the first shelf when I saw him stop and look closely, first at the shelf, then at the ground beneath it, and, finally, at the two adjacent coffins.

"This wants looking into, Jervis," said he. "These two coffins have been moved quite recently. The thick dust on the shelf has been brushed away—you can see some of it on the floor—but there are clear traces showing that both coffins have been pulled forward. And, if you look closely at the coffins themselves, you will see pretty evident signs of their having been opened at some fairly recent time. This right-hand one has been opened quite roughly, with inadequate tools. The other has been treated more skilfully ; but if you look at the screws you can see that they have been withdrawn and replaced quite recently. Parts of the slots have been scraped bright by the screwdriver and the edges of the slots are burred up, particularly on the left side, showing that they were difficult to turn, as you would expect in the case of an old screw that has been in position for years.'

"For what purpose do you suppose the coffins were opened ? " I asked.

"Why suppose at all ? " he replied, "when the coffins are here, and Polton has a whole burglar's outfit on his person ? Let us get the lids off and see what is inside. I take it that the damaged coffin is the one that was opened first, so we will begin with the other one. Have you a practicable screwdriver about you, Polton ? "

The question was hardly necessary, for Polton had already extracted from some secret and illegal pocket a good-sized ratchet screwdriver with a hollow handle containing several spare blades of different sizes. Having taken a glance at the screws, he fitted in a blade of the appropriate size, and then, as we drew out the coffin to the front of the shelf, he fell to work on it.

" The last operator wasn't much of a hand with the screwdriver," he grumbled. " He's scraped away half the slots."

However, by bearing heavily on the tool, he got the screws started, and, as they came out one by one and were put tidily on a clear space on the shelf, we brought the coffin a stage farther forward to bring the next one within reach. When the last of them had been extracted, the " case-opener " was produced, and its beak inserted under the lid. A slight tweak raised the latter, and it was easily lifted off.

As Polton drew it aside and exposed the interior of the coffin, I uttered a cry of astonishment.

" Why, there are two bodies ! " I exclaimed.

" Skeletons, I should call 'em, sir," Polton corrected, disparagingly.

" Yes," Thorndyke agreed ; " there would hardly have been room for two recent corpses. But they are not so badly preserved, considering that they have been here for close on a century. Now, let us get the other one open, and don't damage the coffin more than you are obliged to, Polton."

" Am I right," I asked, " in supposing that you expected to find two bodies in that coffin ? "

" Yes," he replied. " That was what the circumstances seemed to suggest."

" And what do you expect to find in the other one ? "

" That question, Jervis," said he, " seems to be answered by the one that we have just opened. Why should a man take a body out of one coffin and cram it into another which is already occupied ? "

The answer was certainly pretty obvious. But the discussion came to a premature end : for, in spite of Polton's care, the damaged lid came loose before all the screws had been extracted. As he lifted it off, I threw the light of my lamp into the cavity ; and though it disclosed nothing that I had not expected, I stood for a while, silently gazing into the coffin with horrified fascination.

The bright glare of the lamp fell on the figure of a grey-haired man, fully clothed, even to a crumpled soft felt hat. His age, so far as it was possible to judge, appeared to be from fifty to sixty, and his neat worsted clothes and the quality of his linen suggested a man of some means, reasonably careful of his appearance. As to how he had died there was nothing to show, save for the sinister suggestion of a smear of blood on one sleeve. I was just turning to Thorndyke to ask a question when the deathly silence was broken by five sharp taps from above, which reverberated through the vault with quite startling distinctness.

" There is Woodburn," said Thorndyke. " Lay the covers on the coffins."

With this he picked up his lamp and went out into the main vault. Following him, I saw him pick his way carefully up the steep and narrow steps until he reached the little platform at the top. There he paused, and threw his light on the under-side of the covering slab. Then, grasping what appeared to be some sort of handle, he gave a pull, first downward and then sideways. Immediately the heavy slab turned on its pivot and runners with a dull grinding sound and a stream of brilliant daylight poured down into the gruesome interior. A moment or two later it was partially obscured as Miller and Woodburn leaned over the edge and peered down curiously into the vault.

" Is it necessary for us to come down again ? " Miller enquired. " The air is a good deal fresher up here."

" I shall want Mr. Woodburn to come down," said Thorndyke. " We have been making some investigations, and I should like to have his opinion on something that we have discovered. Probably you will be interested too."

He was—very decidedly. At the mention of a discovery, his long legs swung, one after the other, over the edge of the sarcophagus, and he followed Thorndyke down the steps as rapidly as was consistent with the necessary caution. Close behind him came Woodburn, all agog with curiosity.

" It isn't so bad here," he remarked, " now that we have got that cover open. We had better keep it open, and let a little air in."

" Then," said Thorndyke, " Polton had better go up and keep a look-out. We don't want any other observers. You saw how the slab was moved, Polton. If anyone comes in sight, shut it at once."

I could see that this duty was not at all acceptable to our ingenious coadjutor, who evidently foresaw dramatic developments in the immediate future. Nevertheless, he climbed the steps and thrust his head out of the opening. But I noticed that one eye and both ears were kept focused on the happenings down below.

" Now, Doctor," said Miller, " what is this discovery that you have made ? "

" I will show you," said Thorndyke, leading the way into the side chamber. " But I may explain that we found that two of the coffins had been moved, and moved quite recently. But they had not only been moved : they had been opened and reclosed. On observing that, we thought it desirable to open them and ascertain why they had been opened. We did so, with this result : we found in one coffin two bodies—two quite ancient bodies ; mere skeletons, in fact."

" Then," said Woodburn, " you may take it that they are strangers to me, and they are not any concern of mine. So we will take them as read."

" Very well," said Thorndyke. " I will not trouble you with that coffin. But I must ask you to look at the other. This is the one."

He drew the coffin a little farther to the front of the shelf and lifted off the lid, throwing the light of his lamp into the cavity. Mr. Woodburn approached with very evident reluctance, holding his handkerchief to his face, and cast a glance of mingled disgust and apprehension towards the coffin. Suddenly he stopped and then started forward with a half-articulate cry. For a moment he stood staring with incredulous horror. Then, in a voice tremulous with emotion, he exclaimed :

" Great God ! It's Mr. Toke ! "

For some moments there was a dead silence. Then Thorndyke replaced the coffin lid, and we went back to the main vault. And still, for a while, no one spoke. On Woodburn this revelation had fallen like a thunderbolt, while Miller, whose theory of the criminal doings at the Manor House was suddenly shattered, was wrapped in the most profound cogitation. At length the latter broke the silence.

" How long do you think Mr. Toke has been in that coffin, Doctor ? " he asked.

" I should say," replied Thorndyke, " that he has been there ever since the day on which he was supposed to have gone abroad."

" Yes," said Woodburn, " I think you are right. I have had all along a lurking suspicion that he never

really went abroad ; that something happened to him
on that last day. I didn't at all like the garage man's
story of that ginger-haired fellow with the red nose."

" Eh ! " exclaimed Miller, all agog in a moment.
" What story was that ? "

Woodburn gave him a brief summary of the incident
of the returned car and the " Ginger Lushington," to
which he listened with profound attention, and on
which he cogitated for a while when Woodburn had
finished. Suddenly he turned to Thorndyke, and
regarded him eagerly and almost fiercely.

" Now, look here, Doctor," said he, " you have got to
tell us what all this means. It is no use for you to try
to put us off. You hold all the clues and you know all
about it. You have followed this case as if you were
running along rails. You knew that someone had been
here. I believe you knew about those sovereigns, and
you went for that secret door as if you knew exactly
where to look for it. And then you came down into
this vault and you went straight for that coffin. I have
no doubt that you knew Mr. Toke was there. Now,
Doctor, I ask you to tell me who killed Mr. Toke, and
who was that red-nosed man."

" You are asking me," replied Thorndyke, " to make
a statement, whereas I can only offer an opinion. But
you can have that opinion for what it is worth ; and I
may say that I think it is worth a good deal, as it is
based on a mass of evidence. I should say that the
red-nosed man at the garage and the murderer of Mr.
Toke are one and the same person ; and that person is
named Walter Hornby."

" What ! " exclaimed Miller. " The villain who
murdered Badger ! "

" That is what I believe," said Thorndyke. " But I
hope that we shall have the opportunity to settle the
question. At any rate, we may fairly take it that the

person who has been frequenting these premises is the person who murdered Mr. Toke."

"And you expect that person to come here to-night?"

"It is only a probability," replied Thorndyke. "You know our reasons for expecting him. It may be to-night, or he may choose some other night. But there is very little doubt that he will come sooner or later to finish up the gold that is left, and take away those sovereigns. But it is quite possible that the next visit will be meant to be the last."

"It will be the last," Miller remarked, grimly. "If I stay here till Doomsday, I am going to have him."

There was a brief pause. Then Woodburn asked:

"Where and how do you suppose the murder was committed?"

"I should say," answered Thorndyke, "that the deed was done at the top of those steps. There is what looks very much like a blood-stain on the brick there. As to the circumstances, I should say that they were roughly these: I take it that Mr. Toke, when he took the car out of the garage, had for some reason to come down here, unexpectedly, to fetch something from, or deposit something in, the gallery; and he had reasons for not wishing to enter the house and break the seals. I think that the murderer must have come to know of this intended visit, and have come on in advance and waited for him in hiding somewhere; that he saw Toke arrive, followed him into the churchyard, and saw him enter the tomb by the secret opening. I suspect that he waited for him to come out, and then murdered him as he was emerging from the tomb. Then he explored the vault, hurriedly broke open a coffin, and, having disposed of the body, made an inspection of the premises, the valuable contents of which may have been known to him. At any rate, he would have found the gold, and known then that it would be worth while to come back to take it away. I should think that the sovereigns were probably an afterthought, suggested by the quantity of gold bullion, which would have been rather unsafe to dispose of in the regular way. Moreover, if I am right as to the identity of the man, we must remember that he was an assayist by profession, and would have an expert knowledge of the methods of dealing with gold. But, as to that, we shall know more when we have seen him. And now we may as well relieve Polton and get back to the house. I don't think we have left any traces of our visit down here, and we must be careful to leave none in the churchyard as we go out."

" No," Miller agreed fervently, " for the Lord's sake don't let us spoil our chances by giving him any sort of warning. At present, we seem to have him in the hollow of our hand. It would take ten years off my life if we should let him slip."

" I don't think you need have any misgivings, Miller," said Thorndyke. " He is bound to come back ; and we are agreed that we are willing to wait for him to come in his own time. We can only hope that he will not keep us waiting too long."

WE made our way out of the vault, one by one, creeping cautiously up the narrow brick steps, and climbing over the side of the tomb into the green and sunny churchyard. Woodburn was the first to emerge, and, as he stepped down on to the grass, he drew a deep breath.

" Lord," he exclaimed, " it is good to be back in the world of living men and to breathe the fresh air. That was a horrible experience ! "

I sympathized with him, though, naturally, my professional training had made me less sensitive to merely physical unpleasantness. For I realized that, whatever misgivings he might have had respecting his client, it must have been a shocking experience to be brought suddenly, without warning, face to face with his murdered corpse. Even Miller was not unaffected by the tragedy that had been so abruptly sprung upon him.

Thorndyke was the last to come up, having lingered to take a final look round and make sure that no telltale evidence of our visit had been left to arouse the suspicions of the hoped-for visitor. As soon as he had stepped out, he seized the displaced slab, and, with a vigorous pull, swung it round into its normal position.

" We may as well make sure, before we go," said he, " that we all understand how this arrangement works from the outside. It seems to be quite a simple device. The slab rocks slightly on its pivot. To release the inside catch, the higher end of the slab has to be pressed down. This raises the other end and so frees the catch. You see that, at present, the slab is quite immovable ; but when I throw my weight on this end, I am able to swing it round without difficulty."

As he spoke, he demonstrated the mechanism ; and when Miller had satisfied himself by actual trial that he had fully grasped the method, we took our way out of the churchyard and walked across to the house. There we were admitted by Mrs. Gibbins in person, who informed us that two officers had arrived, and, further, that lunch would be served in five minutes, and, furthermore, that separate arrangements had been made for Mr. Polton and the two officers.

At the latter announcement Miller smiled grimly. " Artful old puss," was his comment, when she had gone. " Made her arrangements to have Mr. Polton all to herself, and get the latest news. But it doesn't matter. She's an interested party, and it will save me the trouble of giving my men the particulars."

Nevertheless, he introduced us to the two officers, and gave them a few instructions, and then we retired to remove, as far as was possible, the traces of our subterranean activities, before sitting down to lunch.

It was a very leisurely meal ; almost intentionally so ; for there was little more to do in the way of preparation, and a long interval before the next phase of our adventure could be expected to begin. But there was plenty of material for discussion, especially as Woodburn had to be put in possession of the numerous and complicated antecedents of the case. Then the details of the procedure to be adopted in the actual capture had to be considered, and the course that would have to be taken in the event of the quarry failing to appear. As to the former, Miller showed a disposition to simplify the proceedings by making the arrest in the churchyard.

" You see," he explained, " there's a good deal to be said for catching your hare while you have the chance.

If we collar him as soon as he has gone up to the tomb,
we shall make sure of him ; whereas, if we let him
go down, he may disappear into some underground
passage that we know nothing about."

But Thorndyke shook his head very decidedly.
" No, Miller," said he. " That won't do. It is a bad
plan in two ways. In the first place, the churchyard is
not secure enough. He would have quite a fair chance
of escape in that open space, with its various obstructions to dodge among, and possibly a car waiting close
by. In the second place, he ought to be arrested, for
evidential reasons, in the gallery. Remember that we
have got to identify him with the coiner who has used
Mr. Toke's gold, and we are going to charge him with
the murder of Mr. Toke. Now, if you arrest him in the
churchyard, you have got those charges to prove. You
will infer, reasonably enough, that he has come into
the churchyard for the purpose of entering the house by
way of the secret passage. But in a criminal trial, on a
capital charge, evidence is sifted very finely. The
defence would deny the intention, and you would have
to prove it. But if he is taken actually in the gallery,
that fact is evidence in itself of his connection with
the coining, and, by fair inference, with the murder of
Mr. Toke."

Miller admitted the force of this contention. " But,
still," he urged, " we are not dealing with an unknown
man. You say you can prove his identity, which
connects him with a previous crime, and you have got
substantial evidence in regard to the murder of poor
Badger."

Thorndyke, however, was firm. " It won't do,
Miller," said he. " We shall want every particle of
evidence that we can get. At present, all that we have
is circumstantial. But, with all respect to the dictum
of a certain learned judge, circumstantial evidence is

much less satisfactory to a jury than that which is more or less direct."

" Very well," said Miller ; " you know more about court work than I do. But what do you suggest—I mean, about planting my men ? "

" The best plan, I think," replied Thorndyke, " would be to instruct them to hide behind the yew tree—it must be pitch-dark there at night—and to wait for the man to arrive. They should let him go down into the tomb, and, as soon as he has disappeared, they should take up their stations at the side of the tomb nearest the steps. There they would have absolute control of him if he should come up again, as he would be standing on the steps."

" You speak of ' him,' " Miller remarked. " Supposing there should be a gang ? "

" That is very unlikely," replied Thorndyke, " but, even so, there are four of us, without counting Polton. I think we can take our chance. Are you and your men armed ? "

" No," replied Miller ; " we don't much favour firearms in the force. We've brought two or three sets of handcuffs, and, for the rest, we've got a pretty serviceable outfit of fists."

" Well, I took the precaution to bring four automatics," said Thorndyke. " You had better have one. A man who has two murders to his account is not likely to boggle at one or two more."

Eventually, the Superintendent accepted Thorndyke's suggestions, and, when we had finished lunch, the final preparations were made. Thorndyke showed the two officers the secret door, and demonstrated the working of the catch from outside and from within, and then conducted them down the stair-way and through the vault to the opening, at which Polton had been sent to keep a look-out. When they had mastered the working of the movable slab, they were shown the spot behind the yew tree where they were to keep watch later on. Then the whole party returned to the house by way of the vault—to avoid exhibiting themselves to any chance observers in the village.

When the officers had been dismissed to repose and smoke their pipes in Mr. Toke's study, Thorndyke produced a six-inch ordnance map of the district, and invited the attention of Woodburn and the Superintendent to a narrow lane that appeared to run close beside the churchyard, and, presently to open into a by-road at no great distance.

" It seems probable," said he, " that our friend, or friends, make the journey here by car, unless they should be local persons ; which is most unlikely. And if they do, this lane would be an ideal approach, as it would avoid the village street, and be a most convenient place in which to leave the car—quite close to the churchyard and well out of sight. It might be worth while to go and inspect that lane."

" I don't think that is necessary," said Woodburn, " because the same idea had occurred to me, and I took the opportunity to walk along it this morning. And I have no doubt that you are right. At any rate, someone has been bringing a car up that lane, for there were clear traces of one—a smallish car it seemed to be—especially at a place near the middle, where it is wide enough to turn round. I could see quite plainly the marks on the grass verge where he had backed in to turn. It appeared that he entered the lane from the by-road and stopped short a couple of hundred yards from the village street. So he must have gone back on the reverse until he came to the wide part, and then have turned round and gone out by the by-road."

" Were these the marks of a single journey," asked Miller, " or were there more than one set ? "

" At the wide part," answered Woodburn, " on the soft grass verge, there were a number of tracks on top of one another. I couldn't say how many."

" Then," said Miller, " we needn't trouble to inspect it ; which is as well. The less we show ourselves in this neighbourhood the better. I'll tell my men to keep their ears pricked up for the sound of a motor, though if it is occupied by the parties that we are expecting, it isn't likely to be a very noisy one."

" No," Thorndyke agreed ; " but in the silence of the country at night it will certainly be audible, especially if the driver should take the precaution— as he probably would—to turn round as soon as he arrived, so as to be ready to drive straight off in the event of an alarm. So we will hope that he comes in style in his car. It would give a very useful warning to your watchers."

" Yes," said Miller, " and it would be rather useful if they could pass the warning on to us in some way. What do you think, Doctor ? "

" Of course," replied Thorndyke, " it would be a great help to us. But I think we shall have to do without it. Any kind of signalling would be extremely unsafe. It might easily give a warning in the wrong quarter."

Miller acknowledged the truth of this, and the subject dropped. And then began a somewhat tedious period of waiting ; for there were yet several hours of daylight to dispose of before our actual vigil would begin. The Superintendent, being an old hand at this sort of business, retired to the study to smoke and " take forty winks " ; while Thorndyke, Woodburn, and I whiled away the afternoon by making a complete tour of Mr. Toke's collection.

A very remarkable collection it was. The gallery was filled mainly with Bow, Chelsea, and other porcelain figures, while the three smaller rooms were occupied by bronze busts and statuettes and a small collection of choice pottery and enamels. The entire contents of the rooms must have been of very great value, for all the pieces seemed to have been selected with the most fastidious taste and obviously expert judgment, without regard to cost. As we walked round and admired them one after another, they suggested two rather curious questions.

First, was it credible that the man who had acquired and treasured all these things of beauty, with such obvious enthusiasm and love for them, could be a mere fence—a receiver of stolen property? Those ingots in the workshop had certainly looked suspicious. Yet how could one believe it? The man who had cherished all these beautiful things so lovingly was no common money-grabber. Every one of them seemed to cry out in vindication of Mr. Toke.

The second question was, How came it that Hornby —if he was indeed the mysterious visitor—should have left this treasure-house intact? Many of the pieces were quite portable, especially to a man with a car. And, as Miller had pointed out, they could have been disposed of quite safely, so long as they had not been missed. The first question could not be discussed in Woodburn's presence, but the second I ventured to put to Thorndyke.

" I think the explanation is fairly simple," he replied. " There appears to have been here an accumulation of gold bullion. How much we cannot guess, nor how it came to be accumulated. But here it was, and its presence was probably known to, or suspected by, the murderer, though it may have been discovered after the murder. My impression—though it is nothing more—is that the murder was not committed *ad hoc*— as a means to the carrying out of the robbery, but for some reason that is not known to us, and that the gold robbery was, as it were, a by-product.

"Now, the existence of this gold bullion was, almost certainly, known to no one but Mr. Toke. It follows that if the murderer could have simply taken away the gold and then disappeared, he would have left no trace whatever of his having ever been here. The corpse, you remember, is in a coffin in the vault, to which the only access is by secret openings whose existence was unknown to anybody but Mr. Toke. You see the masterly simplicity of the plan. When Mr. Toke failed to return or give any sign of being alive, and leave had been granted by the court to presume death, these rooms would have been opened and everything found apparently intact. There would have been nothing whatever to suggest any crime. It might have been suspected that Mr. Toke had met with foul play. But not here. The scene of his disappearance would have been placed in some unknown locality abroad.

"But now suppose that this man, in addition to taking away the gold, had rifled the collection. Then, as soon as the rooms were entered, it would have been seen that there had been a robbery. But a robbery in conjunction with a disappearance at once suggests a murder. There would have been a search, with the possible, and even probable, dicovery of the body. Obviously, it was worth the murderer's while to abstain from tampering with the collection."

The afternoon wore on and merged into evening. The daylight faded, and, as the twilight deepened and the night closed in on the old house, we felt that the time had come to set the watch. For this was a quiet country neighbourhood where people went to rest early and measured time by the sun rather than by the clock. Accordingly, we went forth in search of the Superintendent, and found him in the act of mustering his forces, preparatory to placing them at their posts in the churchyard.

" It seems a bit early," said he. " But it won't do to be caught napping. Our friends may turn up earlier than we expect. I'll just go out and see my men posted, and then we will make our arrangements."

With this he departed and we proceeded with the preliminaries that concerned us. First Woodburn instructed Mrs. Gibbins to have all lights out at the usual time—which appeared to be ten o'clock—and advised that the inmates should go to bed when they put out the lights (which I suspected to be a counsel of perfection that was not likely to be followed). Then we made out our programme for the night watch in the gallery. Woodburn not only volunteered, but insisted on joining the party; and Polton, when he was offered the use of a spare bedroom, became, for the first time on record, positively mutinous, absolutely refusing to be driven away from the scene of action. So he had to be put on the roster of the " garrison," and proceeded with us to the gallery to take up our final positions, where we were presently joined by the Superintendent.

" Well," the latter remarked, surveying our party with a grin, " if there is only one man, we ought to be able to manage him. Seven of us, all told. Seems as if we weren't taking many risks. Of course, if there should be more than one, we shan't be too many. And now we've got to settle on our stations, because, when once we have taken them, we must keep them. There must be no moving about. Now, we can't lock that door, as there is no keyhole on the inside, so one or two of us had better take post in the first room—the one that is next to the door. The question is, which of us ? "

" I think you had better take that post, Miller," said

Thorndyke, " as that is where he, or they, will probably have to be stopped. They will know that the door is unlocked as soon as they discover that someone is in the room, and, as the secret door will be blocked, they will naturally make a burst for the main door."

" Yes," agreed Miller, " I think you are right, Doctor. Then I propose that Mr. Woodburn and I take the end room, and the rest of you take post in the workshop, where you will be close to the secret door."

These arrangements having been agreed to, Thorndyke made a final round to make sure that nothing was visible that might create premature suspicion. First, he inspected the secret door, and set the catch exactly as he had found it, wiping away the last traces of the dusting powder by the light of his lamp (for we had put on no lights in the gallery). Then he went to the main door, and, taking the dangling remains of the seal, heated the wax with a lighted match (which he carefully shrouded with his hand), and stuck it in its original place so that, to a casual glance, it appeared to be unbroken.

" Now, I think we are all ready," said he, " and it is about time that we took our places."

The existing arrangements did not make for luxury, or even common comfort. The Superintendent and Woodburn found in their room one chair, and collected another from the adjoining room. But in the workshop there was but one hideously incommodious stool, which we all rejected, preferring to seat ourselves on the bench, when we had removed the flasks and other obstructions. It was far from being a comfortable seat, and the shelves behind it offered but an uneasy support to the back. However, Thorndyke reminded us that many a journeyman tailor spent the greater part of his life seated on just such a bench, and added with undoubted truth that it had the virtue of offering a steady resistance to any tendency to drowsiness.

I look back on that long vigil as one of the strangest experiences of my life. It was like that of a big-game hunter, offering a curious combination of tedium and excitement, of wearisome monotony with the need for incessant alertness and the uncertainty as to what the next moment might bring forth, or whether it might bring forth anything. We took our places, very prematurely, at half-past nine ; and thereafter we sat in the dark, conversing little, and then in the softest of whispers, and hardly daring to change our positions. It would have been a relief to smoke, but this was, of course, forbidden, though at intervals, a faint sniff, accompanied by the suspicion of a distinctive scent, informed me that Polton was indulging in the mild dissipation of a pinch of snuff. Once, indeed, the cold touch of a metal snuff-box on my hand was accompanied by a whispered invitation to test the virtues of Brown Rappee ; an invitation which I half-reluctantly declined.

The tardy minutes crawled on with incredible slowness. Sitting there in the darkness, encompassed, as it seemed, by the silence of the tomb, I was able to mark their passage by the chimes of a clock, somewhere in the village, which were borne faintly to my ear across the quiet countryside. The clock struck the quarters ; but each quarter seemed to have the duration of an hour. I fingered the automatic pistol in my pocket and wondered what degree of urgency would induce me to use it. Like Thorndyke, I had a profound dislike of firearms ; and none of our party had seemed to show much enthusiasm when he handed them out. Miller had the typical police officer's contempt for a mere assassin's weapon, and had offered his to Polton.

But Polton assured him that he had never fired a pistol in his life and should probably hit the wrong man ; upon which Miller hastily took it back.

The distant clock had struck half-past ten when the dreariness of our vigil was to some extent mitigated by the appearance of the moon. It first came into view through the curtained window of the gallery which was just visible through the half-open door of the workshop, as a misshapen, coppery disc (for it was a few days past the full), just peeping above the window-sill. Then, by slow degrees, it crept up higher and higher ; and, as its dull copper brightened into a warm, ruddy glow and then to a clear, cold, silvery sheen, the shape of the lofty window became traced on the floor in an elongated, luminous patch, on which the pattern of the lace curtains stood out clearly in forms of delicate shadow.

That shape of patterned moonlight came as a welcome distraction which helped to fill the long intervals between the chimes of the distant clock. Like some solitary prisoner in his cell, I followed its infinitely slow progress across the floor, idly calculating the time that it would take to reach the foot of the pilaster in which was the secret door. At present, the pilaster was enveloped in dense, black shadow, and a wide space of floor separated it from the patch of moonlight. I tried to think of that space in terms of angular distance and time, but failed to reach any intelligible result. Then I fell to thinking about the man for whom we were waiting. Was he now on the road, drawing gradually nearer to his doom—or, perchance, ours ? If so, how far away was he now ? Was he travelling alone or had he companions with whom we should have to reckon ? Or was he, even now, comfortably tucked up in bed in some far-away hiding-place with no intention of sallying forth this night ? Or was he lurking in the village, fully warned by the sight of us to keep out of the way ? To leave us to our profitless vigil until the coming of daylight should send us away, drowsy and defeated ?

The silence of the old house was like the silence of some cavern in the heart of a mountain. Save for the infrequent chime of the far-away clock, there was not a sound. Not a window rattled—for it was a still night—not a joist creaked, no mouse " shrieked in the wainscot " or scuttled through its burrow. None of the ordinary night sounds of an old house were audible. It was as still as the inside of a pyramid.

A few minutes had passed since the hardly audible chime of the distant clock had told out the half-hour after eleven when that deathly silence was, for the first time, disturbed by a sound that seemed to come from within the house. And, even then, it was so faint and indefinite that I doubted whether I had, in fact, heard anything. I listened intently. Then, after the lapse of nearly a minute, it was repeated. It conveyed nothing to me. It was just a sound—infinitely faint and remote, and so devoid of any recognizable character that I was still doubtful. But at this moment Thorndyke silently slid off the bench and was followed—less silently—by Polton. I, too, slipped my legs over the edge and, as I stood upright beside Thorndyke, I asked in a whisper :

" Did you think you heard anything ? "

" Yes," he replied. " It was the slab turning on its pivot. Listen ! "

I strained my ears, but for a few moments I could hear no further sound. Then I became aware of a faint but distinctly audible murmur or rustle as if a number of separate sounds were being confused by echoes. Suddenly it became much more distinct and changed in character ; for now I could clearly distinguish footsteps—soft, stealthy footsteps, mingled with their reverberations, but unmistakable.

Nearer and nearer they came, still secret and stealthy, but now recognizable as the tread of feet on the long stairway. Once, the feet slipped or stumbled, and the sound of some hard object striking the steps, followed by a muttered curse, told me that the man was nearer than I had thought. Suddenly on the side of the pilaster, there appeared a bright thread—the light of a lamp from the stairway shining through the crack of the secret door.

With a throbbing heart I watched that thread of light, drawn on the black shadow of the pilaster, as it waxed in brightness from moment to moment. At last plain sounds from within the woodwork told us that our visitor had come. There was a soft scraping like the sound of a groping hand ; two successive creaks followed by a sharp click. Then the secret door swung open, and a man stepped out into the room.

At first, he was no more than a dim, dark shape, as he stood in the shadow ; but when he moved, I could see that he was hatless, and that he carried a good-sized hand-bag in one hand and in the other what looked like a large electric lamp, the light of which was switched off. From the door he went across to the table and laid his bag on it. Then he walked softly up the room until he came to the door, where he switched on his lamp and threw its light on the seals. Apparently their appearance satisfied him, for he turned away after a brief glance ; but then, as if by an after-thought, he turned back and threw the light on again. Evidently he had detected something amiss, for, after a few moments' inspection, he mounted the steps to examine the seals more closely. As he did so, Thorndyke glided like a shadow from the workshop door to the pilaster, where he halted just in front of the secret opening. Almost at the same moment, looking out from the workshop, I saw another shadow glide out of the door of the farther room without a sound and slip round behind the stranger as he ascended the steps.

At this point, I crept silently out into the gallery, for the reflection from the moonlit floor enabled me to recognize this second shadow as the Superintendent, and I knew that the critical moment had come. It had seemed to me that Miller had moved quite noiselessly, but apparently I was wrong ; for, at the very moment when his arm stretched out to seize his prey, the stranger turned sharply, and, as the light of his lamp fell on the Superintendent, he uttered a sort of snarl, struck out viciously, and wrenched himself away, springing from the steps and racing down the room, closely pursued by Miller and Woodburn.

As to what followed my recollections are somewhat confused. It all happened so quickly and the light was so imperfect that nothing but a general impression remains. I saw the fugitive adroitly catch up a chair and whirl it back at his pursuers, with the result that Miller staggered heavily sideways, and Woodburn, whose legs it struck, fell sprawling on the floor. The next moment, as the man swerved to pass the workshop door, the light of his lamp fell on Thorndyke. I think that in that instant he must have recognized him, for he uttered a savage cry, checked for a moment, and then threw out his arm. Instantly I realized, though I could not see it, that the hand of that extended arm held a pistol, and I started forward. But at that instant something hurtled past me and struck the stranger in the face with such force that he staggered backward. The report of the pistol rang out sharply, and the missile, whatever it was, clattered heavily on the floor.

It had been a near thing ; and, indeed it was not yet over,though Miller had now rushed forward and grasped the pistol arm while I sprang at the other. But our prisoner fought and struggled like a maniac, yet with a settled purpose, for the flash and report of the pistol were repeated again and again, not at random, but always when the weapon could be brought to bear in Thorndyke's direction. Now, however, my colleague, having closed and fastened the secret door, came forward to take a hand with the light of his lamp turned full on the struggling, swaying group, which had now been joined by Woodburn.

Suddenly I heard Thorndyke call out sharply : " Keep out of the way, Polton ! " At the same moment I caught sight of our artificer, skirmishing round at Miller's side, with his eyes riveted on the pistol. Almost as Thorndyke spoke, a pair of large crucible-tongs came into view, reaching out towards the hand which held the weapon. There was a quick but unhurried move-ment, and the tongs took firm hold of the pistol by its flat stock. Then the long handles were quietly raised and twisted the weapon irresistibly out of the prisoner's grasp.

The removal of the pistol brought the struggle virtually to an end. I did, indeed, feel the hand which I controlled thrusting towards the waist-belt. But I had already detected the presence there of a sheath-knife of formidable size, and I easily circumvented the movement. And, when Thorndyke seized both the prisoner's wrists and held them together, Miller was able to snap on the handcuffs. Even then, our prisoner continued to struggle violently ; and it was not until Thorndyke had encircled his legs and pinioned his arms with a couple of document straps (which he had, apparently, put in his pocket for that purpose) that his resistance ceased. Then we sat him in a chair, and, while we recovered our breath, considered the next move.

" I think," said Miller, " I will just run across to the churchyard and relieve my men. They may be able to produce some sort of transport. If not, I shall have to borrow Mr. Woodburn's car. I leave the prisoner in your custody, Doctor."

As soon as he had gone, Woodburn proceeded to light the two hanging lamps which swung by long chains from beams in the gallery ceiling—for there was neither gas nor electric light in the house—when we were able to survey one another and examine our prisoner. Woodburn was the only one of us who had suffered visibly from the encounter, having an undeniable black eye. But the prisoner was a sorry spectacle, and, villain as he was, I could not but feel some twinges of compunction as I looked at him. His face was badly bruised and bleeding ; at which I was not surprised, when I picked up the missile that had struck him and recognized it as Polton's " case-opener." But what most contributed to his forlorn and wretched aspect was his bald head, from which the wig had been dislodged during the fray. It was not a common, natural, and decent bald head, which would have been normal enough, but the baldness was in large patches with separating areas of stubble ; the condition, in fact, known to our profession as *Alopecia areata*.

I picked up the wig and carefully replaced it on his head, disregarding his profane and furious protests. Then I went with Thorndyke to the workshop, where the research case had been deposited, to fetch the little first-aid case that was part of its permanent equipment, and, as I was thus engaged, Thorndyke proceeded to moralize.

" That Alopecia is interesting," he remarked. " I mean, as an illustration of the incalculability of human affairs. If he had not been compelled to wear a wig, he would probably never have thought of personating Dobey. Probably, too, he would not have murdered Badger—at any rate not in that way ; and he might not have murdered Toke. Evidently, the course of his criminal career has been largely influenced by his Alopecia. He had to wear a wig, but he could wear any kind of wig that he pleased, and change it at any time for any other kind that circumstances seemed to require."

"Yes," I agreed ; "a disguise which has to be habitually worn naturally suggests additions and variations."

I took the little emergency case and a basin of water, and we went back to the prisoner. As I was mixing some lotion while Thorndyke prepared a dressing, the patient watched him with a glare of the most concentrated malice.

"Don't you touch me, you devil ! " he exclaimed, huskily, " or I'll bite you. I ought to have settled with you years ago."

In different circumstances it might have been permissible to remind him that he had made three pretty determined attempts. Nevertheless, as a matter of policy, he was certainly right. But for Thorndyke, he would have been, at this moment, at large and unsuspected.

I had hardly finished attending to his damaged face when Miller returned.

"We shall be able to manage quite well," he announced. "My men discovered a car in that lane—heard it arrive, in fact. So I shan't want Mr. Woodburn's. We can take him to London in his own car."

Here the two officers entered, and, advancing up the gallery, took a long and curious look at the prisoner. Then Miller proceeded to make the formal charge.

" I arrest you, Walter Hornby, for the murder of Mr. Didbury Toke ; and I caution you that anything you say will be taken down in writing and may be used against you——"

" Oh, go to blazes ! " interrupted Hornby. " Do you think I am a cackling old woman ? I am not going to say anything."

Nevertheless, in spite of his bravado, I had the impression that the nature of the charge came as an appalling shock. I think he had expected to be charged only with breaking and entering, for after this outburst he settled down into sullen silence and submitted passively to being carried away by the two officers. Only once, as he was borne out, he turned his head to bestow on Thorndyke a look of the most concentrated malignancy.

When the grim procession, accompanied by the Superintendent, had passed out and the footsteps had died away, Thorndyke turned to his faithful henchman and laid his hand on his shoulder.

" It was fortunate for me, Polton," said he, " that you would not go to bed. But for that remarkable shot of yours, I think Hornby would have settled his account with me, after all."

Polton crinkled apologetically and gave a little embarrassed cough as he replied :

" Yes, sir, I thought I might be useful. You see, sir, when I was younger, I used to take a good deal of practice at the coco-nuts on Hampstead Heath. I got to be quite a dab at 'em ; and the Aunt Sallies, too."

At this moment, the gallery door opened, and Mrs. Gibbins entered spectrally, bearing a lighted candle in a bedroom candlestick.

" I've come to tell you, sir," she said, addressing Woodburn, " that I have laid supper in the dining-room. Mr. Miller is coming back to join you when he has seen the other officers off in the car."

It was an undeniably welcome announcement ; and, when Woodburn had extinguished the lamps, we switched on our electric lanterns and followed the housekeeper along the winding corridor.

WITH the arrest of Walter Hornby, this history—which is that of an investigation—naturally comes to an end. In the course of the events that followed, nothing transpired that could be regarded as a new discovery. Certain details were filled in, and certain conclusions which had been arrived at by inference were confirmed by actual demonstration. Thus, at the inquest, it was proved that Mr. Toke had died from a deep knife wound, and the evidence left no doubt that it had been inflicted, as Thorndyke had suggested, just as he was in the act of emerging from the tomb. The wound corresponded exactly with the knife which was on Hornby's person when he was arrested. And, though that knife had been carefully washed, when Polton, under Thorndyke's supervision, unriveted and removed the wooden handle, considerable traces of blood were discovered ; sufficient, in fact, to admit of a biochemical test which showed it to be human blood.

At the trial, there was practically no defence, nor was there any appeal from the conviction and sentence. The prisoner was indicted for the murder of Mr. Toke, the other crime being held back for a further indictment in the unlikely event of an acquittal. But of an acquittal there was never the remotest chance. For, in addition to the profoundly incriminating fact that Hornby had been captured in actual occupation of the murdered man's premises and in command of the secret passages in which the body was concealed, there was

the utterly damning fact that Mr. Toke's signet ring
was found in his pocket when he was searched after his
arrest.

It was unavoidable that the trial and its dreadful
sequel should be a cause of pain to many estimable
people, including his cousin Reuben—against whom
he had hatched such a dastardly plot in the years
gone by. To my wife, who had been almost in
the position of a relative, the whole sordidly
tragic affair was so harrowing that we tacitly
agreed not to speak of it. Even I, who had known
the man in the days of his prosperity and re-
spectability, could hardly bring myself to contemplate his present terrible plight ; and I was
almost disposed to resent Thorndyke's calm, impersonal interest in the trial and his satisfaction at the
conviction and the sentence. For a man so kindly
by nature, this callousness—as it appeared to me—
seemed surprising and hardly natural. I think I must
have given expression to some such sentiments—on the
day, I remember, when the execution had just taken
place, and he was calmly collecting the notes and
memoranda of the case to put away in the files where the
records were kept. His reply was characteristic ;
and, looking back, I am not much disposed to cavil
at it.

" I understand, Jervis," said he, " your personal
discomfort in contemplating this tragedy ; the ship-
wreck of a life that started with so much promise and
had such potentialities of usefulness and success. But
it is a mistake to grow sentimental over the Nemesis
that awaits the criminal. The most far-reaching
mercy that can be exercised in social life is to safe-
guard the liberties of those who respect the liberties
of others. Believe me, Jervis, the great purveyor of
human happiness is not philanthropy, which seeks

to soften the lot of the unworthy, but justice, which secures to the worthy the power to achieve their own happiness, by protecting them from the wrong-doer and the social parasite."

THE END